WEAPON
of CHOICE

WEAPON of CHOICE

by

JANETTE ANDERSON

BearManor Media

2013

For information, address:

BearManor Media
P. O. Box 71426
Albany, GA 31708

bearmanormedia.com

Typesetting and layout by John Teehan

Published in the USA by BearManor Fiction

ISBN—1-59393-393-2
978-1-59393-393-7

Dedicated to
Tom Selleck, Sam Elliott,
Barry Bostwick
and Eric Fleming…
all 10s in my book.

Chapter 1

Men, with faces tortured in pain, lay dying all around him: his men, his unit. The rescue chopper, with a bold red-cross sign emblazoned on the side, hovered above them ready to land on the scorched and rotting earth. From three sides the flames engulfed the old metallic bird, its body glistening in the flame-burned sky. Behind them… Viet Cong.

"Get those men inside that fucking piece of metal!" With nowhere to run, Sergeant Daniel Caulder turned, firing his well-worn M-15 until he emptied the machine gun, and then flung the useless weapon to the ground. Reaching for his companion's means of fire, Daniel stretched down, grabbing the gun from its resting place next to his number two.

Sam lay on the parched earth, blood pouring from his gaping chest wound. Caulder raised the gun and fired, seemingly endless rounds of shells, and the enemy fell to the ground. In slow motion, Caulder gestured to his men to move, and he yelled at the top of his lungs.

"Everyone get into that chopper. Go, you stupid bastards!" Caulder's deep, masculine voice echoed through the jungles of smoke and time. He pulled the black bandana from his head, and bound it tightly round his own shattered arm. Blood dripped down what was left of his army shirt, reaching his scarred fingers, and dribbled to the ground making red pools in the decaying earth.

"Sarge, save your self. Leave me!" Sam's voice could hardly be heard above the noise of war.

"The hell I will! You're too much of a bastard to die."

"Sarge, behind you!" screamed Sam, pointing with his one good arm. The other clutched the wound on his chest.

Caulder turned and with one swift movement brought his hands up around the lone Vietnamese throat. The scrawny opponent hung in his grasp while Caulder, with some difficulty, pulled a large knife from his belt, and, without hesitation, Daniel Caulder slit the captor's throat. Dropping the man to the blood-stained earth, he turned his attentions back to Sam.

Caulder swung the spare gun over his shoulder, and bent down to get his comrade. His arms slid under Sam, and, through his own pain, hoisted his friend to an upright position. In one maneuver, he raised him up and over his shoulder. Caulder groaned under the black man's weight, and ignoring his own pain that seared through his brain, began his seemingly long journey to the waiting craft. He could hear his men calling him and urging him to hurry as he trundled on through bloodied corpses lying in all positions on the ground. Caulder's tired legs ached and his vision blurred, and still he kept going. Sweat ran down his forehead, mixing with filth and grime, ending up misting tortured eyes.

With one final burst of energy, he reached the waiting chopper. Black and white hands reached out and pulled their battered comrades inside the open doors. Caulder remembered someone grabbing his arms, pulling him to safety. Then the world as he knew it exploded. Time stood still, and brilliant, white light blinded him, and he knew no more.

Three tall trees cast long shadows across the sun's rays and blocked the heat of the day from his body. Daniel Caulder turned from his sideward position in his stainless steel pool chair and then sat upright. He stretched his long, muscular legs onto the concrete floor and propped his broad shoulders against the thick cushioned backrests of the chair. Lean and golden brown, his whole body was muscular and well proportioned. He removed his shades, revealing dark, brown eyes and black eyebrows. Running his hands through his thick, black hair it fell back onto his shoulders and hung there, making Caulder very distinguished, but decidedly ominous.

Picking up his familiar brand of cigarettes from the poolside table, he lit one up with his favorite silver lighter, placing the end of the cigarette in his lips. Inhaling deeply, the smoke came down through his angular nose and he blew the rest out through his mouth. It wafted into the hot air and floated there, lingering.

He looked up at the trees, almost accusing them of stealing his sunshine. Tomorrow he would get them trimmed. That was tomorrow. Today, he sat and smoked the cigarette till it became of no use to him, and he squashed it out in the ashtray that also sat on the table. Caulder looked at the table where his drink patiently waited to be consumed. With his strong fingers, he felt the glass... it was warm. He picked up his expensive looking cell phone and dialed into the house.

"Bring me a fresh glass of whiskey!" and he hung up his line. No please, no thank you, just an order.

Still the trees bothered him. He replaced his shades. In doing so, he accidently moved the towel on the side of his chair, leaving his gun slightly visible: black, shiny steel gleaming in the afternoon sun, a weapon of destruction, his personal choice. He made no secret of it lying there. Maybe, he would put it away when his guest arrived... maybe, but generally, he didn't, feeling somewhat lost without it by his side.

Caulder looked at his gold Rolex. Three o'clock. The visitor was due any moment. Caulder relaxed a little as waited for the reporter to arrive. The interview, with the International Times and Sinclair, had been arranged some days ago by his aide. He'd chosen this paper purposely. Picking up last week's issue, from the place he had dropped it on the ground; his story had made front page headlines.

'Riot quelled in top African country. Governor overthrown by army. New leader takes over...' He didn't read the rest, he didn't have to. Caulder had firsthand knowledge.

He dozed in the warm afternoon sun, and his mind was filled with memories. He could see the motorcycle speeding through the open stretches of jungle, could feel the girl's arms around his waist, her hands slipping into his jeans. A smile spread across Caulder's face and then his expression changed. Flashes of fire exploded in his brain, bright lights burning into his skull. Men dying around him with faces of tortured anguish. His men. There was light again, bright, burning, hot in his eyes.

He was wide awake and sat bolt upright in his pool chair. All he saw was the red hot sun and trees parting in the warm afternoon breeze. Nothing more, just the sun. Would nothing make him forget his charred memories and blackened dreams? Caulder thought not.

The black Mercedes cleared at the gate, and pulled into the driveway of the mansion grounds. The occupant of the car drove it through the spacious courtyard. Toni Sinclair looked at the Spanish-style house, complete with opulent splendor, and marveled at the wealth of the man. The assignment was to find out just how he acquired that wealth.

As a Times reporter for the past four years, this was to be the first big story for Sinclair. Toni stopped the car, opened the door and climbed out, taking hold of a brand new briefcase, and walked with a spring in the heel to the front door. The journalist was about to ring the bell, when a well-armed guard opened the door in greeting. He looked the person up and down and then escorted Sinclair through the superbly furbished rooms, where exotic paintings hung from every wall. French antique furniture graced the rooms...and the smell of money lingered in the air. Toni's mind was confused. This open display of splendor was not what was expected and the reporter stared around like a kid in a candy store.

The French windows opened and outside, by the marble pool, Sinclair could see a man thought to be Caulder, stretched out in his chair waiting for the interview. Toni had been briefed about the assignment, but the journalist was not prepared for the man. The bodyguard escorted Toni to Caulder's chair.

"Sir, this is Toni Sinclair," and the dark-haired, bronzed muscle stepped aside.

Caulder's eyes started at Sinclair's feet. High-heeled shoes, black stockings, and a plain grey suit, depicted something other than Caulder was expecting. He pulled the shades from his striking eyes, looked up the body until he made contact with the face.

"Is this some sort of joke?" His deep, masculine voice rang out. "I was expecting a Tony Sinclair... a man. Not a woman!"

"I am Toni Sinclair. It's Toni with an I. I'm sorry I disappoint you. Perhaps you would feel more comfortable with one of my male colleagues doing the interview," she retorted, staring him straight in the face.

He looked her up and down. Glasses and a blonde plait completed the picture. Caulder thought there may be someone pretty lurking behind those rimmed spectacles. Pull the hair down, open the buttons of the pink blouse a little to reveal more cleavage, and there may be hope for her as a woman.

Toni Sinclair still stared at Caulder. She was angry. This was not the first time that her gender had posed a problem, and was most likely not the last. But he was not what she expected. Beside the obvious physical appearance of his body, he was very attractive. She wasn't sure what she thought he would look like in person... but not this. He was extremely good looking, and he knew it. Filled with arrogance and conceit, this fifty-something-year-old man was devastatingly handsome. Her eyes first made contact with his face and she took in every detail from eyes to his mouth. She couldn't help looking down at his body, the black hair on his chest curling a line down to his stomach. His file didn't contain his exact age, only one that was surmised by the intelligence agencies. Daniel Caulder had hidden a lot of things very carefully, but not, it appeared his great physique or his attitude towards female reporters.

She turned to leave.

"Ms. Sinclair," he paused to take a long breath, "as long as you write well... and by that I mean the truth... you can do the piece. There is, however, one condition." He never raised his head or his voice as he spoke.

"And that is?" she inquired, looking down into his face.

"You stay with me for one month. Where I go, you go. If you want the story of the way I make my living, that's the way you'll find it." He replaced his shades with apparent finality of the conversation ending.

"Where you go, I go? Everywhere?" Toni asked a little shocked.

"Everywhere. No exceptions!"

"Deal!" and she put her slim hand out to him.

He ignored it and continued speaking. "Be back here tomorrow at eight a.m., sharp." He lay back in the chair and closed his eyes.

She had been dismissed. Toni retracted her hand and collected her composure.

The all-too-bronzed guard made his presence known again. "I'll escort you to the door."

"Oh, yes. Thank you." Toni stammered. She wasn't used to being dismissed, nor being ordered to do anything.

She turned and walked away, following the muscle back through the house and to her car. He opened the car door for her, bid her farewell and closed it behind her.

Once inside the car she realized what she had done. She'd made a deal to live in this man's life for one month. How would the newspaper react to this news? Were they already aware of what they had sent her into? Now she knew why they had recommended a woman to do the job. She turned the engine on, slightly over-revving as she did. Putting her foot down on the gas, she drove out of the gates at high speed and didn't look back, her hands shaking on the steering wheel.

Toni slammed Caulder's file down on her editor's desk. This time she hadn't waited to be invited into his office, and leaned across the large oak table, looking into her editor's face. "Did you know what his reaction would be before you sent me there?" her face flushed pink.

With an amused expression, Bryan Sinclair looked up at his niece. "Sure, why do you think I sent a woman? You wanted to be one of the Times' top reporters. So, you achieve that title the hard way. Just because you are family doesn't entitle you to preferential treatment. What were his terms?" His eyes gleamed as he leaned back in the chair.

"I have to stay with him for one month, and go wherever he goes for the entire time," Toni replied, as she rescued her glasses from falling off her nose.

Bryan rose up from his office chair. Grey-haired, with a face lined from years in the newspaper business, he moved to the window of his spacious office. The seventh floor offered spectacular views of downtown Los Angeles. He hadn't figured Caulder would be quite so devious. The editor thought he would be more responsive and polite to a young woman, and now he realized he should have known better.

"Uncle Bryan, did you know he would do that?" she demanded banging her fist on his overcrowded desk and looking towards her uncle like he was totally to blame for the last few hours.

Her uncle came back to reality and turned his tired eyes to look at her. "No, Toni. I thought that as a woman you would get farther than a man, but to stay in his house... I'm not sure that's a good idea. Caulder has a personal reputation as well as a professional one. And... it's only the latter one we're interested in for this newspaper." He frowned at her, his eyebrows almost meeting as he spoke.

"I'm a big girl and can look after myself in that field. Anyway, I'm not his type. He made that very plain!" The meeting was still a painful memory, and Toni pulled at the front of her blouse making sure every button was still in the place it should be.

"Don't be so sure about that. You underestimate yourself. You're a very pretty girl, Toni, a little immature, maybe, but he's a very experienced man, and one who apparently likes young women. Didn't you read his dossier?" Sinclair was suddenly concerned for his niece.

"I read it. I also made a deal with him. One I don't intend to break. After all, you gave me the assignment." She pulled her glasses down from her face, folded them and put them in her blouse pocket. "I'll be fine, and if I'm not you can send the troops in to get me out," she mocked.

"That's not funny. You take your cell phone and call me every night. The first night I don't hear, I'll call you... agreed?" He looked her in the face; although he knew his niece well, he was not totally convinced she should pursue this. Maybe this was a mistake.

"Agreed. That's, of course, if we stay at the house. Caulder said 'everywhere', as if he was intending going somewhere within the next month. Or he was just trying to scare me," she reflected on this. Maybe he was just trying to scare her.

Bryan watched his niece. "Did he succeed, Toni?"

She lied blatantly. "No. Should he have?" If she were to get through this she may as well be tough right from the start. Underneath, she was terrified at spending time with this man. But she also needed to fulfill her dreams of being the best in her field. Whatever it took and this seemed to be the way.

Her uncle knew very well how she felt. He hadn't raised her pretty much single-handed for all these years without knowing how her mind worked. If her mother and father had survived the crash they would have praised their daughter's courage.

"Okay, Toni. I believe you. But if he does take you somewhere else, other than that house, you let me know." He moved towards her.

Toni leaned forward, threw her arms around his neck, and then planted a kiss on his cheek with her glossy pink lips. "I love you. Thanks for letting me do this. You won't regret giving me this assignment. While I'm gone, will you water my plants? You still have a spare key, don't you?" She babbled out the sentences staccato style, suddenly full of excitement at going on the assignment.

"Yeah, it's on my key ring. I sometimes think you love those plants more than anything else," he laughed and jingled the key ring that hung on his belt.

"Second only to you," and then she paused. "And about Daniel Caulder... I really can look after myself. See you in a month," and with that she was gone out of the door, slamming it shut as she went.

Bryan Sinclair sat down at his desk, pulled his chair in closer, and studied the dossier yet again. Daniel Caulder was a man probably around his age. Yet, the difference between them was remarkable. Bryan's lifestyle, dedicating his life to the raising of his brother's child, becoming both father and mother to Toni, had prematurely aged him. He had never found the time or the inclination to marry. Publisher and editor of the International Times, wealthy in his own right, and generally a loner, Sinclair was content. Almost!

Caulder was a man with a notorious past and probably a notable future. Also, a man who had never married, but one who had so many affairs with the rich and famous, that his file could not hold the information. Wealthy beyond belief, but through foul means, surmised as a mercenary or maybe even a terrorist, that's what Toni had to find out.

That's the story Sinclair had told Toni, and that's how Caulder's dossier read to the outside world. Why the hell had he sent her? He should have sent a man, not this woman, especially one who had received such a sheltered upbringing.

"God damn, why did I do it?" and he slammed his fist down on the desk. "If anything happens to her… she's all I have." He looked at the picture of his brother and his wife that sat in prime position on the desk. "I had to let go at some point, and this seemed as good a time as any. Only problem is that Toni is no match for a man like Daniel Caulder. I kept her too sheltered through her life. This assignment will make or break her… and me, too." Sinclair picked up the photo and looked at it closely. Toni looked like her mother… right down to the sparkling, green eyes. Even the temperament was the same, bold, daring, and wanting to be treated like one of the guys but, underneath, waiting to be recognized as a woman. His fingers traced her face on the picture, and then as he leaned back in the chair, he replaced the photograph on the desk. He closed his eyes and thought back a piece. How Bryan had loved his brother's wife.

Toni packed enough clothes for the month, and then some. Jeans, T-shirts, shorts, a swimsuit or two, several kinds of heeled shoes, and tossed in a little black dress for good measure. She packed her make-up bag and her expensive perfume. Pens and papers all found their way into the suitcase and spilled over into a backpack. She watered her plants one last time, left a note for her uncle, set the luggage by the front door, and headed to her own familiar, singular bed for an early night.

At six a.m., after a good night's sleep, Toni left her small, comfortable apartment for a mansion, one owned by a man she knew only from a dossier. Little did she know that since yesterday Caulder had her file and everything he needed to know about her.

At 7.45 a.m. she drove through what could only be described as the gates of hell, having no idea what lay ahead of her. Only time would tell. She stopped the car, climbed out, closing the door on her world, picked up her suitcase and moved forward. Breathing a huge sigh, she looked up at the house and shivered in the morning sunlight. The house appeared to be leering back at her; the windows wide open even at that time of the morning. They looked like a thousand eyes watching her, and Toni shivered in the crisp air.

"Well… here we go. God, I'm scared, terrified of this man and he's going to know it. A hunter can smell fear, and that's just what he is!" she muttered under her breath.

There was no more time to be afraid, as the same bodyguard from yesterday opened the large front door, and escorted her into the spacious house. He took her bags from her, and then led Toni into the rather large sitting room where Caulder sat.

"You're early. I like that!" He glanced at his watch, and then looked her up and down. "Ben, take Ms. Sinclair's luggage to her room. Ms. Sinclair, will you join me for breakfast?" He stood up from the very exclusive, black leather sofa. Dressed in expensive black jeans, that looked like they had been tailored to his body, and sporting a tight, black T-shirt with buttons down the front leaving it open almost to his waist, Toni could easily see why Caulder had had so many conquests. He gave the desired impression to women.

Today Toni wore a thin, white linen pant-suit and black high heels. With her hair in a plait and sporting spectacles, she still looked severe. The heels were deceiving, and gave her the extra three inches in height, bringing her up to the five-feet-five inches she wanted to be.

"Thank you, Mr. Caulder. I've already eaten, but I'll have a cup of coffee."

He reached for her arm, and touched her lightly, leading her into the more than spacious dining room. At just over six feet he was still tall, compared to her. "Ms. Sinclair," he paused, "if we are going to be in each other's company for a month, we should start using first names. After all, we both know each other's backgrounds… more or less," Daniel said condescendingly.

Toni looked down at the place settings, and there sat a file marked with her name. He'd done his homework, and she smiled to herself. At least her file was quick reading. She turned to face him and paused just a moment. "Mr. Caulder, I see you had some bedtime reading. I hope it wasn't too boring for you."

He tilted his head just slightly, and a smile shadowed itself across his face. "On the contrary, I learned what a good reporter you are.

You live on your own, drive a Mercedes, love all plants and kids, don't date much, and you're still a virgin at twenty-four..."

Toni glared at him. "What the hell has that got to do with my job here? And how did you find out?" She was furious, her face flushed and her voice raised an octave.

"Like you, I have my sources," and he pulled the cushioned chair out for her to sit down, inclining his head at the seat.

She did as she was requested, and Daniel left his hands on the back of the chair.

He continued. "It has nothing to do with your job, nothing at all. Just a change to have one in this house... and it will make life more interesting."

Immediately, she rose up from her chair, turned and confronted him, her breasts almost touching him. "Mr. Caulder! I have no intention of sleeping with you or being any kind of challenge to you. You, sir, are arrogant and conceited... in fact you're exactly what your dossier said you were and then some. You may have a personal reputation, but you don't have to prove that to me. I'm only interested in the wealth you attained from your profession..." She was flustered. "No, I mean... in what you do for a living. So take me off your female hit-list. I intend to stay a virgin until I find the right man to change that status, and for some reason I don't foresee it being you!" She tried to move from the table, but he had her trapped between it and the chair.

He pinned her there, not moving an inch. Leaning down into her face, he almost yelled at her, his breath crisp and clear on her face, and his long hair dropping forward. "Then, Miss Sinclair, why the hell are you here? You could have turned down this job. I'm sure your uncle gave you that option last night. But you see a way to make a name for yourself through being here." Caulder was angry and it showed. "So, let's get one thing straight right now. What I tell you to do while you're with me... you'll do it! Regardless! Do you understand? It may save your life." He paused and turned slightly away from Toni but, as an afterthought, turned back and continued, "And don't unpack too many things. We're leaving here in three days."

"Leaving? Where are we going?" She looked astounded, her face turning a shade of red.

He leaned towards her and looked into her face, his eyes searching hers. "Do you really think I'm going to tell you that? I assume you have a passport with you?"

She nodded in the affirmative.

"So, tell your uncle you won't be calling him after a couple more days!" And he turned to his chair at the table, and started to sit down.

Toni stared at him. "How did you know that? What makes you think I would be calling my uncle? I'm not a child!"

"Then stop acting like one!" Caulder pushed his long hair from his eyes and glanced at her body. "Oh, by the way, black suits you," and he sat down in the hard back chair.

Toni stopped in her tracks. The only black things she wore were her shoes... and her underwear. Speechless, she turned away from him and headed for the door. She opened it, and, in her path, stood Ben, the very dark-haired, bronzed muscle.

"Let her by," Caulder called to his man almost condescendingly. "And, Toni, remember what I said. Everything I tell you! Ben will show you to your room." He had dismissed her once again, without Toni even realizing the fact, and proceeded to pour a cup of coffee for himself.

One flight of stairs and Ben stopped at a door almost at the top of the stairs. Opening the door, he showed her into a spacious room. "This is yours while you are here. If you need anything there's a phone by your bed. Just dial two for my line. Bathroom is through that door," and he pointed to the left of the bed. "Everything you need is in this room. Mr. Caulder will expect you down at ten sharp." And Ben left her alone.

Toni sat down on the side of the palatial bed which seemed to be covered by a pretty patchwork comforter that hung to the plush, grey carpet and fused itself in color. The bed was big enough to sleep five, which didn't even seem to faze Toni. This was all too much wealth for one man to have acquired by honest means. She leaned back on the giant, fluffy pillows. Was she out of her depth? Doubt was now creeping in fast.

Toni looked at her wrist watch. Nine a.m. She had one hour to kill before she was due back with Caulder. She glanced around, viewing red and pink flock wallpaper, red velvet curtains, and a small redwood table, complete with a welcome fruit basket sitting in the middle. A couple of bottles of spring water stood next to them, and a seemingly full ice bucket alongside of them. These windows were closed, causing the room to be warm, and Toni fell asleep.

She was rudely awakened by the phone on her bedside table leaping into action. In a blur of panic, she grabbed the line.

"Toni speaking…"

"Ms. Sinclair… Mr. Caulder said ten o'clock, and it is ten fifteen. He'll be at the pool." Ben hung up the line which made a distinct click as he did.

"Oh, my god!" she exclaimed. "That's a great start." She removed her suit and left it on the bed. Grabbing T-shirt and tight, black shorts from her now open luggage, she pulled them on and rushed from the room going back through the house pretty much the way she had come into the place.

She found Caulder. Not at the pool… but in the pool. He was gliding through the water with great ease. She watched him as his athletic prowess shone through. He took in air and kept on swimming, his tan, muscular body glistening in the water as he continued swimming, fully aware she was watching him.

Toni sat down in one of the pool chairs. She knew he would do what he wanted, and would come out when he was ready, and not before. She lay back in the chair and looked down at her body. It was so pale… so pale, it was embarrassing. Perhaps three days in the sun would help her. She thought not! Three weeks, maybe.

Her sunlight was blocked as a shadow cast itself across her. Toni looked up and Caulder stood in front of her, water dripping from his body, a body she had a job not to look at with some admiration, and directed her eyes away from the skin-tight swimming trunks he wore.

"Did Ben tell you ten a.m., Ms. Sinclair?" His annoyance showed very clearly.

"He did, and I'm sorry. I was awake early today and…" She was not allowed to finish.

"Then, please be punctual in the future. Can you swim?" He questioned her like a commandant.

Now she was on the defensive. "I swim. Maybe not as well as you, but I swim! Why?"

"Because where we are going you're going to need that accomplishment."

"And where might that be?" She pushed him.

"I'll tell you on the plane and not before. Now... show me!"

"I'm not dressed for swimming," Toni retorted.

"You think that clothes would stop you in the real world? Jump in the pool and show me. Do it!" Caulder was losing patience with her and was asserting his authority. "If you don't, I'll throw you in the damn pool!" He bent down and leaned towards her, a gesture that let Toni know he was serious.

She raised her hands. "Okay, I'll go," and jumped up from the pool chair which made a clanging noise as it fell backwards.

Diving in the deep end of the Olympic-sized pool, her clothes impeded her flow. Almost straight away after only a couple of lengths she was struggling, and she gave in, swimming to the side. She clung to the pool wall, pushing her long hair out of her view. Immediately he appeared in front of her standing tall on the side of the concrete patio surrounding the pool.

"I said swim, damn it, not stop! You stop when I tell you and not before." He dived in beside her and surfaced. "Now, start again. Keep up with me."

Toni thought he would never quit. Six, seven, eight lengths... she felt like she was about to explode. Keeping pace with him was too hard for her, and Daniel knew she was struggling. As she turned in the eight feet of water, she could not maintain the stamina she needed. Exhausted, she stopped swimming. Lack of a good solid breakfast and fatigue overcame her and she sank to the bottom of the pool, bubbles streaming up through the water. She was cold, as well as tired.

Caulder left her there until he thought she had had enough, but not wanting her to drown, swam down and under her legs, taking hold of her by the waist. Pulling a struggling young woman to the surface, he held her head above the water. As Toni gasped for air, her hair fell across her face and any eye shadow that was left smeared from her eyes. Caulder swam to the side, still keeping a tight hold on her waist, and pulling her with him. He removed the hair from Toni's face while she twisted in his grasp, still struggling for air.

"I have you!" he yelled. "For god's sake stop fighting me, you're not going to drown. In a real situation you'd pull us both under."

She relaxed in his arms while tears streamed down her face… tears of anger. "Why did you do that? You know I cannot compete with you!" she screamed at him.

He hid his amusement very well. "You're not trying to compete… just to survive. And you'll have to do better than that," and he put his hands round her backside and pushed her over the side onto the concrete. He was strong… very strong. Pulling himself out of the water, he sat down beside her.

She was still semi-choking, while trying to maintain some sort of dignity.

He looked at her, grabbed the back of her hair and wrung excess water out with his hands. "We have three days to get you into some sort of shape. Three days, Toni. You asked for this assignment… where I go, you go… and where we are going is very different from anywhere you have ever been before. Three days, young lady, and you will be a lot stronger and tougher than when you arrived here. And in a month's time, even your uncle won't know you. This, Miss Sinclair, is my promise to you. You will also have been privileged to see a side of my life that no one has survived to talk about. Out there," and Caulder pointed at the pool, "you showed me you had guts. I assumed you would stop after a couple of laps and you didn't, you kept going and didn't quit like most women would. And this morning at breakfast, whether you knew it or not, you also gained my respect. Now all you have to do is prove what your dossier tells me. Go get changed into some sweats and meet me in the gym at noon. Eat first, though. Ben will fix you some food. We don't want you fainting."

She stood up and turned to leave him.

"Toni," he called to her.

She looked back at him, water dripping from her now tight- fitting clothes that showed exactly how slim she was.

"We may make a woman out of you yet," he said with a wry smile and dived back into the pool with the grace of a great white whale.

The three days were to be an eternity for Toni. Caulder pushed her hard. The first day was rounded off with climbing ropes in the gym, a day in which Caulder quickly dispensed with her fear of heights. When she neared the ceiling, he began swaying the rope backwards and forwards. She screamed... loud. When she didn't scream anymore, he let her down. His reward to her was dinner and an early night, similar, she thought, to a master with his new puppy.

In her room, Toni fell into the steaming, hot bath trying to ease her exhaustion. Her arms and legs were covered in bruises, and her back ached without remorse. The inside of her hands were raw and she didn't know whether to laugh or cry. Lounging in the hot water, Toni was aware of her cell phone ringing. She reached out of the bathtub and retrieved it from the top of the small white table it lay on.

"Toni Sinclair."

"Where the hell have you been? I've waited for your call." Her uncle's tone was one of anger.

"Sorry. I just got back in to my room. Daniel has been putting me through some sort of training. We're leaving in two more days, and I have to be ready."

"Ready for what?" asked her uncle. In the back of his mind he was considering the fact that it was already 'Daniel.'

"I don't know what." She continued. "He won't tell me... not until we are on the plane." She lounged back in the water; cell in hand, while sweet smelling bubbles foamed around her body.

"On the plane? Get out of this now, Toni. You don't know where this is going!"

"No way! I want to be in on this one. He said it will make a woman of me, and, because I have guts, he will give me the story," she exclaimed.

"You're woman enough. Get out, Toni, before it's too late! Think what you have just said. You called him *Daniel*, and you're leaving with him in two days? You've only been there a day. You don't know this man." He yelled down the phone.

"Somehow, I don't think…" and her voice was drowned out by a sudden and increasing noise.

"Toni, can you still hear me? What's that noise?" Sinclair demanded.

"Hold on…"

Stepping out of the bath, she pulled a large, white fluffy towel around her and rushed to the bedroom window. She watched as a helicopter landed in the floodlit gardens. She saw Caulder walk to the open door of the chopper and lift a young boy down onto the ground. In the glaring lights she could see a child of nine or ten years of age, seemingly darker skinned, with long black hair. The two bowed to each other. Caulder took the child by the arm and turned back towards the house, while the chopper departed into the night air, leaving Toni totally mesmerized.

"You still there?" Her voice was almost a whisper, fearing that she could be overheard in her own room.

"What the hell is going on? Was that a chopper I heard?" Sinclair realized he was whispering back to her.

"Sure was. Something is going on out there. See what you can dig up on a small boy," and she gave Bryan a description of the child, as she glanced back through the window.

"Toni, stay in your room tonight. I know you! Don't go snooping around down there. I'll see what I can find out and call you tomorrow night. Just be careful. We don't know whether Caulder is mercenary or terrorist. Not that there's much difference in my book. What we do know, is that he's a dangerous man," and he hung up the line.

Toni considered her uncle's words. Maybe he was right. So much had happened in one day.

Seven a.m. and her alarm brought a swift reality to the new day. She showered, dressed, and was downstairs by seven-thirty. She arrived at the breakfast table, only to find Ben and the servants in the room. Ben stood up to greet her.

"Miss Sinclair, Mr. Caulder sends his apologies. He has some business to attend to. I will be your trainer for the day. He asks that when we have finished, you be ready for dinner by eight p.m. You will find your dress hanging in your closet. He also asks that you wear your hair in a feminine fashion, and please do not wear your glasses. But I see you're not wearing them today." Ben offered her a seat.

Toni found she was disappointed at Caulder not being there and tried to hide the fact from Ben. "I only wear glasses for reading and paperwork." She changed the subject. "So, what's first?" She sat down in the seat offered to her.

"First, you eat," inclining his head towards the food. "Then at nine we will go for a five-mile run. After lunch, we go to the gym for the rest of the day. We'll finish work at six."

He sounded more like a drill instructor than a bodyguard. Toni figured this was to be the day from hell with this thirty-year-old man.

"Now eat! Eggs, fruit, oatmeal… drink the orange juice. It's good for you! We need to build you up a little. Where we are going you need all the stamina you can get!" and Ben proceeded to make her a plate of food that would feed an army, and he also made sure she ate every bit.

She struggled to get the food down not being used to eating this much. She glanced up at Ben who was watching her every move, and now she felt like a bug under a microscope. When they left the table, Ben ushered her outside. He also made sure she wore the right running shoes, and was totally kitted out for the day.

Ben turned out to be twice the taskmaster that his boss was, making her keep a much better pace than Daniel had. While running in the grounds, Toni noticed security that was not there yesterday. It reminded her of a prison camp, and as she went to mention it to Ben, she thought better of it. She glanced sideward at him once or twice and thought he reminded her of someone she knew, but she couldn't place the resemblance. One hour turned into two and Toni was tired and it showed. She was having difficulty in keeping up with Ben, and more than weary, she could not make it happen. They ventured outside the grounds but not far enough away that the house and grounds could not be seen, and more to the point the security could still see them.

When finally lunch time arrived it was not much more than cheese and grapes. If it wasn't hard enough before lunch it became so now. Toni and Ben returned to the gym of yesterday to climb more ropes and lift weights.

"Not again! I did this yesterday!" Toni sat down on the hard wooden floor, he legs splayed out in front of her. She rubbed the back of her legs. They ached... badly.

"Are you going to sit there all day, or what? We have to finish this training this afternoon," said Ben looking at his sports watch and back to Toni, "and you have to be ready for dinner tonight."

She heaved herself up from the floor, and let out a sigh. Ben noticed.

"What was that for? You asked for this, Toni. If you want to quit, you better quit now, before you get in too deep. Well?" Ben stood with his hands on his hips quite resembling a drill sergeant.

"I don't quit. Not ever!" she retorted, pouting her lips at him.

"Then get your butt up the ropes there and show me what you are made of!"

She did it. It hurt, but she made it up there. She also knew he was watching her closely and that he would report this back to his boss. Wasn't a smart move letting him see the weak side of her.

At last it was six o'clock, and she climbed the stairs to her room with a glow on her cheeks and a body that ached.

When she finally reached her room, all she wanted to do was take a bath and lie on the bed. She flopped down on the comforter and lay there, starring at the ceiling watching the ceiling fan whir round and round, reminding her of the chopper of last night. What the hell was she doing trying to compete with these guys? She pulled her hands in front of her face. They were raw, and she was overwhelmingly tired. And she cried, big silent tears, that ran down her face and onto the pillows. She wanted to pack her bag and leave right then, flee the magic kingdom of Daniel Caulder and she could not, as defeat was not something her uncle would not tolerate, and neither would she.

She dried her tears, glanced at her watch and decided she needed to move... and now. She slid off the bed, moved to the closet and opened the door. It creaked just a tad. Toni held her breath as she looked at the dress hanging there. A long, black gown with low neckline and capped sleeves, and sporting a designer tag that Toni recognized, and one she could never afford.

Laying the dress on the bed, Toni headed for the bathroom. Running the water into the giant cream tub, Toni wondered what was the truth behind all the stories she had heard and who was the boy she had seen. Stepping into the water, she leaned back against the rim of the tub. She had a feeling that tonight she may find out more than she really wanted to know at this point. Bubbles foamed around her and she closed her eyes, hoping the aching would stop long enough for her to enjoy the evening.

It was getting dark as Toni sat in front the oak dresser and applied way more make-up than usual. Using half a bottle of perfume on her neck and arms, she thought maybe that was a little too much. She pulled her hair up on her head, looked at herself, and then considered just leaving it hanging down. Proud of her long hair, which was now cascading down her back, she pushed it behind her ears. Long, sparkling earrings hung to her shoulder and now all she needed to complete the picture was the dress itself. Toni slid into it. It fit to perfection. Toni laughed. "Man has good taste, and knows how to please women," and Toni laughed at her own joke.

Standing in front of the full-length mirror, Toni looked at this new woman. "Not bad, even if I do say so myself. Hope the great white hunter approves." She smoothed any wrinkles from the dress, tided her hair, and left the room at seven forty-five.

Descending the stairs, she walked slowly along the brightly lit corridor towards the sound of voices. Pictures adorned the walls, and seemingly ancient tapestries hung above the doors. Toni was marveling at these when, from the shadows, Ben stepped out in front of her. He was wearing a black dinner suit and bow tie. Was this the same Ben from the gym? She hadn't realized just how good looking he was till then. He was the muscle, and Caulder's right hand man. He was Ben, the gym instructor, Ben, the bodyguard and, now, Ben, the tuxedo.

"Miss Sinclair," and he offered her his arm, as he afforded her an admiring glance. He opened the door and escorted her into the room filled with people, causing it to look like a banquet of thousands. Peering into the room, Toni could see the table was aglow with candles and exquisite dinnerware. From the ceiling hung the chandelier glistening with blazing crystal lights and it lit up the room like Christmas.

Her instructor of the day stood watching her. Miss Sinclair was stunning, completely transformed from the sweaty girl of the gym class. He noted the make-up she wore and the way the dress hung on her body, but she was still a little too pale for his liking. The dress only enhanced that fact, but gave her a rare beauty. She reminded him of a rose waiting for the honey bee to deflower her, and that prompted him to look across at his boss. He'd been Caulder's number 2 for almost ten years now, and he knew his boss well. He turned his attentions back to the lady, one who stood in awe of her surroundings.

"Miss Sinclair, you're a very pretty woman, very innocent and demure. I, for one, would like you to stay that way as long as possible." He glanced towards Caulder who was busy talking to a group of gentleman in the nearby corner.

Toni stared at Ben. "Thank you for your comments," and she followed his gaze to Daniel. "But I assure you I do not intend to give your boss any particular pleasure... if that's what's on your mind!" She turned towards Ben, with Caulder now behind her.

"It's not just him..." and he stopped speaking very abruptly.

Toni blushed. She knew what Ben was saying, making her green eyes twinkle at the compliment.

"Did Ben say something to offend you, Toni?" A stern voice behind them interrupted the conversation.

"On the contrary, Ben was very flattering," Toni was quick to defend as she turned in the direction of the now familiar voice.

"Indeed!" Caulder looked directly at her. "Not hard to see why." He put his hand out to her.

Ben immediately let go of her arm, like he had been electric-shocked into doing so.

Caulder took her hand, and as he moved closer to her, the smell of her perfume filled his nostrils. "You look exactly as I imagined you would in that dress. When you get back to your room, you'll find a few more things for the trip." He studied her figure and the shape in the dress she wore, looking her up and down. "All you need now is a little sun on your body," and his other hand very gently touched her arm.

Toni never flinched when his skin touched hers. She looked up into his eyes, eyes that gave nothing away. She thought how accomplished this man was and her stare lasted longer than she intended it to.

The black tux he wore fit him like a glove, and Toni found herself more attracted to him than ever. His hair hung over his collar, and his muscles bristled through the tight shirt.

"Let me introduce you to some of the guests, especially the one that will interest you the most." Daniel paused. "Before I forget, our trip has been brought forward a few hours. We leave tomorrow at noon. Ben will tell you what you need to take."

Ben nodded in agreement. Daniel Caulder continued speaking, and watched Toni's face for a reaction as he said the next sentence.

"There will be five of us on the flight to start with, counting you and me, and then Ben, Sam, and the Prince. You'll be the only woman, Toni, and you'll be traveling as my fiancée."

Now she flinched! Composure was lost. "I'll be what?!" she stammered, looking at him like he was insane.

"My fiancée." He wasn't sure which statement she meant, so he opted for the fiancée. "Surely even you can manage that? Don't worry; you'll be safe with me. You have my word, but I want you where I can keep my eye on you at all times. It's for your own good." He was matter of fact and all business, even though inside of him he found her reaction distinctly funny.

Toni had no choice but to believe him.

Daniel carefully slipped his arm further around her shoulders. "And now let me introduce you to my son." Without any hesitation, he escorted her across the room, one brimming with wealth and an effervescent quality of power.

If Caulder was trying to impress and surprise her, he had succeeded… and then some.

Toni began to think she was losing it, and felt like she was propelled along by some magic hand and a destiny she had no control over.

"Toni, this is my son… he is the Crown Prince of Yaoundé. You can call him Dana."

Chapter 2

Toni was speechless. There had been no mention of any son, let alone a Crown Prince.

The boy looked at her with the same deep, brown eyes and the angular nose that his father had. Only the skin color was different. The child was very dark, almost black.

"I see you are surprised. Not in my dossier is it? And that's how it's going to stay. Right?" Caulder was in complete control of the situation.

"Ah, right. Whatever you say." She was shocked and could not collect her thoughts together.

"Dana, this is Toni Sinclair. She will be accompanying us on the trip back to your country," explained his father.

Dana looked at her. Even at his age he could appreciate a beautiful woman. "Toni, it is my greatest pleasure to meet you. My father tells me what a good reporter you are, and that you will be a fair judge of me," and this ten-year-old put his hand out to her, with his English quite impeccable.

Toni considered curtseying to him. Instead, she returned the boy's handshake. "I'm privileged to meet you, Your Highness." Her mind was racing. She thought of the story in last week's paper. No one knew what happened to the boy when the government of Yaoundé was overthrown, and the new army had taken control. Now Toni knew where the new leader and the boy were. They stood in front of her. He and his father. "I hope I will meet your expectations." She was struggling, wallowing in a sudden lack of knowledge.

Caulder saw it and stepped in to save her any embarrassment. "I am sure that you will, Miss Sinclair... I'm sure you will. And now, Dana will introduce you to some of the guests. And, Miss Sinclair, you *can* call him Dana."

Toni looked at Caulder. Fifty he may have been, but tonight, dressed in a black tuxedo, he could have passed for forty. He was a perfect specimen of manhood, and his child only enhanced the virility of the man. As Caulder walked away from them, Dana watched Toni with some amusement.

"My father is very attractive to you, Miss Sinclair?" He said it as a child who had seen it all before.

"Yes..." and she paused reflecting that he was indeed. "No... He is a very professional man, and you, well, you were a total surprise!" That was the truth! She regained some of her composure.

"I'm sure I was. Now, would you like to meet some of the people that support my cause? They can all be trusted as I'm sure you can." Those eyes looked at her. The Caulder eyes.

She could not resist them, for the child had immediately captured her heart. And that was Caulder's plan.

Toni fitted in well. Her uncle had brought her up to know the rights and wrongs at a dinner party. She could converse with the best... and on their level. She knew how to use the appropriate cutlery for the right courses, which wines to drink and how much, and she was well versed in current politics and polite conversation.

Caulder observed her from his seat across the table from her. He sat with his hand propping up his chin, and his elbow resting on the table, while she sat by his son, with whom she was becoming well acquainted. That was the plan. Toni wasn't just going as his fiancée, but as Dana's companion. He'd had someone in mind for the job until Toni had arrived for the interview. He knew she wanted the story badly enough to do almost anything. He wondered just how far she would go for that reason, and the thought amused him. Leaning back in the chair, he pulled out a pack of his favorite cigarettes. Immediately a servant was at his side with a light. When lit, he puffed hard on the weed, and the rings drifted into the air, joining the ever growing haze of smoke.

Ben saw Daniel watching her. He never would, or could, compete with his boss. But this time, for some reason, he wanted to. To try for her affections would be his demise, unless for some reason Caulder did not show an interest in the girl, and judging by the way he was watching her that would not be the case. Yet Caulder had given his word, and one could die by Caulder's word.

Toni was finding dinner interesting. Dana was more than good company. It was like conversing with someone her own age. He discussed the politics of his country, and spoke of his mother. According to Dana, Caulder had met her eleven years ago while on a mission. She was the king's youngest wife, and Caulder had found her more than attractive, the pair becoming lovers. When the king was assassinated, as Dana was born, Caulder assumed responsibility for the baby, a child that was born with more than just Caulder's features. The young princess had given birth to their child and had tried to hold onto life, as well.

The son now sat before Toni. His mother's story only brought tears to Toni's eyes. He had no mother… just like herself. Dana realized what he had said.

"Toni, you are like me? You have only one person to look after you?" the child asked, his eyes piercing hers.

"I am exactly like you. My uncle and your father are nearly the same age. Dana, I hope that you and I will become good friends on this trip. If ever you need someone to turn to… well, I…"

He put his young hand on hers. "I know what you mean. Toni… I may only be ten, but my life is as an adult… I am here for companionship to you, also." He turned his attentions across the table to Daniel. "Father, may I talk to you for a moment?"

Dana stood up and moved away from the table, as did Caulder. He was the father, but Dana was the Prince. They talked for some minutes while Toni watched with interest. Caulder towered over the child, being almost a foot and a half between the two sets of eyes, yet they held each other in a hypnotic stare.

Dana returned to the table and a servant held the chair out for him to sit down. "That is partly why he picked you, because of your background. I shall retire now, so goodnight, Toni. I will see you at noon tomorrow." He leaned forward and kissed her on both sides of her face. One was the mark of friendship the other was the kiss of a little boy.

Toni was overcome by the moment. If it were all an act to gain her trust, it was a good one. They had just made sure she would not say a word about the omission in the dossier…not to anyone. Toni played with the linen napkins, twisting them and turning them in her fingers as if she was unraveling some sort of knot. She was immediately aware of Caulder sitting down beside her.

"I need to talk to you in private," he announced.

She started to rise from her chair.

He laid his hand on her shoulder to stop her rising. "Not here. Come to my suite at midnight. Ben will show you the way." He thought for a moment. "No, perhaps that is not a good idea. I will come to your room, and then no one will be suspicious."

"And what's that supposed to mean?" she inquired. "Do you often visit that room?" She looked him in the face as she spoke.

"Frequently," and he rose from the table and left her with her thoughts, returning to his own seating.

Toni stayed there, not quite knowing where this was going, but she had to admit that she was enjoying the company of some of the people there. At eleven-thirty she excused herself from the palatial dining room. Caulder noted her departure with a sideward glance. The party had decreased in numbers and the staff of the household went about their professional duties. Toni needed some air. She walked through the long hallway and went towards the main door, where an unfamiliar man stepped in front of her.

"Miss Sinclair, you cannot go outside," an unfamiliar voice boomed at her.

"Why not? And who are you?" Toni was alarmed by this dreadlock-sporting gentleman.

Tall, black as coal, and built like a rock, Sam stopped her in her tracks. Dressed in dark grey clothes, a holster and gun hung about him, which only increased the ominous manner he conveyed.

"My name is Sam, and I did not mean to frighten you. I am number 3 in the household. Mr. Caulder does not want you outside at night, not on your own, anyway. If you wish, I can get Ben to take you out by the pool."

Now she knew who all five traveling companions were. "No, don't do that. I'll just go to my room." She glanced at the clock on the wall. It was twenty to twelve. She smiled at him and turned on her heel.

Toni had no idea how she got back up the stairs and to her bedroom. Her uncle was right in saying she should have left. Now… it was too late. She turned the handle on the door and entered the room, reaching for her cell phone as soon as she shut the door. Toni dialed Bryan's number.

"Bryan Sinclair."

"It's Toni. I think that you were…" she whispered.

As if on cue, the door of her room opened, and Daniel Caulder stood in the archway. Toni looked at him in the light. If she betrayed him now, she was also betraying a ten-year-old boy. Caulder walked towards her and stood opposite her, never even attempting to take the phone from her.

She paused, and looked up into his face. Smelling his expensive cologne, she could feel the intensity of the situation.

"Toni, are you there?" Sinclair yelled.

"I'm here. You were right when… you sent me on this assignment. Maybe a woman can seduce him into telling the truth." She paused and stood defiant. "A woman will get farther than a man. And about the boy I asked you to investigate, he belongs to one of the servants here. No need to dig anything up on him, not that there is anything to find." She paused. "I'm leaving tomorrow with the rest of the team. There is another woman for company, so I'm sure I'll be fine. Perhaps we were wrong about Mr. Caulder. He's really not so bad." The whole time she kept her eyes focused on Caulder. She swore she could see him smile. "Okay, so if there's any news I'll call you. Otherwise, I'll see you on my return."

"Toni," asked Bryan, "are you alone?"

Her reply was too quick. "Of course! Whom do you think would be in my room? You know me better than that. You take care. And water my plants for me." She disconnected the call, setting the phone down. Toni had done a thing she had never done before… she'd lied. She turned away facing the windows.

Caulder breathed a silent sigh and took a step towards her. "Why did you do that?" His tone was gentle, almost unbelieving.

There was no reply.

"Toni, I asked you a question. Why didn't you give me away?" he asked, a little more urgently.

"It was Dana I did not give away. Not you. My opinion of you has not changed, Mr. Caulder."

"Then turn around and tell me that!" He put his hand on her shoulder.

She shut her eyes, and took a deep breath. Focusing, she turned towards him.

"It was for your son." The emphasis was on 'your son'. "I cannot betray such a beautiful child. I would have no compunction in betraying you, or the society you live in." She never flinched in her commitment.

His eyes narrowed as he spoke. "You're lying, Toni, and not very well. But we'll leave it at that… for now. You believe what you want, as long as it saves my son's life. I watched you with Dana. You will be good for him. He is only used to being around men, and now he will have some female companionship."

"You speak as if I'll always be with him. It's only for a month, remember? Or do you have some other scheme that I don't know about?" She flushed with anger.

"No, no other scheme. Would you like there to be?" Daniel was amazingly calm.

"No, Mr. Caulder? Dana is your real son, correct?" She knew she was treading on thin ice.

"You know the answer to that. But to allay your suspicions… yes, he is. And, before you ask, I did not have anything to do with the king's death." He was beginning to tire of the interrogation. "So, Miss Sinclair, I bid you goodnight." His hand still rested on her shoulder.

"I thought you wanted to ask me about something." Her brain kicked into gear, and she shook very slightly under his touch. "But you already know the answer, don't you?"

"Yes, I do." He bent down as if to kiss her on the cheek.

Toni turned quite accidentally and his lips caught her on the mouth instead. It was a shock for them both, one that was not expected.

It didn't appear to faze Caulder, a man who was quite accustomed to kissing women. "Tomorrow at noon, Miss Sinclair," and he left the room and, while closing the door behind him, he opened a new chapter of his life.

Toni touched her mouth with her fingers and tears ran down her face. Her uncle's words echoed in her ear. 'Get out now, Toni.'

Now... was too late.

Noon came quickly. Two choppers landed on the lawn, silver, hovering birds in a flawless, blue sky. They came to pick them up, and fly the party to a private landing strip way out of Los Angeles... exact final destination unknown. Africa was the only apparent place on the horizon. Toni, the boy, and Ben flew in one chopper, while Caulder, Sam and the luggage in the other. Toni clutched her familiar back pack to her like some kind of security blanket. Daniel had hardly spoken to her that morning, being constantly preoccupied with the arrangements.

Toni was a little uneasy at being in the helicopter, and even though a fairly large craft, she still felt like a sardine in a can. Used to only flying on passenger planes, this was a new experience and one she was not readily enjoying, her hands shaking as she clutched her belongings.

Dana was fully aware of his companion's nervousness. "It's only a short trip by chopper to the airport. There we board a 737, which is one of father's private jets. From there we go to Brazil, via Panama, where we pick up more people... you would call them 'mercenaries.'" He smiled quite proud of himself for giving such a full description.

Toni blinked, wondering if she had heard him right.

"Are you surprised, Toni? You wondered which of the two my father was... mercenary or terrorist... now you know. But he fights for a good cause. I would call him a missionary," stated the young man with some finality. "I have to take leadership of my country and

I can only do that with help. Papa's army is in control right now, but an absent leader is no good to anyone."

Was this boy really ten years of age? Toni wondered how he knew so much, but then he had Caulder for a father. What Toni was really sure of was that she was flying into a lot of danger. She looked straight at Ben, whom she knew had been watching her.

"Don't worry, Toni! Mr. Caulder knows what he's doing. You're safe. He wouldn't risk taking a reporter with him and getting them killed. Not good for business… or for his reputation. Just sit tight. The longer plane ride will be much better." Ben leaned back and closed his eyes, pulled his safari hat down, and shut out the look that Toni was giving him.

She was not totally reassured by his words. As she peered out over downtown Los Angeles, she spotted the Times building below her. If only her uncle knew what she was about to do. Perhaps it was better he didn't.

They landed at an airport that she had never seen before, on a side-area that Toni had never even heard of. Caulder's jet stood ready, its bodywork shimmering in the noonday sun, adorned with black and gold paintwork. The group disembarked from the chopper, and Toni was ushered across the smoldering tarmac and onto the plane. She took a seat by the window… not just one, but three seats. Toni could stretch out across the luxurious cushions and sleep if she so wanted. This was the way to travel in an up market and refurbished jet, a far cry from the economy class she was used to flying.

It was from here she saw Caulder. He and Sam were supervising the loading of food supplies, followed by the luggage. Toni was told to bring her backpack filled with shorts, T-shirts, some long cotton pants and two long-sleeved shirts. No pens and papers, no glasses, nothing bulky or heavy: no unusable objects. In her wind-breaker jacket she had pushed a small tape recorder and cassettes. Her camera hung round her neck. Ben had made sure she wore hiking boots, and extra socks peeped out from the over-stuffed bag. Underwear was kept at a minimum, and one swimsuit was allowed. In her jacket she carried her passport. .. and a box of tampons. From inside the box, Toni removed one tampon and had hidden a tube of mascara in the empty space. She had been told no make-up, a comb, yes, and bands for her hair. Toni pushed the tampon box deeper into the pocket of the jacket, and suddenly found her thoughts interrupted.

"I'll sit in front of you," Dana offered, "then we can talk or we can sleep," and the boy sat down. He sat cross-legged in the plush seating and peered through the window at the events outside.

"Dana, what's in the boxes?" Toni asked, as if she couldn't guess.

"Just medical supplies for my people. We'll negotiate for the guns in Panama, and pick them up in Brazil."

Toni didn't know whether to laugh or cry. Mercenaries and guns... both in Brazil! And then there were the medical supplies, obviously some kind of cover for carrying cash.

Suddenly, Caulder reached his hand over the seat and onto her shoulder, startling her as he did. "You okay? Ben will bring you anything you need. My pilot tells me the weather is good, so it should be a fairly smooth flight. It should only take a few hours to get to Panama. We'll stop for a short time while I meet with someone. You will not leave the plane, nor will my son. Now, try to get some rest."

She looked up at him. He was dressed all in black, this fifty- year-old mercenary, and a man twenty-six years older than her. But still she found him attractive. His grip was strong, and she could feel the power in his arm the same as she had the other day in the pool. As he spoke, she felt the grip tighten.

"I'll be at the front end of the plane if you need to talk to me. Dana, look after Toni for me," and he handed her a blanket. "Curl up and keep warm. Make the most of the sleep you get on these flights," and he left her.

Toni watched Caulder walk away down the plane.

"You rate highly with my father. Normally, he does not travel alone," and Dana curled up into a ball.

Toni was well aware what Dana meant. She pulled the blanket around her, covering her bare legs. She'd worn shorts with her jacket, and the air conditioning was chilly. With the plane high in the air she tried to keep her eyes open, and make sense of the events of the afternoon. Slowly, with the roar of engines in her ears, her eyelids closed and she fell asleep.

Not long after Caulder stopped at his son's seats. Dana was sleeping. He covered the little boy with a fluffy blue blanket and watched him awhile. There lay a future king.

Caulder turned his gaze to the girl. Her blanket had slipped down from her body, and he pulled it back up and around her shoulders, making sure she was warm. She stirred in her sleep and moved her head. Her dark eyelashes fluttered; she did not wake, but Dana did. He watched his father, and witnessed tenderness towards the woman that he had not seen his father display before, and it intrigued him.

Ben saw it, too. He sat a couple of rows back and across the aisle, studying maps. Caulder was not aware Ben was watching him, and he stepped back into the aisle while Ben lowered his head. His boss sat down beside him.

"Should be in Panama within the hour. *Mr.* Sung will be waiting on the runway with his usual henchmen. Keep the girl and my son well away from the doors while Sam and I meet Sung. You stay by the door… just in case I need you."

"Yes, sir, Mr. Caulder. How many men did you want to take with you?" Ben still fiddled with the maps.

"Six should be enough. We already have an army out there. These guys will take us to Cameroon. Sung promised us guns and men to be picked up in Belem. Guns will go under the medical supplies. We have to keep control of Yaoundé at any price. It's my son's inheritance at stake." He started to rise from the seat.

Ben stopped him, with a slight touch of the hand on his boss's arm. "Mr. Caulder… about the girl… she's so young and vulnerable…" He didn't finish the sentence.

"She is, Ben. And, one way or another, this trip will make a woman out of her." He laughed, cutting his eyes at the younger man. His tone changed. "Ben, do you have some intentions towards her?" He looked him in the face.

"Towards Toni? Should I?" Ben was surprised that Caulder had picked up on it… but then he had the same interest.

"No. But you're very concerned for her." Daniel studied his companion's face. He had figured his number 2 did have eyes for the girl, but he would let things take their own course. Ben was more her age and Caulder was fully aware he was near her uncle's, an uncle he thought he knew all about.

"Concerned, that's all," and Ben changed the subject, looking down at the charts as he spoke. "Been checking the flying times. Not too far. Just to be on the safe side, we'll refuel at both airports, as we'll be carrying extra weight pretty soon."

"Leave all that to you. That's what I pay you for. I'm going to the back of the plane to rest." When Caulder said rest, he meant to think… and should not be disturbed, and he wasn't until they neared the airstrip.

Touching down on the shimmering tarmac of the private landing strip, Caulder could see a limo waiting in the shadows. First from the side and then from the front as the plane taxied to a halt. Dana and Toni were awake, both with their noses pressed against the windows, watching and waiting, while Caulder and Sam left the aircraft.

Pulling into the early evening light, the driver opened the door of the limo. Out stepped a well-dressed Oriental gentleman, flanked by three dark-suited bodyguards. Caulder approached them with a certain caution. Sam hung back just a little, yet, to Toni, it seemed that Caulder could have taken the whole party on himself, and dispensed with them with equal efficiency. She watched as deals were made and money changed hands.

"Sung," whispered Dana, wide eyed. "He controls the men here. Papa does not ask where they come from. The guns will be the Chinese equivalent to an AK-47 Russian Kalashnikov."

"How do you know all this, Dana? You're just a boy! You should be playing with toy pistols… not the real thing!" She was horrified and it showed by the expression on her face.

"I know it, because papa teaches me. And because that is my destiny," he replied without hesitation.

"To get killed?" she retorted looking him n the face.

"No, to be king." He was so matter-of-fact and leaned back in the seat and waited for take off.

Once again, everyone settled back in the plane, and they took to the air. It started to rain, and with turbulence really high, it was a bad take off. Immediately, Toni felt sick. Her head swam and she had this huge over whelming urge to throw up. Dana saw it immediately, and leaned across the seating to attract his father's attention.

"Father, Toni doesn't feel well!" Dana called down the plane, concern in his young voice.

Caulder stepped out into the aisle and moved towards Toni's seat, bending down beside her. "Put your head between your knees," he stated, pushing her head down as he spoke. "When did you last eat?" Caulder asked her.

"Last night," the reply was muffled.

Daniel looked towards his number 2. "Ben, fetch them some food." Daniel turned back to her. "Are you going to make a habit of fainting on me?"

"Only when I try hard," she laughed and promptly threw up into the sick bag. She leaned back in the seat, her face pale and drawn.

"Feel better now? Here, drink this." Caulder offered her a bottle, and held her hair out of the way while she glugged it down.

"What is it?" she asked, and peered inside it.

"Bourbon! Just drink it down," Daniel commanded.

"I don't drink..." she protested.

He cut her off. "Yeah, I know that. On this trip you will be glad to drink! Now, take a swallow." This time he wouldn't take no for an answer.

Ben returned with crackers and fruit and handed them to his boss.

"Eat, young lady. Dana... you also." Caulder sat down next to her making sure she did. "Remember, I'm fully aware of what you don't do. It's what you can do that interests me!" He offered her the bottle again. Then he picked at some of Dana's fruit and swallowed down a handful of grapes.

Toni was embarrassed. "If this is bourbon, it's awful!" she commented and made a face. Her eyebrows wrinkled and her mouth curled at the ends.

"Don't argue with me. Just drink it." As she raised the bottle to her lips, his hand tipped the end of the bourbon until there was a steady stream to her mouth. He only let it go when he thought she'd had enough.

"Are you trying to get me drunk?" Her head began to swim worse than before.

"Not trying... succeeding!" came his reply. "This way, you'll sleep all the way to our destination."

The drink hit her hard. "Mr. Colder, Caulder... I don't want to sleep. I want to see..." She couldn't focus.

Caulder put his arm around her back. "You need to sleep. Here, put this pillow behind your head." He pulled her feet first down the seats. She offered no resistance, instead smiling at him with a rich and full smile, one that made a deep impression in the black hole he called a heart. Daniel leaned over her and wrapped several blankets around her in cocoon fashion.

Leaning closer to his boss, Ben asked, "Not just bourbon in that bottle is it?"

"Nope. Sure isn't. Suggest you don't drink from it unless you want to sleep for about eight hours! I just added a small ingredient to it." Caulder had drugged her. "She'll wake up with a headache, nothing else. No lasting effect."

Daniel waited till he was sure she was under. Pushing the pillow further under her head, he let his hand slide down her face and linger just slightly longer than was necessary. He felt the warmth of her young skin... Ben was right. She was young... and very desirable.

Ben knew by that one single action, he had no chance against his boss where the girl was concerned.

Once this episode was over, the flight to Belem was uneventful. The men discussed plans for most of the time, while Dana watched out for his new friend.

At two a.m., Brazilian time, the jet landed safely at a private airstrip outside the city of Belem. Passports were shown... money greased palms... no questions were asked, and Toni was still out cold.

The night air was far cooler than normal for July. Sam and the pilot stayed on board the plane... ensuring that no one would mess with the cargo with Sam on board. A limo drew up alongside the landing strip, and transported the party to the hotel. Toni was blissfully unaware that Caulder carried her in his arms from the plane to the car, and then again from the car to the hotel.

The establishment they had picked was auspiciously low key, in a seedy neighborhood out back of the town. Caulder had been there many times before, had always paid well, and this time would be no exception, ensuring they had the most private of rooms. Two men and a woman were not unusual. A child in tow, maybe. After signing in under an assumed name, Ben picked up two sets of keys. Dana ran up the stairs ahead of them, while Caulder hesitated and hung back. Still he carried Toni in his arms. She weighed nothing to him, and she was easy to lift up the winding stairs. At the top he stopped, and spoke quietly to Ben.

"I'll put Toni to bed, and then join you in your room. Be just a few minutes. Don't want her to wake and not know where the hell she is. Ben, just dump the backpacks in our room. Dana, go with Ben." He pushed the room door open with his boot, and carried her to what passed for a king-sized bed.

Laying Toni down on her back, he pulled her jacket off and put it on the chair. Unlacing her boots he laid them by her backpack. He covered her with thread-bare blankets, and then went to check his own backpack. He noted the dirty couch on the way, and also the beetles that climbed around the walls. Finding the windows were secure, probably due to the dirt and grime that held them together, he sat down to write her a note.

'If you wake, we're next door… room 115. Daniel.'

He propped it on the bedside table along with a spare key. Daniel locked the door behind him, and moved to the next room, gently knocking on Ben's door.

Ben opened it slowly and let his boss into the room, speaking quietly as he did. "Dana was asleep in minutes. Toni wake up?" he whispered.

"No. We just have a few things to settle, and then we should call it a day… or night." Caulder looked at his watch. Three a.m. already. "Okay, we leave tomorrow at ten. Make sure the new guys know their place, what they're to do and have them report to you. Don't involve me unless necessary… and make damn sure they keep away from the girl, and my son. Do any of them speak English?" As he spoke, Caulder moved to the bedside and stroked his son's hair. Daniel Caulder was very vulnerable where Dana was concerned.

"A couple of them. The others speak a mixture of French and Portuguese," Ben replied.

"Make sure they understand that I'm the boss and the girl's with me, not for their pleasure. Otherwise, complications could set in." Daniel lit up a cigarette and took a long hard drag as smoke wafted into the air.

"Sure, boss." He felt no other comment was necessary.

For half an hour they talked, and then Caulder returned to his room. He was very tired, and without thinking he lay down in the semi-dark on the bed. Then, he remembered Toni. In the half-light he could see her. A strange thought occurred to him. He'd never slept with a woman in a bed without making love to her. This was a first! He stifled a laugh, and slid his gun under the pillow, turning away from her as he did. She was too tempting... even for a man as tired as he was, and he slipped into an uneasy sleep.

Toni woke as light streamed through the ragged curtains. The first thing she saw was a huge beetle crawling on the blankets right towards her face. She screamed! Caulder woke immediately, and pulled his gun from under the pillow, his finger ready on the trigger. She screamed again... at the sight of the gun.

"What the hell are you screaming for? It's a beetle, Toni. The thing is more scared of you than you are of him. I'll shoot it if you like." He was amused by her reactions. "You're going to see lots of those and worse before you see home again. Go get showered! We have to be downstairs for breakfast. We don't want any more of your fainting episodes today." And he replaced the gun on the pillow, and lay back watching her. "You didn't scream like that when you saw the gun at the house," and he laughed.

"What gun? I didn't see any gun... where was the gun?" Toni was horrified and it showed, as she stared blankly at him.

"On the table by the pool, first day you came to the house. Maybe the newspaper fell on it. Now, go do as I tell you and shower!"

She slid off the bed, aware that some of her clothes were missing and not wanting to know how.

"By the way, the bathroom door doesn't close and the bath is full of..." he yelled to her as he sat upright on the bed.

She screamed... again, very loudly.

"Found the rest of the beetle family then!" Daniel rushed into the bathroom after her.

She grabbed a grimy, once-white bath towel and wrapped it around her body.

He dispensed with the intruders by gathering them up and flushing them down the disgusting filthy toilet. "Now, try the shower. I have my back turned."

She climbed into the tub and turned the handle. Ice-cold, mud-colored water poured from the faucet. "It's freezing!" she yelled. "How do I get warm water? It really is freezing! Daniel, help me!"

"Move over!"

"What?" She screamed at him more than just spoke to him.

"You heard me! Move over and turn around." He pulled his shirt off, and clad in just pants, he climbed into the tub. And he saw her body in front of him. "Damn it, girl! I told you to turn around. I don't care what I see... but you might just care what I see of you."

She did as she was told. But he had seen... and now he wanted.

They made it to breakfast at nine. Ben could sense a tension between the two... one that was not there last night. Dana was too busy to notice, and continued to eat the food offered.

Daniel ate ravenously while watching both Dana and Toni. "Both of you," and Caulder pointed to his son and Toni, "eat! The next meal will be in Cameroon."

Toni played with hers; this kind of food alien to her palate, and the food went round and round the plate instead of into her stomach.

Daniel turned to her. "Young lady... didn't you hear me? Eat or I will force it down you! You need some meat on those bones of yours. You are too damned thin!"

She turned crimson and Ben glanced from one to the other.

Caulder never flinched. "Okay, so let's go. You," and he pointed to her, "bring yours with you. Ben, get her some fruit."

And with that they left the breakfast table, and gathered their belongings. He didn't speak to her again until they reached the plane where Sam was standing on the tarmac waiting for them, along with six dark- skinned men. Tough, rough and ready for action, the men stood waiting for their orders. Dressed in dirty combat clothes, they definitely looked like the mercenaries they were. Toni shivered at the prospect of being with these kinds of men.

Caulder noticed her tension and took Toni's hand in his, while whispering in her ear. "This was what I was telling you back at the house. Whatever I tell you from now on…you obey me without question. You understand?"

She understood very clearly. She looked at the way the men were looking at her. Blonde hair and fair skin…and right now, fair game to them. She tightened her small hand around his large sprawling fingers. Toni watched as one or two wiped their mouths on the back of their hands, and she could not miss the look in their eyes.

Caulder could just hear her voice as she whispered to him. "Without question," and she stayed as close to him as body contact would allow, following him across the tarmac and up the steps to the plane.

On board the aircraft, she sat down in a seat away from the men, and Dana sat down with his father in the row across from her. She was uncomfortable with the atmosphere and it showed. Pulling a blanket around her, she huddled down as if to protect herself wishing now she had more on than shorts.

Daniel watched her awhile before speaking. He leaned across the seating. "Toni, get used to the situation. These men will be with us the rest of the trip, and are our bodyguards from the airport to the town. It's a rough drive to our headquarters, and these guys will get us there in one piece. Yaoundé may be ours, but there are still rebels in the suburbs. The damned place is surrounded by tropical forests." He paused and thought for a moment. "You allergic to anything? Snakes, spiders, mosquitoes. We already know about your fear of beetles." He couldn't resist the last statement, and sported a smug smile.

She peered out of her blanket with disgust at his joke. "Funny! Don't know about the rest. Never been in a tropical forest before. How do I know what I'm allergic to? Except ice-cold mud water," she retorted.

"Touché. Seriously, are you allergic?" Caulder tried again.

"I'm being serious. I don't know." She objected.

"Great! Don't you get regular shots?" and Daniel raised his voice slightly.

She looked across the row at him, catching the stare from his eyes. "Only when people give me shots of doped bourbon!"

Caulder looked surprised and raised his eyebrows at her.

"My head ached too much to be a hangover. I'm naive... not stupid!" and she crossed her legs in the seat, letting the blanket slide up quite unintentionally to reveal her legs.

He was amused by her and he also took time out to look at her legs. "You're okay, kid. Stick with me. You're gonna be just fine!" and from where he sat... she was exactly that.

"Oh, you bet I'm going to stick with you. Wherever you go, I'll be right behind you. You can bet your life on that!" His sarcastic, domineering attitude towards her had created a new spirit in Toni... which was exactly what Caulder intended.

"I hope it doesn't come to that, Miss Sinclair," and Daniel leaned back in the seat.

Dana watched with interest. He'd never seen his father play games with a woman before. This was a first and Dana was enjoying it, and he was very amused.

At the other end of the plane it was a far different story. Serious business was being discussed. Sam and Ben enlightened the mercenaries how to conduct themselves in Mr. Caulder's company and also in his companion's. Ben spoke in a universal language so that all would quite clearly understand, and what he couldn't convey in words, he conveyed in gestures and pictures. What they didn't understand from Ben, Sam made it very clear to them by his own means.

After so much flying in the last two days, these few hours seemed endless. It was still light, and Toni could see out of the windows. A great view... if you liked clouds. A dryer July heat over the Atlantic had made giant puffy marshmallows for the plane to cruise on. The altitude was high, but comfortable. Once or twice on the trip, she caught sight of water. With a sigh, she slumped back in her seat, her head resting on the window.

"Are we bored?" Caulder questioned her, moving out of his row and into hers. He sat down in the seat next to her, resting his arm on the rest separating the seats.

"No. I was just wondering if we'll ever see land again, let alone reach a destination."

"Honey, you'll see land like you've only dreamed of very soon. Toni, look now... down there." He took her by the shoulders and made her look back out of the window. "It's the shoreline of Cameroon. See the harbor of Douala? Not long now and we'll be down." He said it with affection... not just for her, but for his beloved Cameroon.

That was his first term of endearment to her. Daniel Caulder had not meant to say it. It just slipped out.

Toni had heard it. She could not help it.

Toni considered it was a good landing in view of the state of the runway. Cracks made long ago by mortar shells had never been patched and the wheels of the plane slid over them, bumping the jet as it did. Gathering her backpack and helping Dana with his, took a few moments. Daniel became impatient and hurried them from the plane, and down the waiting steps.

Once on terra ferma, Toni could see old and beaten-up trucks approaching at a very fast speed. She glanced across to Daniel, who was standing with his small group of men, and was constantly talking and seemingly waving his fingers at them all. Toni adjusted her backpack and waited for instructions. It was hot... really hot, and flies hovered around her. She pulled her jacket from her body and stuffed it into the side of the backpack.

Dana moved by her side, smiling. "This is my father's real love. Being out here with his men and having a goal. You will discover that for yourself very soon."

She looked at the boy as though she was missing something, and she frowned.

Ben approached Caulder, leaning his head towards him, and gestured across to the men they had hired. Tony could not hear what they were saying, even though she tried to. She stepped away from Dana, and tried even harder to listen.

"I already figured as much. I'll take care of it right now," and Daniel moved towards Toni. Without warning, he leaned down and took her in his arms, pinning her to the fuselage. "Kiss me like we have just spent the night together."

"What?" she exclaimed.

"Is that your favorite word? Just do it, damn it! Surely even you can manage that." Putting his face right by hers, he kissed her long and hard. When his lips touched hers, she felt electrified. She knew this was an act… but the act was real good, too good. His strong arms held her a moment more than needed, and then just as fast, he let her go. She stood there realizing they had an audience.

Applause rippled though his men, with laughter and talk that needed no apparent translation. Daniel could not lose face in front of these people, and even Toni realized that.

"Thank you. Not bad for a cold-hearted virgin." Caulder was crude.

She raised her hand and he caught her arm before it moved six inches from her body. Looking into her eyes, Daniel could smell her femininity, and Toni could sense the feelings of being the prey, and him the hunter.

"Do you really find me that repulsive?" The way she had responded to him, he doubted that very much, and he ushered her into the waiting vehicle.

Toni rode in the larger truck with Dana. Sam and some of the mercenaries rode with them. Everyone else took the other truck, which made her more than curious over the split. She understood the action on the runway, but not this, and also noted that the provisions and equipment went with Daniel.

Daylight was almost non-existent as they left the airstrip. This was no regular airport or landing, and certainly no regular route to their destination.

They drove out into what passed for a street, war-torn and decidedly muddy, and then turned away in the direction of the jungle. The trucks, being old, were inconspicuous in the undergrowth, and trucks moving slowly through Cameroon, was not a new thing.

Toni pulled the canvas back and peered out the back of her truck, and then stared back at Dana looking somewhat shocked. "Are we going through there tonight?" She looked astounded as they entered the density of trees.

"Of course! Where else would we be going? This airstrip is miles from Yaoundé. Now all we have to do… is get there." Dana stated, quite unconcerned.

"But, I thought that this all belonged to you and that the runway was by the capitol! You know, palace-round-the-corner type thing."

"Oh, no, Toni. This is just the beginning of the adventure… not the end. Tonight, my father will make camp in the jungle. We will sleep where he says we do."

"**What**?" she exclaimed, more loudly than she meant to. "Out there? Not in some hotel?" Her face was ashen. The thought of spending the night in the bush was inconceivable.

"Papa is right, '*what*' is your favorite word. No, Toni. Tonight you will sleep where the animals sleep, and tomorrow bathe where they do. This is a new beginning… the first day of the rest of your life!"

And, as the trucks pulled away, Toni saw the color pink shade the African sky. The moon rose through the splendor of evolution, and stars she had never noticed before graced the skies. She leaned down on her elbows and looked out in wonderment at a night she had never seen before, and a world she had never known.

Chapter 3

The darkness of the trees was dense, and the coolness of the night hit hard. Toni could hear noises like she had never heard before and never wanted to hear again.

They'd camped in a fairly safe area of the jungle, with trees surrounding them, and a couple of men on guard duty. A fire was built and Toni, wrapped in a huge blanket, huddled by it, her legs tucked under her. Dana sat with her, trying to explain the rudiments of cooking over an open fire.

"You hold the fork over the flames till the meat is cooked, like this... Toni, are you listening to me?" He nudged her.

She was flustered. "I'm sorry, Dana. I've never heard these kinds of noises before. What are they?" Her head was bobbing around like a fish in a goldfish bowl.

"Elephants in some far off-place... as I was explaining..." and Dana tried to continue.

"What?" She pulled the blanket tighter, not noticing the visitor.

"So, we have a new name for you young lady... 'What'... from now on you'll be called 'What'." Caulder was standing right behind them. "Elephants, just like Dana said. Maybe some human cries in there somewhere and the noises of bugs. Does it scare you, 'What'?"

"Course not!" she retorted. "And my name's not 'What'! And what bugs?" she asked , half turning towards Daniel.

He ignored her question. "It is now. There's bread and fruit over there if the meat's not to your liking." He dropped the bag he was carrying onto the ground by her making a thud as it did.

Dana laughed out loud. It was funny to a ten-year-old boy.

Feeling that Caulder was making a fool of her she stood up, letting the blanket fall to the ground, and then turned toward the bush.

"Where the hell are you going?" he demanded in a very loud voice.

"I need to pee, or is that also a joke?"

Caulder clicked his fingers and Ben appeared from nowhere. "Go with her."

"Mr. Caulder, I said I needed to pee!" Toni protested, really irritated with this man.

"I heard you. That's why Ben goes with you... or would you rather I escort you?" He stood with his hands on his hips... gun hanging in his shoulder holster. Mercenary was the first word that sprang to mind.

"Let's go," and she turned to Ben.

They walked in silence to the cover of the bush, where Ben was the first to speak. "Why are you so angry towards Mr. Caulder?"

She turned to face him, her cheeks flushed. "Because he treats me like a child!"

"Didn't look like that this afternoon on the runway. Think he made it quite clear to everyone where you stand." Ben was trying to hide the laughter in his voice.

"Oh, really... and where is that?" she argued... her face now red with anger.

"You want I should draw you a picture? Get wise, Toni. If you don't want him to treat you like a child don't act like one. He has enough with his son and this power play out here. Help him... don't hinder him. You asked for all this. You invited yourself into his life, not the other way round."

"How dare you talk to me like that!" she yelled at him.

"I'll talk to you anyway I damn well please, Miss Sinclair! Now, go and do what you came out here to do, before they send a search party for us," he screamed back at her.

But Toni didn't move. Instead, she broke down crying.

"Hey, I'm sorry. I didn't realize how scared you are. You're terrified, aren't you?" His tone was soft and there was a frown on his face.

She nodded yes.

Ben put his arms around her, and she leaned on his chest, her tears running down onto his open shirt. Holding her tightly to him, he stroked her hair until her sobs became quieter, smelling her hair, and the last odors of soap on her skin. She looked up into his face, and the moment was tense. Toni pulled away from him instantly, as she realized he did not see her as just a friend.

"What are you afraid of? The jungle, the trip, what's ahead of us... what scares you so much?" He'd been blind, and he continued, "Or is it Daniel Caulder that scares you so, and the way you are beginning to feel for him?"

Her eyes were wide. "It's the jungle that's all... just the jungle with its noises... nothing else." But she wasn't looking at Ben. Six feet behind them was Caulder. "I'll be back," and she disappeared.

Ben watched her scurry to a patch of undergrowth suitable for latrines... so did Caulder, and made his presence known. "Anything wrong, Ben?"

"Mr. Caulder!" Ben was startled. That's why Toni had lied. He wondered how much his boss had seen... and heard, and he considered he had been so focused on Toni, that he hadn't even heard Daniel approach them.

"Nothing, sir. Just waiting for Toni."

"Fine. See you back at camp."

Daniel Caulder walked away. He was a commanding figure, someone not to cross, and a man who feared nothing. No wonder the girl was scared of her feelings. Ben watched his boss go, and turned his attentions back to waiting for Toni.

After eating, and planning the next day's drive, sleep was a natural progression. Still, the noises of the night disturbed Toni. She was contemplating what animals might disturb her dreams when Sam appeared before her with an alarming statement.

"Miss Sinclair, you and the prince will sleep in the smaller truck.

No need to spend the night on the ground." He was so matter of fact about it.

"Thank you, Sam. I wasn't looking forward to sharing my sleeping bag with a snake," and stood up, collecting her jacket and blanket, and followed Dana.

Sam laughed. "And the boss will be sleeping in same truck with you!"

"From one kind of snake to another," she murmured, with head bent.

"You say something, Toni?" Sam asked, knowing full well what she had said.

"Nothing, Sam," she replied and moved towards the truck.

She knew that in the jungle one slept in one's clothes: more or less. When Toni climbed in the vehicle, she found a small sleeping bag and then a double one. Dumping her back pack at the end of the truck, Toni crawled around trying to figure out who should go where.

"Dana, you and your…" But Dana had already crawled into his bag right behind her, and Toni did not get to finish her sentence.

"Great!" She dropped her discarded jacket and boots. Underneath, she wore a T-shirt with her shorts. There wasn't much room between sleeping-bags and boxes at that end of the truck for moving about. She climbed into the only available bag and lay in it, staring at the canvas roof, pulling the quilted cover up round her neck. Then she heard voices from outside.

"Keep two men posted throughout the night. Three-hour shifts. We should be safe enough, but we have some special cargo. Sung knows where we are, and I still don't trust him. We paid him and I'm sure the other side did, too. Wake me at six. Remember, Ben, all our lives depend on us staying safe… all our lives!" He made the point crystal clear.

When he climbed into the truck, Toni closed her eyes. Daniel removed his boots, and placed them as quietly as he could beside the bag. Pulling out his revolver, he laid it near where his head would be, and then climbed in the bag beside her.

Leaning back on his folded, arms he whispered to Toni. "'What', are you awake?" As he spoke, he watched the ants crawling around the roof of the truck. He hoped the girl had not noticed these little creatures.

No reply.

He turned to her, and as he did his long hair touched her face. "Toni, I'm sorry for earlier tonight. I wasn't trying to make a fool of you. It's just that you're young and vulnerable in my eyes, and I tend to treat you like Dana. I've never been around someone like you before and you're so easy to have fun with." He paused when there was no answer, and he became irritated. "For god's sake, woman... I'm trying to apologize! Okay... so pretend to be asleep. Tomorrow is another day. Sweet dreams, 'What.'" He turned away from her, pulled more than his fair share of the sleeping-bag over him, and fell into a much needed sleep.

Toni had heard every word he'd said. When his hair touched her face, she knew exactly how close he was to her. She had felt his warm breath in the cool night air, and now she was more frightened than ever, frightened to believe in him. Frightened of getting involved in something she was losing control over, and terrified of being hurt by this man.

When Daniel awoke, she had rolled over to his side of the bag. The night was cold, and unintentionally she had turned to him for warmth. Instinctively, he had put his arms around her and she nestled under his chin. He could feel her body through the thin clothes she wore, her breasts pressed against his chest, and he could feel her nipples harden when she touched him. It aroused feelings inside him that he knew should not be there, being more than old enough to be her father.

Her eyelashes fluttered as she slept, and she moaned in her dreams. He'd noticed the change in her skin color the last day at the house. Another few days in the suns of Africa, and she would be a blonde with a tan. He didn't want to move and spoil the moment of just holding her in his arms. Just then the flap on the canvass of the truck moved. Daniel instinctively reached for his gun, hammer cocked and ready to fire. Ben's head looked in, and he stopped in his tracks. Caulder motioned with the gun for Ben to step back from the truck, and he released the hammer. Ben closed the flap and moved to the side of the truck, his mind filled with thoughts of what he had just seen.

Not waking his two companions, Daniel let go of her, slid out of the sleeping bag, collected his boots, and jumped down into the early morning light, gun still in his hand. Ben glared at Daniel.

"What the fuck are you looking at? I didn't touch her, Ben. We'll let Miss Sinclair make her own choice," and he walked away from the trucks, and down the bank towards the nearby river.

This time, Ben had no comeback for his boss.

At the river, Caulder removed his clothes, dumped them on the riverbank, and sat down naked in the water. Cold, fresh, fast-flowing water billowed over him, and he put his head under the spray, and tossed his hair back onto his shoulders. It felt good to him, but he couldn't cleanse the thought of her from his mind. This was not good. Tonight, she would sleep somewhere else... not with him, and not by Ben.

He wasn't sure how many minutes he sat in the water, but gut instinct told him someone was watching from a patch of bush. He was in arm's reach of his pistol, but he had the feeling this person posed no threat to his safety.

"Come out where I can see you," he demanded, his voice rose an octave or two.

"I'm sorry," she stammered, stepping out into the clearing by the bank. "I saw the river and I wanted to wash. And before you go yelling at Ben, I slipped away. I'm sorry, it was wrong." She bowed her head.

"You bet your damn life it was! Are you trying to get killed?" He stood up in the water, and reached for his clothes, water dripping down his body.

Toni didn't flinch as he stood naked in front of her, pulling on his pants. He shoved the gun down the back of his black pants, threw his boots over his shoulder, and then stood on the bank. "Get in," he demanded of her.

She stopped herself from saying that word again. He'd seen her naked before. She laid clean underwear on the rocks, removed the dirty ones, and stepped into the water. With her hands covering her breasts, and the water past her waist, she spoke softly to him.

"Caulder, last night in the truck... I heard what you said. It's me who should be apologizing to you. Ben was right. I was acting like a kid, and it's time to grow up. Dana is the child here... not me. I'm sorry for the trouble I seem to be causing."

Her long hair cascaded down her back. She wore no make-up, and she was nothing like any of his women. No plastic Barbie doll from a movie screen; no one rich and famous; no nothing. She was 'What'! He watched her a few moments longer before he made his next move.

He stepped back down into the water. "Follow me."

She turned to get her clothes.

"Leave them," he snapped, and picking up his shirt from the ground, threw it to her.

She did as she was asked, caught the shirt, wrapped it round her, and followed him through the cool water to the next clearing.

The waterfall came into her line of sight, while sparkling in the morning mist, with foliage around it glistening in the sun-kissed dew. Dana was right. This was the beginning of the rest of her life. This was a place she could only dream about.

Toni's eyes were bright with fascination. In front of her was a whole new world. She could see the monkeys in the trees, and their chatter became music to her ears. She watched as they swung on the vines, their dexterity amazing her. She was aware of none of this last night; all she knew was fear. Today, Caulder introduced her to his world, a world full of bright lights and beauty. She looked again at the waterfall, its colors changing before her eyes.

"It's beautiful. I'm so glad you shared this with me. This obviously has some special meaning for you." She tried not to pry.

"It's where I met Dana's mother and it's also the place where Dana was conceived. It was her secret place to escape to when we were in this part of the country... and it was our place." He looked at their reflection in the water, and then raised his head. "And now I share it with you."

Was this the same Caulder? She moved towards him, his black shirt tight against her wet skin. She reached up on tiptoe, gently put her hands on his shoulders, and kissed him on his cheek. "Thank you," she whispered near his ear. To her it was innocent.

What the hell is she trying to do to me?' he thought.

He grabbed hold of her and looked into her eyes. Temptation was almost too much as his body pressed against hers. She felt him tense against her, and for a fleeting moment her fear was back. He was holding her by her wrists, and it hurt. She squirmed in his grasp, and as if coming to his senses, he let her go, staring at her like he had never seen her before.

"Get dressed… go on! We have a long way to go today. Go, Toni!" and he almost but pushed her out of his way.

She ran back through the water, tears blurring her eyes, and water splashing up her legs. She ripped his shirt from her, and pulled a clean vest and shorts on, totally unaware that Ben had witnessed the whole scenario. He had seen her body, also, and the way Caulder had looked at her. Ben also understood why his boss was looking at her not just with lust in his eyes, but something else that he couldn't quite place right then.

Suddenly, without any warning, a helicopter noise cracked the air, looming overhead and a spray of bullets hit the water like giant hailstones. They missed Toni by inches.

"Get down on the ground. Lie flat!" Ben screamed at the top of his lungs.

Caulder turned towards the noise, and ran back through the water towards the girl, bounding through the spray to get to her. At first he thought she had been hit. Bending down, he scooped her up in his arms as if she weighed nothing.

"Ben," Daniel yelled, "Get back to camp and move that truck out! Get Dana clear. Take the first truck and move." He saw Ben hesitate. "Now, damn it! I've got Toni. We'll catch up to you. Go!" Caulder was yelling as the chopper circled for a second attempt at the ground.

When Ben hit the camp, the men were already heading for the truck. Sam grabbed Dana up in his huge arms, and whisked him into the truck. The mercenaries kicked at the fire, and breakfast stayed just where it lay. Those were the only things they left behind, except Caulder, his companion, and a couple of mercenaries for the second truck.

With blinding speed truck number one took off into the jungle. One of the remaining men jumped into the driver's seat of the remaining truck; the other had his rifle ready. He watched and waited for his boss to come racing through the trees, carrying a bundle in his arms. As Daniel reached the back of the truck, the mercenary opened the flaps for Caulder. Literally throwing the girl inside, he jumped in after her. At breakneck speed the truck roared off down the well-worn tire tracks, swerving through the trees like they were on an obstacle course.

The chopper closed in on them, lowering its self as close to the trees as it could. Caulder, reaching inside the truck, pulled an M60 machine gun over to the back flap, loading it at the same time. The Brazilian mercenary had another, and with no words spoken, leaned side by side with Caulder.

When the helicopter reached the desired level, the two men opened fire. Both men knew they had to take the craft out, or they would not survive. It hovered above them, with noisy chopper blades causing dust, and just clipping the trees. Debris swirled in the air, as a burst of gunfire from Caulder's machine gun hit the pilot, and a combination of other bullets hit the gas tank. The chopper blades spun uncontrollably, and the bedraggled metal bird dropped to the ground with a sickening thud, and burst into a ball of orange flames.

Toni lay between the boxes of guns stacked in the back of the truck, exactly where Daniel had thrown her. All she could hear was gunfire, and the sound of men screaming in death. She put her hands over her ears and held them there, tears streaming down her face. She didn't know it would be like this… she didn't know! What she did realize, however, was that she was in the way. Caulder had been paying attention to her instead of his real task. She had distracted him long enough for him to let his guard down. Still, she sat there with her hands clasped around her ears and her eyes tightly shut. Maybe it would go away… but it wasn't about to.

Daniel dropped the now empty gun on to the floor of the truck and, nodding to his companion, turned to look at Toni.

"Toni!" and he physically pulled her out from between the boxes. "It's over… for now. It was a patrol…" he realized she couldn't even hear him. He pulled her arms down by her side. "Toni? Are you hurt? Did you take a hit?" and he pulled her clothes in all directions trying to find out if there were any marks on her.

She was crying hysterically.

"Toni, stop it, stop it… now!" He shook her hard. "Crying won't help any!"

When she didn't stop, Caulder raised his hand and hit her across the face.

Immediately she stopped crying, opened her eyes and stared at him. "I could have got you killed with my own stupidity. I came down there to find you. Ben was right, I am hindering you," she screamed at him, tears and finger marks staining her face.

He yelled back at her. "Ben had no right to tell you that. Damn him! You're not in the way, just not used to playing war games." His fingers brushed hair from her eyes, and he rearranged her clothes for her. Obviously she had not been hit.

The truck slowed down taking a more leisurely route through the trees. Daniel sat Toni upright and backed slightly away from her. The whelps down her left cheek grew deep red, and it didn't make him proud, having never hit a woman before today.

Caulder continued. "What we have to do now is to change your appearance. That chopper may have radioed back that there is a girl with us. White-skinned girls, especially with your hair coloring, are rare and valuable out here. If they were on Sung's payroll, he will be looking for you. That's why you had to stay in the background in Panama, or they could be rebels from 'round here, but somehow I doubt that. The pilot was Chinese. My guess is Sung's playing both sides of the fence." He thought for a moment, and glanced round him.

The truck came to a complete stop, and this gave Daniel time to form a plan of action. He turned to his ally from the gun battle. "You, out… and leave the flap up. Stay out front, just in case," Caulder yelled in French, hoping his companion understood him, and turned his attentions back to the girl. "Get out of those clothes!"

"No, Mr. Caulder, please, I…" she begged on her knees, scraping them on the dirty wood as she did.

Not asking again, he leaned forward, expertly undid her shorts, and pulled her vest over her head. She tried desperately to hold on to her clothes, grabbing at the shorts, but failed miserably against him. Dropping her clothes on the floor, he pulled some underwear, long green pants, small, tight vest, and a shirt from Dana's backpack. There wasn't a lot of difference in Toni's and Dana's size.

Daniel forced the underwear and pants up her legs till they reached her waist, and then pulled the vest shirt on to her slender body. He bound the shirt around her with a leather belt, and tucked a gun into it: a loaded gun. She stared at him in disbelief, but if she thought that was bad enough, she was not prepared for the next step. From his sheath he produced a knife, its blade glinting in the dim lighting of the truck. She knew what he meant to do.

"No, Mr. Caulder, I beg you don't do it..." She screamed at him, and put her hands up to her head, clinging to her hair.

He grabbed her arms with one hand, pulling them down, yelling in her face. She could feel his breath on her cheek.

"Do you want to live or die... or worse? You want to be captured by Sung and his men? They have ways out here for women to die. First they rape them, then they torture them..." his look was fierce. He brandished the knife in her face.

"Stop it, please! Let me do it," she begged and she tried to grab for the knife.

"There isn't time. We're in the jungle, not a beauty parlor!" Letting go of her arms, he grabbed a handful of hair and cut it roughly, watching her golden tresses fall on the truck floor. Handful after handful till her hair was way shorter than his, while she clutched at the curls as they fell. Daniel stepped back.

"Not bad, not bad at all. You still have a shape on your head. Makes you look like someone Dana's age." He admired his own work. After rubbing dirt from his own boots onto her face, he held up a pan for her to look into.

Someone she didn't know looked back. Her eyebrows gave her face shape, and her eyelashes were still dark. He'd smeared dirt across her cheeks, down her neck and across the shirt. But her hair! It was gone and a Peter-Pan-type person looked back at her. She didn't look at Caulder. Right then she hated him, and everything he stood for... and he saw that hate in her eyes. French and English voices brought her back to reality. Someone was calling him.

"Papa, are you there?" The other truck returned when they saw the fireball over the trees. Dana had climbed out and run to the back of his father's truck. "Papa?" And he peered inside.

"I'm fine, Dana. It's okay." Caulder opened the flap and jumped to the ground hugging the boy to him.

He was watched with interest by the rest of the group.

"Where's Toni? Is she with you? She is okay, too? Yes?" The child's concern was touching as he tried to peer into the truck.

Caulder let go of his son, turned around, and pulled the flap back on the truck. "Out," he yelled at her. There was no movement, and he was becoming impatient. Climbing up into the truck, he picked her up in his arms, and bodily took her to the entrance, dropping her out onto the ground as he did.

No one said a word. Ben stared at her. Gone was her femininity, her ladylike ways. In front of them was something resembling a young boy, and Ben could see the hate on her face, hate for Daniel Caulder, and maybe for them all. Daniel broke the silence.

"Ben, you take her in your truck for the rest of the day, and from now on refer to her only as Toni. Make sure that everyone understands. Tonight she sleeps by Sam." He discontinued the conversation, and started to turn away from the situation, but instead he looked at her. If anything, in his eyes, she was even more beautiful. "No taking off those clothes to bathe, no anything, unless Ben or I are with you. You understand me? You understand everything I'm saying to you? Do you?" He leered at her, his eyes full of venom. It was the only way he knew, to be hard and cruel, even to a woman.

"Yes," she mumbled, with her head down, staring at the ground.

"Can't hear you!" Caulder screamed at her, hands on his hips.

She raised her head high looking into his face. "Yes," she yelled back at him. "Whatever you say, Mr. Caulder, sir!" Now, she was screaming.

"That's better. Now get going." It was more the reaction he wanted. Now, he could turn away from her. In the heat of the day, Toni Sinclair had become one of them... whether she liked it or not. All this humility in front of his men was degrading for her. Yet, she had requested this assignment, for better or for worse.

As the day progressed Toni rode with Ben, never leaving his side. He leaned on his rifle at the entrance of the truck, a pensive look on his face. Toni slumped down on the floor, leaned back against the boxes, and with the movement of the truck, fell asleep. They still had many miles ahead of them, and riding in jungles was unpredictable. Several times the trucks stopped. There were enormous hindrances of large trees and rock masses, now fallen into the path, presenting problems for the two trucks. Several times his men removed the problem, just like Caulder seemed to be doing with anything else that stood in his way.

When they camped that night, and a fire was made, Sam showed Toni how to handle a gun. But Toni was not a novice. Her uncle had bought her a gun a year before, and she'd taken lessons. Dana was impressed at her knowledge and her spirit which now seemed to be back on course.

When she went to the bush, Ben went with her. Their friendship grew by the hour, and that's just what Caulder wanted. Toni was happy round Ben, safe and secure, with him posing no threat from a man to a woman. At supper, she sat well away from Daniel and spent her time with his son. She was explaining to him why she had become a reporter, following in her uncle's and father's footsteps.

Caulder sat down on the logs next to Ben, and watched her in the firelight. He swatted mosquitoes from his neck, and then pulled out his cigarettes and lit one. Circles of smoke wafted up into the night air. Ben saw him watching the girl. He knew the signs when his boss was interested in a woman.

He interrupted the stillness. "So, boss, who do you think was behind today's little skirmish? Think it was Sung?"

"Not sure, Ben. I noticed someone had been trying to use the two-way radio. I left some fine tape over the dial, and this morning it was missing. Think we may have a traitor amongst us. One of us is leading a double life… excluding Toni. We know she is!" He tried to joke, but the thought was very serious. "It's not you or Sam, so that leaves the six men. One of them is working for the rebels. Whether they gave away the girl… I don't know. If that chopper was Sung's, he may know the girl is with us. It depends if the pilot radioed the information back to base before he was killed. If he didn't, she may be safe because no one can use the radio anymore. I made sure of that. They can't reach the outside now... but neither can we. We have no choice but to plod on. Dana has to be in Yaoundé as soon as possible. The longer he stays away the more power he loses. Our army can only hold the pretense for so long; then the people will want to see their leader. Amazing how one little boy can hold such a key. No one in Cameroon is sure that he's not the king's son. And that's how it must stay. I'm his protector... that's all."

He squashed the half-smoked cigarette between his fingers, dropping it to the ground, and continued to watch Toni. Then his gaze switched to his son. Sam had trimmed the child's hair at Dana's request. He'd wanted it to look like Toni's, he said, to make her feel better. He was dark-haired... she was blonde. He was dark skinned, and she was not. What they were was, more or less, was the same size. And what Sung may not know, was that the child was his. He looked at Toni sitting, talking in the half light. He glanced back to Dana. The two were laughing. Dana was taking the fear from Toni. Darken the girl's hair; dye her skin with oils from the jungle, and at a push from the distance of a balcony...

Ben watched Caulder. He could almost read his mind. "Let's hope it never comes to that, boss."

"Let's hope, Ben. Let's hope! But it would work; you know damn well it would!" So, plan B was hatched.

Plan A, was to go straight through to the capitol with eyes carefully watching the six men. Meanwhile, Caulder had conceived an idea to catch the traitor by using Toni as bait, a plan he thought he might just be able to execute. Now it was time to sleep... away from the girl. But sleep didn't come easy. His mind was full of things that it should not have been.

After little sleep, morning saw Caulder awake early, and discarding his crude bedding, he crossed the clearing to where Ben lay. Tapping him lightly on the shoulder, Daniel's other hand was across his number 2's mouth, while his mouth formed words. "Follow me."

Ben rose up and left his bed and followed his boss.

Away from the rest, and in the nearby trees, Caulder told Ben of the plan. "Just lead her and Dana into the bush. Not too far, but far enough for the traitor to follow. Take the Brazilian, Andre, with you. He's not your man. Don't think he would shoot his own comrades, especially when he had a better shot at taking me out."

Andre proved to be Caulder's gun companion from the previous day, and had now secured number 4 position in the ranks. "Take the backpacks like you're going on for food. Make it look good. It has to be realistic, or the traitor won't be convinced. Dana will follow you; Toni may put up a fight, but we have to catch this man. I kept thinking about it last night. You know he'll have made plans to meet with someone, somewhere. As much as I'd like to know with whom, we cannot wait that long. He may do it without our knowledge, so let's just force the issue now. All you have to do is keep them out there. When you're far enough away from camp, go on with Toni. Leave Dana and the Brazilian back a piece. Leave the rest to me! Nothing will happen to any of you." Caulder turned away.

Ben had his instructions and a pretty fair idea of what his boss intended to do. He returned to camp and, looking for his charges, found them packing some bags.

"Okay, Toni and Dana, let's go get breakfast. Come on, you guys, get going. Chop, chop. We have a long walk ahead of us. We're going to get some fresh meat. Dana, if you want, you can kill an animal for us. Good fresh meat." Ben made a huge production of the event. He hustled and bustled like some mother hen, watered his chicks, and collected their backpacks for them, dumping them by the pair's feet.

Toni had had cramps in her stomach all night. "Ben, I need the bathroom…" She wasn't sure which term to use… girl's or boy's room! All she knew was she needed the bathroom and fast.

"Okay, Toni. We'll wait for you over by the fire. Don't be long! And don't go where I can't see you."

"I also need my jacket from the truck," she added, almost embarrassed, her head bent.

"To go to the bathroom? Just go, Toni. You can get your jacket afterwards." He was becoming agitated.

"Problem, Ben?" asked Caulder… ignoring Toni.

"No problem, boss. Toni needs her jacket." He raised his eyebrows at Daniel.

He turned to her. "Your jacket? What the hell do you need that for?" Even Caulder was suspicious.

"There's something in the pocket..." She hung her head even further. "I just need it, that's all. Can I get it?" She shuffled her boots round in the dirt.

"No. I will!" and Caulder walked towards the truck.

"No, Mr. Caulder. It's private..." She trailed after him, following every step. "Mr. Caulder..." She had taken to calling him that again. She felt Daniel was too familiar.

He climbed into the truck bed, leaving the flap open, searching around until he found her jacket. Toni climbed up behind him, and stood watching him. Shaking it hard, the tape recorder fell out of the pocket. Was she the spy? He doubted it. She was a journalist with an assignment. But to be on the safe side, he took the tape out anyway. Feeling in the other pocket, his hand touched the box. He pulled it out and looked at Toni's face. This was what she needed. He opened the box of tampons and pulled one out, only it was the tube of mascara instead. He stared at it and so did Toni.

"So, what else do we have hidden in here?" He tipped the contents out onto his large hand. Convinced they were the genuine article he pushed the majority of the tampons back into the pocket. He threw the mascara on the floor and it rolled across the truck.

"That's something you won't need. Boys don't wear mascara.... anyway; you're beautiful enough without it." He handed her a tampon and almost laughed at her.

Grabbing it from him, she hissed in his face. "You son-of-a-bitch! Don't you think you've degraded me enough? Short of having me grovel at your feet and licking your boots, what else could you do? No, don't answer that!" she screamed. "You'd find something! Your dossier was only half right!"

This time he laughed at her.

She hit him across the face.

And he let her.

He laughed again.

She hit him again and again, her fists then beating on his chest. Without warning, he put his arms around her body and pinned her arms to her side. "All out now! Are you finished? You're even more beautiful when you're angry."

Her green eyes flashed at him. He was destroying her day by day...in her eyes. In his...she was becoming a woman.

"Let go of me," and she struggled in his grasp. "You may be the boss out here, but I'll see you in hell back in L.A. The pen is still mightier than the sword."

"Funny. That's not the impression you gave yesterday at the waterfall. I thought we were making progress and that you actually liked me!" He looked directly down at her. She was so tiny compared to him, and her blows had hardly hurt him. Suddenly he had this overwhelming desire to kiss her, a desire he fulfilled.

She tried to struggle, but his grip was too strong. She didn't have to like his kiss; unfortunately she did. And this time it was no act. His kiss was strong and powerful, just like him. Warm and sensuous and full of promise as to what making love with him would be like. When he stopped kissing her, her eyes were shut.

She came to her senses. "I still hate you. I'll always hate you for doing this to me..." She faltered.

"Yeah, sure. I could feel the hate in you...especially from your body. Yes, ma'am. It came through real clear." He let her go and climbed out of the truck, dropping to the ground.

She followed him down still clutching her possession in her hand, and disappeared into the bush.

Ben and Dana stood waiting. Caulder passed by them and, with a nod of his head, kept going.

Toni came back to Ben within five minutes. She still looked shaken. "I'm ready."

"You okay?" asked the number 2, genuinely concerned for her.

"I'm fine...just fine. One of those women things...you know. A couple of days and...well, you know." Now she was really embarrassed.

"Is that why you wanted your jacket? God, I'm so sorry. I would have told you to go..." Now he felt like an idiot. Ben himself had caused her embarrassment.

"It's okay, Ben. I got what I wanted in the truck..." she stammered. "I mean from the jacket." She was flushed and decidedly uncomfortable.

Ben had a feeling that wasn't all she got in the truck. They'd all heard her yell.

Finally, when Toni had done what she had had to do, and gathered her things together, they moved out, a party of four moving east toward Yaoundé. After a good mile they stopped. Ben whispered to the Brazilian. He laughed and pulled Dana to one side. They stood in the long grasses and waited.

"Come on, Toni. You and I have something to do. Just walk with me and pretend you like me better than Mr. Caulder." Ben half glanced at her, with the feeling she would not object to that comment.

"Right now that wouldn't be too hard," Toni muttered under her breath.

"Then do it!"

"What is it with you guys? Do you all think I'm here for your sexual pleasure? I didn't think you…"

"Don't think… just walk. We're being followed." He suspected they were and now he was sure. He'd told Dana and his companion to stay very still. He knew that Andre would not disobey him. "Keep walking, Toni." Ben put his arm around her and she responded back to him.

Her heart was beating fast, letting her body know how scared she was. They kept going through the long grass and Toni tried not to stumble.

"Who's following us…" His kiss stopped her from talking.

She tried to respond and failed.

He noticed.

From behind them, the branches cracked as heavy boots trod the earth. Birds flew out from the bush and two men approached them. Not one, but two traitors! Someone must be paying well. Ben turned around and saw them step out behind him and Toni. He pushed Toni to the back of him. Clinging to Ben's shirt, she saw Caulder some feet back. With his gun glinting in the morning sunlight, he crept up behind the men and shot the one in the back of the head with a silenced berretta. The man fell with a thud and lay there in the bloodied grass. Then Daniel swung his powerful arms around the neck of the other, his muscles flexing in the black T shirt he wore. The man begged for mercy in some language that no one seemed to understand.

"On your knees!"

Nothing.

"Ben, tell him!" yelled Caulder.

Portuguese flowed from Ben's tongue. The man dropped on the hard ground begging for his life.

Caulder produced his knife. "Ask him who he's working for."

Ben asked.

He received no reply.

"Ask him again, damn it! I want an answer. Tell him I'll cut off his ear." Caulder brandished the knife by the groveling man's head, and cursed loudly in French.

Something incoherent came from the captive's mouth.

"What did he say? Never mind." Caulder grabbed the guy by the hair and wrenched his head up. "See this?" and he pressed the knife into his neck. "This will kill you if you don't give me a name. A name, damn it! Who are you working for?"

The face looked up and spat at the American. Caulder wiped the saliva from his cheeks, still with the blade in his hand. Then he slowly pulled the knife across the traitor's face. The writhing man screamed in pain and blood gushed out of the cut. "You get the idea now?"

"Sung… Sung," he screamed.

"Thank you," and Caulder pulled hard on his captives hair, and without any hesitation… he slit the man's throat.

Toni threw up where she stood… down the back of Ben's shirt, and onto the ground, tears blurring her eyes.

Ben removed his shirt and turned to her. "What did you expect, Toni? Mr. Caulder did what he had to. He was protecting us all. Now we can go on knowing the group is trustworthy." So precise and so matter of fact.

She stopped retching, and she stopped the flow of salty tears. She watched as Caulder wiped the blade clean on the man's clothes, then replaced it in his sheath. Standing up tall, Daniel looked to Ben.

"She okay?" he asked, never even glancing at Toni.

"She will be, boss." Ben escorted her back to Daniel Caulder.

Toni stumbled through the grass not even able to speak to him, nor even look him in the face. She'd watched him kill two men with his own hands. They walked in silence back to Dana and the Brazilian.

When she reached him, the child slid his hand into Toni's and held it there as if trying to comfort her. Then he whispered in her ear. "Told you my father had a goal. Now you have seen him as he really is…achieving that goal. Nothing will stop him, Toni. Not traitors, not Sung, not anything…not even his affection for you!"

Chapter 4

When the group returned to camp, they found far more than they bargained for. Three hired hands waited patiently, with a lot of bad news. They conveyed it both in languages and by sign work to Ben.

"Aw, fuck! God damn, those bastards." Ben turned to Caulder, an exasperated look on his face.

"What? Is it that bad?" His boss demanded, waiting for an explanation.

"Worse! Before they left here, they sabotaged the trucks beyond repair. We have no transportation, meaning we can't take the guns and supplies," Ben replied.

"Did no one try to stop them?" he asked, waving his arms at the men. "What about these three idiots? Aw forget it! We'll carry what we need," replied Caulder. "Pack everyone's backpack with supplies. Take out anything of a personal nature; just take medical supplies and food. I'll keep the money on me. Everybody carries a rifle… and I mean each person including Dana and Toni. Make a litter for the machine guns. You and I will take turns pulling it. Destroy everything we don't take with us. Burn it!"

Ben was astounded. "Boss, it's too much. Dana and Toni aren't strong enough to carry all…"

She interrupted him. "Don't make excuses for me, Ben! If Mr. Caulder thinks I can do it, then I can do it. I can carry my share." She stood defiant, proud and stubborn, trying not to let them see her cry.

Ben threw her a rifle which she caught despite its weight. Toni swung it over her shoulder and stood there like the soldier she was becoming. All she had to do now was to carry the backpack, the water, and her camera... but she'd manage it. She wouldn't let Caulder see how close she was to breaking. Just when she thought he couldn't make her feel any worse... he'd succeeded... again.

Daniel watched her struggle with the backpack and the rifle. He was well aware how he was breaking her spirit. If she was to survive this, she had to be tamed till she would obey his every command. It wasn't a macho thing... it was survival of the fittest! He carried on watching her while he strapped the litter to his shoulders, along with his backpack, a holster and the rifle. A canteen of water hung from his belt, along with his knife and revolver.

Toni looked at Daniel. The all-American hero! She wanted to laugh out loud, hysterically. But it wasn't funny!

Dana was overloaded and Toni had offered to carry his rifle. "No, Toni. I can do it. Like you, I will show Papa," determination written all over his face.

Caulder watched with interest. He knew the girl was tired and distressed about the dead men... still she offered to help her young friend. Maybe, just maybe, she was teaching his father something.

As they filed out, she looked back and saw her clothes burning on the pile, tears filling her eyes. She wiped them away when she thought no one was looking. She had been allowed to take her jacket, pockets still stuffed as before, with one added exception. A film she had already used lay hidden in the lining. She figured no one knew it was there.

By late afternoon, Toni was both hot and tired. Water was plentiful, but the more she drank the more she needed to urinate. She didn't know why, but she could not get enough water. The moisture should have stayed in her and it wasn't. Perhaps the time of month had something to do with it. She only knew she was beginning to dehydrate.

They plowed on... Caulder in the lead, Ben bringing up the rear. Ben had been watching her, knew by her frequent visits to the bush that she was losing moisture. He also knew his boss would not stop, not for any reason. He was a man obsessed in reaching Yaoundé.

Ben tapped Sam on the shoulder. "Sam, take over from me at the back, would you?" Without waiting for an answer, Ben moved up the ranks until he was level with his boss. "Mr. Caulder, Toni's not doing well in this heat. Could we camp early tonight? Give her a break?" He pleaded on her behalf.

Caulder kept up the brisk pace, glancing back at the girl, and then looked ahead. "And what about tomorrow and the next day? When it's still as hot, and the mosquitoes are biting her and she's still not feeling good? What then? Dana is holding his own," and he continued to look ahead of him.

"That's the point. She is a girl and right now..." Ben was becoming a little exasperated with Daniel.

Daniel cut Ben short. "Yeah, I know what's right now. Okay, today and tomorrow, she gets a break and that's it. She better be over her aches and pains by then. That suits you, Ben?" His look was fierce, and he left Ben standing, staring at him and marched away into the long grass.

By seven, they'd made their camp. Caulder had wanted to go on through the night and camp at dawn. But in all fairness, he knew that neither Toni nor his son would make it. Toni leaned back against a tree for support, away from the men. She remembered drinking down half a canteen of water and that's all she remembered as she dropped to the ground.

Dana watched her as she slithered down the tree. "Papa, Toni is sleeping over there. She looks kind of strange." The boy pointed in her direction, and was most concerned that something was very wrong.

Caulder dropped what he was doing and rushed to where she lay on the hard ground. She was out cold. "Not again. Is she gonna do this the whole trip?" He put his soiled hand on her forehead. She was burning up. "Good god. She's on fire... Get some blankets, this isn't any female thing!" Daniel undid her shirt and removed it, checking her upper body as he went. Nothing. He tried to pull her pants legs up but they were firmly attached in her boots. Taking his knife, he cut them from her legs. He was looking for bite marks or scratches, and found what he suspected on her lower thigh... a huge welt caused by a spider bite. "How the hell did this happen? She must have felt pretty damn sick." When he cut out the poison with his razor-sharp knife, she didn't even move. As blood tricked gently, making rivulets down her leg and onto the ground making it appear the tree was weeping blood.

Dana turned away, trying hard not to vomit.

"Okay, that's got rid of it. Pass me some rags. Need to keep this clean," and Daniel fussed over her like she was his child. When he finished bandaging her leg, he wrapped Toni in the blankets to keep her warm. He looked up at his son. "I'll stay with her. Dana, do what Sam tells you. Ben, get me some food and take over the operation."

Sitting down on the ground, Caulder acted as a pillow for her body. She lay across him totally unaware of whom she was with and he held her tightly in his arms, gun resting by his side.

He whispered close to her ear. "Hey, lady. You really do make my life interesting. You gonna keep this up all the way to Yaoundé? You know, don't you, that you're changing my..." He stopped speaking, and leaned back against the damp tree. Food smells wafted from cooking on the fire. This would probably be the last night for hot food as firelight would be dangerous from now on. He listened to the noises the animal kingdom made. In the distance he heard a lion roaring for its mate. Must be antelope nearby, and water. Day after tomorrow they could follow the river. It would lead them right to the capitol. Couldn't stay on the roads anymore... too easy a target. His mind was wandering, as he was suddenly disturbed by cracking branches.

"Food, Mr. Caulder?" Ben offered him a plate and a mug of hot coffee. From his jacket, he produced a hip flask. "Want something to add to it?"

"Sure," and he pulled his arms from under the girl and took the food. "Tomorrow we will stay put. Give her some time. Just hope infection doesn't set in. Maybe it's time we all took a break." He paused while Ben tipped more than just coffee into the tin mug. "Ben? Today, when I killed those bastards, there was a look on this girl's face that went through me like a knife. She hated me," and he swirled the mixture of coffee and whiskey round in the old can.

Ben drew a long sigh in the night air. "No, boss. She doesn't understand, that's all. You and I do, but she doesn't. Probably never will. But she doesn't hate you...I assure you of that," Ben raised his eyebrows at his boss and then left them alone.

Toni woke at dawn, with her mouth dry and her eyesight more than blurred. She tried to focus on the sleeping person holding her. It looked like Caulder, but this person was far too gentle. She felt warm and secure in his arms, but her leg ached as she tried to move in the cocoon of blankets she was weaved into. Still she tried to move, but her movements woke him from the shallow-bottomed weary sleep he had succumbed to.

"Toni, don't move...lie still. You had a bite on your leg. Why on earth didn't you say something?" and he reached for the canteen of water. "Like some?" He held the vessel to her lips and tipped it slightly for her.

She had nodded yes, and gulped it down.

"Easy, easy, not too much or you'll need the bathroom. And I don't think you can manage that right now." He pulled the water back from her mouth and set it by his side, paying attention to her again.

That triggered the button in her head. She needed to go for another reason, and she tried to convey the reason to Caulder.

"Toni, you can't get up. You want to black out again?" Now he was concerned. He didn't want her to get sicker and die on him...for several reasons.

"I have to go, Daniel! There's something I need to take care of," she murmured, hardly audible.

"Okay, then I'll go with you. Need something from your jacket?" This time he wasn't so dumb about what was happening to her.

He carried her to the undergrowth, setting her very gently down on her feet. He held Toni tightly, turning his head away; and then let her go for a minute while she did what she had to do. Toni had never shared such intimacy with anyone, let alone a man like Daniel Caulder.

"Ready?" he asked her. He felt a sudden surge of guilt that this was mainly his fault this girl was in the situation she was.

"Yes," and she felt the faintness again. She swayed just slightly, tilting his way, almost falling on him for support.

With his strong muscular arms, he picked her up like she weighed nothing and started to carry her back to camp. She automatically leaned on his chest, her head resting on his shoulders, and inside of her there was a feeling she didn't quite understand.

A new confidence and respect had arisen between Daniel Caulder and Toni. He'd been the perfect gentleman... not his usual style. Caulder was with her when she hallucinated and when she almost convulsed. It was his fingers under her tongue that stopped her from swallowing it. When her fever broke, he was by her side. He had washed and fed her. Everything was done together, away from the others. They had only one barrier left between them. They were two people growing together... whether they liked it or not.

Three days later, they broke camp. Following the Sanaga River from the west bank, they planned to cross at its lowest point and make a right. The altitude increased, as did the density of the rain forest. It was hot, very hot, and the thunder clouds loomed in a far off place.

As night crept upon them, the temperature decreased, and also the darkening clouds gave them cover. Now, she knew why Caulder was traveling at night. It was easier on them, especially her. She was right behind him as they marched on in military fashion, and most of her belongings swayed to and fro on the litter. Maybe she would stop hating him... maybe. But when she closed her eyes, she could still see dead men walking. Hating him came very easy.

At two a.m., they came across a village nestled by the river. The inhabitants were long asleep, and that's how it needed to stay.

The leader turned back towards the group. "No one make any noise. Step lightly!" whispered Caulder.

The party made their way on by, treading as lightly as possible to get passed and away from the danger.

Toni was amazed at the state of the shanties of the natives that passed for homes. The hovels had rusted tin roofs, and torn cloths passed for doors. Poverty was the word that sprang readily to mind. The stench of garbage and excrement reached them down by the river, and a primitive graveyard added to the odor. As they walked by the fringes of the town, Toni could see tiny crosses of children dead at birth.

Caulder's keen ear heard her exclaim.

"Keep going, Toni. That's standard out here." He reached his hand back to her. She looked at his arm extended in friendship. She hesitated, and he kept his arm outstretched so she moved alongside him and slid her hand into his, uncertain as to why he had done that.

By dawn, they had covered several miles and passed many such villages. Places that had many secrets and the river that held them all. Toni thought they would never stop walking. Her feet ached and her heart was heavy, but still she clung to Daniel's hand finding some kind of reassurance there.

As the sun rose, Caulder stopped the trek. He waved for the party to crouch down in the grass and pulled Toni down with him. Ferns brushed against their legs. "Look across the river."

In front of them was a herd of elephants taking in the cool water of the Sanaga. Out from the mother elephant stood a calf not more than a few months old. He splashed in the water with his baby squeals of delight piercing the morning air. He shot water at his mama, and she swung her trunk as if to scold her infant. Toni was fascinated. Her grip tightened around Caulder's hand. Slowly, he released it and put his arm around her shoulders, and she never noticed, being so absorbed by the sight in front of her. They watched together as the bull moved in on his mate. The majestic leader of the group stood protecting his female and his young, and then threw his head back and a loud, wondrous noise hit the sky. He'd picked up the scent of his worst enemy… man!

They watched till the herd moved on and Toni was both happy and sad all in one for she had never witnessed anything like this before. She kept on watching till the herd was just a dot on the horizon, a horizon of early morning rays and the dawning of a new day. This was reality and life at its finest. Her eyes were moist as tears trickled down her face and she felt Caulder pull her closer.

"Hey, come on. They're happy and safe." He looked into her eyes and wiped the tears that sprang from them. As he did his hand brushed her face and he could feel her warm breath on his fingers… this time, he followed through. He touched her lips with his fingers and then he very gently leaned forward and kissed her. This was no kiss of urgency... just one of a man for the woman he wanted.

For them, as it was for the young elephant, they had crossed over the barrier and had tasted a new side of living.

Ben watched the proceedings from the back of the line. He'd taken out binoculars to watch the elephants, and now he watched man instead. Pangs of jealousy swept through his heart, like he never thought he could posses. He'd watched Daniel and Toni grow closer in the last few days... how could he not? But he knew his boss well and he didn't want to see Toni used and abused. She wasn't like the others. This girl was warm and gentle and certainly not the kind of woman that hung round the place. Who was he kidding? He knew that this time his boss genuinely cared for the girl... he knew because of the way he tended to her... the same way Ben had seen him do for Dana. That's how he knew.

As for Dana, the boy had crept up behind his father. When he saw him kissing Toni, he retraced his steps almost embarrassed. Sam caught him on the way back, touching him lightly on his arm.

"Anything wrong, Dana? You look a little upset, partner." Sam's voice was soft and low, not his usual demeanor.

"Not upset, Sam, not at all. They were kissing, Sam. My father was kissing Toni and she kissed him back. I hope that Papa will keep Toni and she will not go away like the others," and in his voice there was a hint of hopefulness.

It was then Sam realized just how much Dana missed a mother in his young life. "Sit down, here in the grass. Let me explain something to you. Your father is a man who enjoys life and, as you know, likes women. You're not a child anymore, Dana, so I'm not talking to you as one. I think this time, Miss Sinclair may change the way your father feels. You might find that he may just keep her around."

"Really, you think so?" and the boy clapped his hands lightly in glee and dropped back into his place in the line.

They pressed on just a few more miles. Toni took her place back in line unaware that half the world had seen him kiss her... and this time not for show of strength. But she was confused. One minute he degraded her, the next he was kissing her. What kind of signals was he giving her, and more to the point what kind was she giving back.

As they walked, the sun burnt hot on their backs. Soon it would be time to camp in the shade. But right now, Toni was hot and she removed her jacket, followed by Dana's borrowed shirt. She was wearing a very tight cutaway T-shirt underneath that she had saved from the backpack. All was fine… till Caulder turned and saw her.

He yelled at her. "Boys don't have boobs! Put your damn shirt back on!"

"It's so hot. Please, no one can see me," she argued, sweat pouring down her body only emphasizing even more that she was a female.

"I can!" and he turned to her and grabbed the shirt out of her hands, ripping the sleeves from their stitching. "Now, put it back on!" and he almost threw it at her.

She did as she was asked. "I didn't think you'd mind…" She didn't get to finish.

"I mind! I mind that half these guys can see you like that." He caught himself. Jealousy rang through with the very words he spoke.

"What business is it of yours anyway? I don't belong to you!" Once again she was on the defensive; all the good days were a fleeting memory again.

"No, you don't. Not yet." He turned away from her and surveyed the river. This would be a good place to cross.

"I beg your pardon? I think 'never' would be a better word." Her face was red with anger, and she grabbed his arm. As she did, she felt his muscles tighten, and he looked down at her hand. She let go immediately.

"Never, Miss Sinclair? That's a long time," and his eyes narrowed at her as his authority reigned supreme.

"What's that supposed to mean?" she argued back with him.

"Whatever *you* want it to." And he turned back to business, totally cool and completely in control, and left her standing staring at him as he started to make camp.

They would stay here a few hours and then go over when it was a little later in the day, after everyone was rested. Even Daniel had to admit this was tough going. He sent some of the men to find fruits that they might enjoy, mindful to keep an eye on both Toni and his son.

As she dozed in the afternoon sun, her mind was full of the morning's events. Dana lay by her side, his face still covered in berry juice and his young head on her lap. They'd eaten well and now they slept a fitful sleep but, at least, sleep.

Close by Caulder and Ben sat talking. "This is as good a place as any to cross. We'll all get an hour sleep. Then we'll take the belongings over a bit at a time. Machine guns go first and the rest can follow." He looked into the distance peering at the sun. "There's a storm heading our way. Perhaps we should cross now?" He looked at the men. They were tired and so was he. "I guess a couple of hours won't make that much difference." His tone changed, and he looked down at the ground. "Ben, there's something I want to tell you. If ever you need help, turn to Sam. He will look after you and Dana. Always watch out for Dana because he's…" A loud clap of thunder stopped him talking as the African skies spilled their contents and water spewed forth like some sick, rabid animal. A flash storm was unusual this time of year.

"Dana, Toni, wake up! We have to cross… now." Caulder yelled at them both, while he grabbed anything around him that they needed.

Men ran in all directions gathering things to the water's edge. Guns, food, blankets, and canteens… anything they could lay their hands on and stacked them onto the makeshift litter a couple of the men had reinforced for crossing the river.

"Sam, you and I will take the litter across, and then we'll come back for the rest." Daniel was driven to get across.

They dragged the now laden litter to the water's edge. Caulder stepped in the water, one hand firmly attached to the litter, pulling it with him as he went. Very unsure of his footing, he trod carefully. Sam followed with the guns and the other end of the litter. They crossed gingerly, step by step, and with great care. It was raining hard now. In just those few minutes the current in the river had become ferocious and it flowed dangerously from the storm that racked the skies. Still Caulder and Sam kept going. The water was higher than Daniel bargained for and once or twice he lost his footing, slipping and sliding as he went, almost losing his grasp on the litter.

Toni stood watching on the bank, a new fear inside her. Rain poured down her face and soaked her clothes in seconds. Much as she thought she hated this man, she was frightened he would drown. Then she remembered the swimmer in him. She watched with baited breath as the two men made it to the bank, Dana standing close by her side. They could just hear yelling from the other side of the fast growing river.

"Sam, stay here! I'll go back and take this rope from the litter with me. Wrap the end around a tree and make a line. It will help the girl and my son to get across." He was dripping water and yelling at the top of his lungs. As he dropped back into the water, Daniel disappeared under it. He wanted to see the depth for himself.

Toni heard herself say his name... 'Daniel,' and she clasped her hands to her mouth hoping no one had heard, glancing around her, and then looking back into the water to see if she could see him.

Daniel surfaced halfway across, and then swam back to the shoreline, climbed out of the water, looking cold and very wet. Pushing his hair from his eyes, he handed the end of the rope to Ben. "Okay, get the guys to go across. Hold the rifles above your heads and the backpacks. You can do it. Go!" and he leaned back on a nearby tree, exhausted from the water's flow, but watching every step the men made.

They managed it, like he hoped they would. One or two of the plastic lined backpacks were no worse for their wash in the water. Then it was his son's turn.

"Okay, Ben. Take Dana across; put him on your back. I'll bring your things. Get going... now!" He could only just be heard above the water's mammoth roar, and Daniel lifted his son up onto Ben's back.

The child perched there, and in his eyes he showed fear, fear that his father could quite clearly see. Dropping into the water, they clung to the line as they inched their way along, hand over hand. Lightning flashed around them, and the thunder was worse than the lion's roar. Caulder could see Dana hanging on to Ben, trying to be brave yet failing like any little boy would. He waited till his son was safely across, climbing up the bank and then turned to Toni.

"It's your turn, young lady. You go in front of me. Sam and the men are pulling the line high in the water. Hold on to it and I will be right behind you," and Daniel gestured at the line as he ushered her towards the water.

Toni buttoned her jacket and pushed the film as deep in the lining as she could. It was in a waterproof container, one that she hoped worked. Her camera had gone over with the litter. It was now or never for her.

"I'm ready, but just in case I don't make it..." She turned to Caulder, suddenly realizing what she felt for him. "I..." and she paused, dropping her head slightly so he wouldn't see her eyes.

"You what?" he yelled above the river's roar, almost amused by the look on her face, and looked down at her.

"Nothing. It doesn't matter," and she turned away, shocked by her own emotions. Rain splattered her face, and she tried to wipe it away.

On impulse he grabbed her by the shoulders and pulled her back to him, looking down into her face. He held her tightly to him, and through the pouring African rains he kissed her passionately, his hands moving down her body holding her with no chance of escape. She responded desperately to him, her arms on his back. Then, he threw his head back and laughed. "At least you don't hate me anymore! Go, Toni!" and he let go, ushering her into the water.

She slipped and slid as she scrambled down the bank and looked back up at Daniel's face. Toni was terrified and he knew it as he waved at her to continue.

Clinging to the lifeline, she fell into the swirling mass of water, putting one hand over the other as she crossed to the middle of the rushing torrent. Sam pulled hard on the rope and tried to hold it, as the others joined him taking up the extra line. Toni was three-quarters of the way there when the rope, now fraying from use, started to slacken. She felt it, and also the panic inside of her.

"Hold on to it, Toni! Mr. Caulder, cross now. The ropes almost gone!" yelled Sam, who could hardly be heard.

Caulder saw her struggling and he glanced back to the bank realizing there were still supplies there. They could stay. He swung his and Ben's rifles crisscross on his body, and then he followed her sliding into the water's edge. He knew the line would not take both weights and hesitated before dropping into the flowing torrent. Ben was closer to Toni, and he reached down grabbing her hand, and only when he knew she was safe did Caulder let go of the slippery grass on the bank.

A hundred and eighty pounds of man was too much for one rope. Halfway over, it snapped. Daniel grabbed for the secure line and hung on to the end, as the men on the other side pulled as hard as their bodies would let them. Toni was now up on the side of the river bank and she stood there crying, almost hysterical, shaking from the cold and rain. She made a break as if to run down the bank and Ben grabbed her as she tried to get back in the water to help Daniel.

"Toni, Toni!" Ben screamed at her. "Take care of Dana! He needs you more than Caulder does. We'll get our boss out!"

The boy stood on the shore shaking while he watched his father struggling in the swirling current. Toni pulled Dana to her and cried with the father's son. He clung to her, his arms encircling her waist. "He'll make it, won't he, Toni? Tell me he will!" and he buried his head against her body.

She looked up to the sky. "He has to, Dana. He just has to. Your father can't leave two people who love him." Toni didn't know what she was saying and clung to the child as if she would lose him also.

Dana knew what she had said.

But in the water the weight of the guns was pulling Caulder under. He realized he had to let them go, and somehow he ditched them both, one at a time, and still managed to cling to his lifeline. And, then, in one split second, the lifeline was gone. It slipped from his fingers and he swam upwards against the fast flowing downwards current. Even with his ability for swimming, he was losing the battle of his life and he knew it. As if in slow motion, his life flashed before him and some of it he didn't want to lose, like his son and the girl on the bank... he tried to focus and desperately held his arm out to his men. As Daniel swam near to them, Ben stretched his hand to him.

"Come on, boss. Grab my hand!" But Caulder's hands were too wet and each time he tried to take a hold, he slipped back into the water, draining him of his strength.

"Boss," shouted Sam, "behind you!" But it was too late. In the panic no one noticed until the log hit Caulder on the back of the head with a whopping thud. He lost consciousness instantly and dropped below the surface.

Toni let go of Dana and the pair rushed to the water's edge trying to get a glimpse of Daniel Caulder.

Without anyone giving orders, Sam and then Andre jumped in the raging torrent together. Ben yelled in any language that came to his head, and two of the men seized both the boy and his friend.

"Keep them back!" screamed Ben. "Don't let them near the water, either of them!"

The Brazilian came up for air first and then plunged back under the current. Sam swam deeper and saw Caulder's outline near the river bottom. Only his foot, caught in a vine, had stopped him from being carried downstream. Sam pulled at the weed and tried to free his boss… He failed miserably. What he needed was a knife. Then he saw the other man swimming through the murky water. Sam gestured to Andre as to what was needed, and Andre pulled a long-stemmed blade from his belt, dived lower in the current and cut the weed away from its captive's foot.

Ben still waited on the bank, pacing up and down. "God, where are they? He's been under too long." Ben let his thoughts run to his mouth. Then he saw them all surface, scrambling through the mud, slipping and sliding back into the muddy water. It took four of them to pull Daniel on shore. Their boss was dead weight, and Sam and Andre lay back on the soft wet ground totally exhausted.

Ben dropped to the ground and felt for a pulse on his boss's neck. Nothing. "He's not breathing! Help me get that jacket off him!" He knew instinctively that he had to get the dank water from Caulder's lungs. Ben had learned CPR sometime back, and now he had a use for it. For some unquestionable reason, this man had to live. He placed his hands on his boss's chest and pushed hard. It didn't work… nothing happened, so he put his mouth onto his and held Caulder's nose, trying to breath life into him. He pushed hard again on the chest. "1001, 1002, 1003! Come on, boss, breathe! For god's sake, someone help me with him!" He tried again and this time water spewed from

Daniel's mouth, running down his face, but still he made no movement.

Lying on his back, Caulder's chest was caked in mud and Ben tried to listen for a heart beat. He couldn't find one. "Damn it, don't you die on me! Damn you, Daniel Caulder, you-son-of-a-bitch. There are two people over there that love you. Don't you leave them! Damn you, don't do this to us!" And he hit Caulder hard on his chest, again and again, waiting for a reaction. He brought his fist down hard and tried to revive this man, knowing that the longer he stayed out the worse it got. Daniel Caulder was turning blue.

Dana cried in Toni's arms. She couldn't watch anymore and turned her head into the child's hair. She whispered into his ear and to her God. "Take me, instead, not this boy's father." It was then they heard a coughing sound.

Caulder was choking. They turned him sideward and more water and grime billowed from his lungs, and he heaved and retched until he could heave no more. Opening his eyes, he focused on the boy now bending over him as Dana flung himself down on his father.

"Papa, papa!" he cried. "We thought you were dead." And the boy hung on like the grim reaper would appear and claim what was rightfully his.

With help Caulder sat up. He held the child to him. "We?" and his voice was labored.

"Toni and I," whispered Dana. "But you didn't, Papa, because Toni prayed for you and because we love you," and the child was crying and tears of joy flowed onto his father.

"We? You and Ben?" Daniel struggled with his speech.

"Ben, papa? No, not Ben. Toni," the boy replied looking questioningly at his father as though he should understand exactly what he meant.

"How do you know that, Dana?" Daniel whispered.

"She told me."

"Who else did she tell?" Daniel was shocked at the statement. But knew his son would never lie to him.

"No one. Is it a secret, papa?" asked the innocent child.

"For now, Dana, for now." Caulder looked across at her, shaking in the pouring rains… afraid of her own shadow.

"Ben, help me up. We have to move away. The river's rising, and I lost the rifles. I couldn't hold them." He still had trouble speaking and as spoke his hand searched his waist touching the money belt. At least that had proved waterproof.

Sam and Ben helped him behind the trees, his legs still a little wobbly. There was little shelter, but the rain showed some signs of letting up. Toni and the rest of the men gathered up the belongings. Through the mists of rain, Caulder watched her pile the rifles together, watched her in torn and wet clothes, her short hair lying flat on her head. She had no make-up, just a rosy glow from the sun, and she struggled with the weight of the guns but still she soldiered on. She would not be defeated. As she moved, she caught sight of him watching her, and turned away from his gaze. Caulder wiped the rain from his eyes with aching fingers and carried on looking at her, captivated by her tenacity to survive and prove herself to him. He had taken her pride and her dignity, all she had left was her virginity… and that he intended to take, very soon.

Finally, the storm cleared, and back came the sunny skies, and with it came the heat. Huddled together for so long in the rain, all of them were glad to dry their clothes. Toni stayed with Dana while Caulder's men looked out for him. She felt like an intruder in a man's world for they could do what she could not. She couldn't drag him to safety, or change his clothes. She wasn't strong enough, and she knew it. But what she could do was love him, from a distance… and look after his son. And now she had admitted it to herself… She did love this man… what kind of love, she had no idea. It was a new experience for her, one she wasn't so sure she liked.

In the early evening light, they ate. Fruit, breads, and berries. For some reason, she was hungry and ate more than usual. Tonight, under the cover of darkness, they would move on.

Daniel sat watching her and his child. "Mr. Caulder, I think you need to rest more. That took a lot from you today. Most men would have died."

"But I'm not most men, Sam. We'll wait till nine, then we'll go on a ways; I just don't want to stay here." And he shivered, pulling a damp blanket round him. "Maybe we'll find a village up ahead. How's the girl?" he added, low under his breath.

"She's in better condition than you. But then you know that, don't you? Mr. Caulder, Daniel, Dana and I had a talk about Toni. He misses a woman's companionship. He wants you to keep her." Sam never looked at his boss as he spoke.

"Does he? He told me that Toni told him she loved me! Quite the day for confessions!" His manner changed instantly to one of much more concentration. "Speaking of which, I almost told Ben…"

"Don't do it, boss," interrupted Sam. "He couldn't handle it right now. He's fighting over his emotions for Toni. He sees you as some sort of competitor, only he knows you're winning. Don't add to that. He may turn on you," and Sam hesitated before he spoke again… "And the girl?"

"I have to tell her about Dana's mother. Then we'll see. Quite some mess, eh, Sam? What's that phrase? What a tangled web we weave, when first we practice to deceive. Yeah, well in this case, it fits! As for Ben, we should have told him long ago." He still coughed from the bilge deep inside his lungs.

"No, we shouldn't! What he doesn't know can't hurt him. But Dana has a point. Are you going to keep her?" Sam was blunt. He'd been with Caulder too long not to be.

"Any reason I should?" He looked his friend in the face, his eyes piercing into Sam's, and he gave nothing away.

"You're the only one who can answer that, *Mr. Caulder*. So we'll be ready by nine, boss." Sam stood up and walked away leaving his boss to think.

Nine was good. They walked just a few miles before they found a small village. Sam had been right. Caulder did need more time to recover from his ordeal. The natives were sympathetic to the cause, and Caulder's money played a large part in that sympathy; also the fact that the women in the village had never seen a white girl before. Caulder found it amusing but also disturbing that she was causing so much attention, and it was hard to hide the fact she was female. They fussed around her like mother hens with an abandoned chick.

Finally Daniel walked to where she stood and taking her by the shoulders, ushered her away to one of the shanties on the outskirts of the village. It was small, with two rooms, and he'd paid plenty to get it. Caulder needed to talk to her, just the two of them, and he'd given the group instructions, especially Sam, who knew just what to do. He moved the curtain door back for her and Toni stepped inside the hovel and walked around the rooms. It was an alien way of life to her, and yet there was something familiar about it. There was a strange odor in the room and one she could not identify.

He watched her smelling the air.

"It's something they burn to keep the insects at bay," he lied to her. He knew exactly what it was, sweet and sickly all in one go. But to introduce her to the world of drugs right now would have been a stupid move and not one he had in mind. "Toni, you and I need to talk."

She turned to face him, her eyes locked onto his face. She thought he looked tired and older than of late, but still there was an attraction to this man she could not understand. "Is that why we're on our own in here and everyone else is together. Or is there some other reason?" She was also tired and it showed on her face and the way she moved her body.

"Sit down. I need you to understand something," and he pointed to the only place to sit, that being a bed and one that was very close to the dirt floor. Colored blankets lay strewn across it, and pillows filled with hair made back rests.

She did as she was asked.

Caulder noted her nervousness, so he stood, actually making her more unsettled than ever.

He began. "Toni, when I met Dana's mother, she was young like you, maybe even younger. She was beautiful and I… well, I fell in love with her." He paused on purpose to give his words time to sink into her brain.

Toni was shocked and it showed by her expression. Caulder in love? Not possible. She kept on staring at him like she didn't believe him.

"Yes, I know that must come as a surprise to you. It did to me, also. But she was so beautiful and full of life. She had spirit and she made me laugh. She also made me fall in love with this country. As you well know, my dossier is full of indiscretions and affairs, but this time it was different. I was really in love for the first time in my life. It was strange to me, but it was a feeling I wanted to last for ever. She was overjoyed when she found she was pregnant with our child. Her beauty only grew, and her silk black skin pulsated with radiance. But, as you know, she was married. We would often return to the waterfall where Dana was conceived. You know the place. We were in our own world there. Free from the trappings of royalty," he paused again, as if he was back in time… with her. "On the same day the king was assassinated, she gave birth to our child there. Everyone thought it was her husband's baby she carried. Even after he died, that lie lived on… to most people."

She listened intently. Why was he telling her all this?

He continued, a certain pain on his face for memories of yesteryear. "She had wanted to go there that day, like she had some sort of premonition about what was to happen. She begged me to stay with her and I didn't. I went back for help. When I returned with help, it was too late. She'd managed to give birth, and died. As you see, they saved my son. I killed her, Toni…" He could not continue, and started to turn away from her.

She stood and put her hand on his arm. "Daniel, I'm so sorry. I had no idea. But you didn't kill her." And then she hesitated knowing she had to ask. "Are you still in love with her now?" Her voice was hardly audible.

She dreaded his reply, feeling that if he said yes, her world might just fall apart.

He collected his thoughts, noting she had called him Daniel and turned to her. "No. I told you for a reason; to let you know why my son is so important to me." And now he hesitated. Once this was said there was no going back for Daniel Caulder. "And it's not her memory I'm in love with… it's you!"

Chapter 5

In the light of the fire, Caulder could see her clearly. Toni was speechless and her face flushed. But he had been known to say those words before… especially when he wanted to take someone to bed. She turned away from him and walked towards the cloth door.

"Where are you going?" he questioned her.

"To join the others…"

"Is that what you want, Toni? Really want?" He was fighting his own emotions, ones of anger and frustration.

She hesitated. "Yes…"

"The truth, young lady! Damn it! Tell me the truth! Dana told me that you're in love with me. Or was that something you said for his benefit? Do you want to leave? I'll ask you for the last time."

"Yes…" she stammered. "No, I don't know anymore. Just that I have to get out of here!"

But Caulder was quicker and coming up behind her, he encircled her with his arms. She tried to free herself, but he was way too strong. He held her tightly to him and she struggled to be free. He leaned down and kissed her neck, feeling her shaking in his arms. "Toni, don't be frightened of me, please! I know it's your first time… and I won't do anything you don't want me to… but I want you and you want me! Give in to me, or at least into your feelings for me. You know you want this as much as I do!"

Toni realized her uncle had been correct. She was naive, and had no idea how to make a man like Caulder happy.

"How the hell do you know that?" she demanded.

He moved his hand across her breast. "This is why." And he touched her raised nipple.

Pulling her top down from her arms, he let it drop to the floor. Turning her around to face him, Caulder touched her face. He pulled her tighter to him, pressed his body against hers and kissed her. She tried to pull away, fighting her own emotions.

As he kissed her, his hands slid the T-shirt down from her sunburned shoulder until her breasts were revealed. He looked down and was more than aroused by her, but now he knew he had to take it slow and easy.

"Caulder, please don't! You know I'm a…" Her green eyes flashed and she tried to move.

"Toni, listen to me. I know. And I also know you have a great body. I've seen it before, remember?" he whispered.

How could she forget? "But it's different… and I'm afraid."

"Afraid? What the hell do you think I'm doing? I'm making love to you, not raping…" And he stopped mid-sentence. He raised her face with his hands and kissed her again, slower and more gently than before. "I can't hold back anymore, Toni. It's now or it's never for us. Say you don't want this; I'll walk away from you and never touch you again."

Her struggles subsided and to him this was a green light. Daniel picked her up and carried her over to the bed, pulling her boots and socks off, then her pants. She lay on the bed, a kind of fear in her eyes and yet, also one of wanting.

"I do want you, Daniel. God, I want you!" She'd used his first name and her breathing was hot and heavy to his ears.

He stood up and removed his clothes, his muscular body glistening in the firelight. He was magnificent in his manhood… and he knew it. Leaning across the bed, he slowly removed her T-shirt. He slid his hand down her body and she felt a surge she had never experienced before. Without her even realizing it, he removed her panties. His mouth covered her breast and his hands searched her body.

Toni felt as if she couldn't breathe. She was choking on her own ecstasy. This man lived up to his reputation and more. She slid her arms from around his neck and slowly he moved down her body, continually kissing her untouched skin. When he reached the coarse patch of hair, he kissed the lips that awaited him and tasted the soft fluid of his woman.

Already heady with the smell of pot floating in the night air, Toni was on a plateau she had only dreamt of. Her hands clung to the bed and she fantasized in eroticism. She was totally conscious of what he was doing to her and yet she wasn't.

He moved back up the bed and pushed her legs either side of his body. "Bend your legs, Toni. Come on, honey. Bring your legs up a little. That's my girl." His tone was soft. He slid his hands up her thighs and under her back. Caulder didn't need any guidance. He slipped his fingers in first, not wanting to cause her pain, and looked at her face. There was no pain, only pleasure. Lowering his body onto her... he took away the virginity she had treasured so long.

He hadn't lied to her; he was in love with her, very much in love. But today was the last time he could tell her that. He knew by what he had just accomplished she would always be his and he would always be hers. Daniel made a pledge to himself... there would be no other woman after her, and he also knew he should have restrained himself. He had not been fair to her or to himself. Somewhere down the line he would have to say goodbye.

Toni cried out, not in pain, but pleasure. She had dreamed of something like this, only between silk sheets and with wine and candlelight. The only part of the dream fulfilled... was the man.

She opened her eyes and looked at Caulder. Sweat ran down her face and he wiped it away with tender fingers. She released the grip she had on his back and gradually became calmer.

"You okay?" and he kissed away her tears. He wanted her to be okay. He knew that he should have respected her wishes and not forced his attentions on her, but his need for her was great.

"I'm fine," she murmured. She looked him in the eyes "Are you? You nearly drowned today, and now look at you."

"I'm feeling just great for a dead man." He pulled himself gently off her body and lay down beside her.

Toni turned on her side and put her arm around him, as he protected her with his arms, and, if needs be, his body. That's how much he loved her.

"My, Toni, how you've changed. You're not the same person that came to my door a couple of weeks back. You did want to make love, didn't you? Toni, if your uncle could see you now," and he glanced down at her body.

She looked at her naked body. "Thank god, he cannot. Or he would kill me… and you. And to answer your question… yes, I did. I wanted you more than I have ever wanted anything in my life. I think I wanted you the first time you touched me. I never knew it would be like this, Daniel. I didn't mean to accuse you of…" She stopped speaking.

"I know you didn't. It's okay, really," and he stopped her from speaking. "Honey, you need some sleep. Tomorrow is going to be a long day." And he let out a sigh.

"What about you? Don't you need sleep? We're sharing the same day, aren't we? And you think something is going to happen, don't you?" she whispered, still curled into him.

"Smart girl. I made love to you because it's what we both wanted… you and me. Because we share feelings." But he didn't say 'love' again. "Yes, we're going on, and yes, I think something is going to happen in the next few days. We're getting closer to our destination and Sung's men will be waiting for us at some point. At first light, Ben and I are going to change your skin and hair color. Dana and you will look similar. When we are near Yaoundé, Dana, Sam, and I will go on. The rest of you will stay at a safe house on the outskirts."

She was startled by the news and sat upright, staring at him. "Why, why do we split up?"

"It's safer for us all, especially you."

"You mean I'm a decoy while you take Dana to his people, right? Was this the plan from the start?" She was afraid of the answer.

"No. The thought occurred to Ben and me the night I cut your hair. You're not a decoy, just a distraction. In more ways than one," and he turned his head towards her, smiling at her.

"Then, Mr. Caulder, can I distract you every night till we part?" She was heady from the odor and the ecstasy, and now she wanted more… much more.

At four they dozed a little. Toni ached. The man's body had been heavy on hers, and he'd made more than a lasting impression in her body.

Six a.m. saw daylight, and Ben came to the cloth door. He didn't know what he expected to find, but certainly not what he did. He listened before entering, craning his head at the doorway.

"Honey, calm down. Come on… Toni." Daniel was trying to let her down gently. "We should have stopped the last time. It's too much for you," and he rocked her gently.

Her cries turned to laughter. "I want to spend every moment making love with you. You took me in my sleep, didn't you? I didn't dream it, did I?"

"No, you didn't dream it." Caulder turned serious. "Toni, I should never have brought you here. Please, take care of yourself. I don't want anything to happen to you," and he swung his legs onto the dirt floor making large footprints as he did.

"Daniel, nothing is going to happen. Why are you so worried?" she asked, draping her naked body around him.

Caulder was trying to concentrate and Toni was making that task harder by the minute. "Because we have many enemies. Even in the village, we have them. If ever you need help, go to Ben or Sam… but especially Ben. I think he has feelings for you."

Ben cringed in the doorway.

"Don't be silly. You'll be telling me next that he's in love with me, too." She leaned around him and looked at Daniel's face. "He isn't, is he?" She was shocked.

He raised his eyebrows and shrugged his shoulders.

"Oh, I hope not. He's just my friend. I never looked at him like that. You were right when you said this trip would make a woman out of me," and she giggled.

"Yeah, I noticed," and his eyes scanned her body. "Some woman. Okay, time to get up…"

"You already did that…" and she laughed, a laugh that was precocious.

As she stepped out on to the dirt floor, he caught her on the backside. "Go and get washed. There's water in that bucket over there. Do you need any help from me?"

"Yeah..." she replied and turned her naked body towards him, taunting him with her young flesh.

Caulder slid off the bed and picked her up. Her legs went around his waist and he had her against the mud walls. "You learn fast, young lady," he whispered.

She struggled to speak. "I have a good teacher..." she murmured, her eyes closed, and Toni moaned with pleasure.

Ben could stand no more. He stepped out in the morning light... a different man. He wanted to vomit, but it would not come. Standing in the air, he knew he had to go back and face them. He had told Caulder he would help with Toni's change. His boss had managed that all by himself!

Ben was lost in thought as he felt someone tugging on his arm.

"Something wrong, Ben?" the young boy asked.

It brought him to his senses, very rapidly. "No, Dana... nothing. Where are you going?" He was aware he could not let the son go to the father.

"To papa and ask him where Toni is." Dana was looking to Ben for answers, his face turned up to the older man.

"That's not a good idea, right now. Your father is busy..." 'He was busy, all right' thought Ben.

"Have you seen her?" The child looked at him, questioning the number 2.

Child? He was no child. But Ben had affection for him that he could never explain.

Just then Caulder appeared at the door. He was dressed in pants and boots; his gun and holster hanging from his shoulder. "Good morning to you both. Dana, I hope you slept well? Ben, are you ready to help change the lady?"

Ben's reply was taut. "Didn't you spend the night doing that?" He stopped. "I'm sorry, Mr. Caulder, that was rude of me and also none of my business. I was out of line."

So, he knew, and Caulder could see the hurt on the young man's face. "No, Ben. It is your business. The lady made her own choice... more or less. But if anything happens to me, you look after her. That's an order. Come on, let's go get this done."

His son looked from one to the other with a puzzled look on his face.

"Dana, you can come, too," Caulder added, trying to hide what was really going down and Daniel ushered his son towards the target.

Inside the shack, Toni wrapped a blanket around her half clothed body and waited for her lover to return. Her feet rested on the floor, her toes playing in the dirt. She wanted her first time of making love to be in a hotel somewhere; to be wined and dined and whisked off to bed. Silk sheets, music, champagne… the works… and the man, he had to be magnificent. That part of the dream was reality. Caulder had left her with an insatiable thirst for sex with him. One night with him was better than ten years with someone else.

Daniel stepped inside their room first to make sure she had clothes on. Satisfied he let the others enter. "Okay, Ben. You and Dana can come in. Honey, stand up against Dana."

She did as she was asked, just glancing at Ben, a little embarrassed at the comments Daniel had made about him.

Ben could immediately see the difference in Toni. She was a transformed woman and when she looked at Caulder… she positively glowed.

Toni realized Ben was staring at her and she pulled the blanket tighter round her, leaving her shoulders and arms bare.

Caulder moved to within an inch of her and lowered the blanket just a little, without revealing anything he didn't want anyone else to see. "Face, neck, shoulders and arms," he pulled the thread bare cover up above her knees, "and legs. Good strong berry juice and some of those hand made oils should do it. Has to be fairly dark and must not come off easily. We'll do the same on her hair." He ruffled her short hair. "There's just a couple of things that we can't do anything about."

She hit him playfully on his arm and Daniel laughed at her. Dana noticed, and he was glad. Perhaps Sam was right… maybe his father did intend to keep her.

They worked on her for over an hour pouring the juices through her hair and the oils over her skin. Caulder rubbed it well into her legs and arms. He allowed his son to make up her face. Then they stood back and admired their work each from a different perspective.

"Can I look?" she asked tentatively turning her face up to Daniel.

"Shall we let her?" asked Caulder, looking at his son.

"Yes, papa. She looks like me... now we can be brother and sister," and there was a gleam in his eye.

Ben thought to himself that that comment was positively incestuous.

Caulder looked around for a mirror, wiped it clean on his pants, and then held it up in front of Toni's face.... And waited for her reaction.

She never made a sound, just stared in disbelief. She blinked but the image didn't go away. She wanted to cry, but to do that would be to undermine Dana and his country.

Caulder handed her the rest of her clothes. "Toni, pull your T-shirt as tight across your chest as you can. Here, let me help you." He'd seen the look on his lover's face. Tonight he would reassure her she was still as beautiful... brown or white.

Ben turned Dana away while she dressed and then Dana looked back at Toni.

"Okay, let's see now. You look great... hardly tell the two of you apart. Toni, you go with Ben and, Dana, you stay by me. From now to Yaoundé the two of you have changed places."

Dana looked at her. "Toni, I want to thank you for your help."

"I'm glad to do it, Dana, for you... and for your father." She dropped her stare, looking down at the ground so that tears would not escape her eyes.

Caulder whispered in her ear. "Stay close to Ben. I'll see you tonight," and he winked at her.

She nodded in agreement, as she stood in the early morning light. Inside... she cried silent tears, knowing she would never be the same again.

They left the village at nine, somewhat later than intended. Now it meant traveling in the daylight... not a good idea. Several hours into the trek, they stopped to rest and drink water. Toni sat away from the others, leaving only Ben near to her. She rested her face on her hands being tired... very tired. Lack of sleep now caught up with her and she had much to think about, especially last night. It was then, disturbing her thoughts, that she heard a sound she thought she would never forget. It was the sound of a baby crying... but no ordinary crying. She recognized the cry as that of a dying baby. Without thinking of her safety, Toni rose up, ran through the bush with the grass brushing her legs and branches stroking her face. There was no fear in her for her safety.

"Toni, come back here... now!" Ben yelled at her, but she was gone like some crazy person. He jumped up from the ground and grabbed for his gun. "Toni!" he screamed. "Boss," he yelled at Caulder, "she's gone! I can't stop her!" and he gave chase after the girl.

Caulder turned from where he sat. "God damn you, Toni, come back! Toni, it's a ploy... Toni!" His voice trailed into the distance.

But she was way ahead of them. The two men went after her, but she kept running as the crying became louder. Breathless, she entered the clearing, and it was there she saw him... the baby elephant with its foot in the trap. Blood gushed from its leg turning green to red. Totally unconcerned for her own well being, she ran to him. He howled in the wind like a banshee and his cries melted her heart. He thrashed to be free, but the steel chain was merciless to its captive. By his side, lay the body of his mother. The rest of the herd was long gone. Toni dropped to the floor and pulled at the chain that held him. She was helpless and she looked into his eyes... eyes full of fear and pain, and the suffering that lingered there. And then she knew no more as a blow, to the back of head, dropped her into unconsciousness and no more pain.

"Get the boy, now." yelled Sung.

His friend did the rest and picked Toni up bodily, throwing her over his shoulder like she weighed nothing.

"Let's depart. Mr. Caulder will be right behind his son." Sung and his men headed for their jeeps, dumped Toni in the back and roared away towards Yaoundé. Somehow he knew who the boy belonged to. Someone else on the outside knew as well.

As the trucks disappeared into the distance, Caulder and Ben reached the elephant still swaying with pain. Caulder raised his rifle, aimed and fired a single shot and the baby joined his mother. He lowered the gun and began to search around for some signs of his woman.

"Toni, for god's sake, where are you?" But he already knew she was gone. "He has her. My god, he has her! Some bastard back at the village betrayed us…Someone loyal to the rebels. Sung has her!" screamed Daniel to anyone that would listen. There was an indescribable fear on his face and an aching in the black hole he called a heart.

"Mr. Caulder, Daniel!" and Ben grabbed his shoulders almost shaking him, not a smart thing to do on any given day. "Boss, listen to me. Does he think he has her… or your son?" Ben tried to get the man in his grasp to concentrate on the situation.

"Oh, my god, he thinks he has Dana," he gasped and broke free from Ben's hands. "What the hell will happen when he finds out that it's a girl he has?" Then he saw the blood by his feet and, bending down, touched it with his finger tips. It was warm. They'd probably hit her from behind when she was trying to help the calf. Daniel wiped it on his pants leg.

By now the rest of the group had caught up with them and Dana ran to his father.

"Papa, where is she? Where's Toni?" He was crying and yelling all in one go, his eyes searching the surrounding terrain.

"Sung has her. He's the only one they would have contacted. He's been on both sides of the fence… and I will kill him in a way that he'll wished he had never been born. It was you they were after, Dana. They were looking for you!" Father and son clung to each other, each with their own grief. It was an act that bonded them together for eternity, but separately was tearing them apart.

Caulder let go of his son and kneeled down in the grass, leaned on his rifle and bent his head.

Sam squatted down in the grasses beside him. "You really love her, don't you?" he questioned his boss.

"That obvious?" and Daniel didn't look up.

"Yeah, boss. To everyone." He glanced sideward at Ben, getting the message to Caulder.

"What have I done, Sam?" Daniel whispered softly, so only Sam would hear.

"Nothing a good father would not have done," and he paused as he searched for the inevitable question. "What plans do you have?" He put his hand on Caulder's arm, an unspoken bond between them.

"Sung will go on to the capitol and then he'll stop... and wait. As long as she keeps her cool, she'll be safe, I hope. We have to get there as fast as we can, so keep everyone moving. I don't know how long she can hold out. Toni doesn't know how to react to him and his ways."

"Boss, for someone who just slept with her, you sure don't know her. The lady has a lot of guts. She kept quiet about the bite, she kept pace with us all the way here, and she survived a whole night with you." Sam waited for the explosion.

Daniel couldn't look up. "Is that supposed to make me feel better?" he mumbled.

"Yeah," and Sam laughed. "She has more courage than you give her credit for."

"I don't doubt her courage, but Sung is big into heroin. And that she will never survive!"

Sam knew his boss was right. Sung used heroin like it was going out of fashion. When he discovered he had the wrong person, there would be no telling how far he would go... especially with a woman.

Caulder stood tall. "Okay, listen up. We'll go on day and night till we get to his camp. He has to be by the capitol. We'll find him and take him out, but no matter what, we have to get the girl out and get my son back in power. We can't radio to our army and we're not far enough in for them to find us. Another day or so and we may come across them. So that's it. Ben, translate, and then let's go." He picked up his guns and strode off in the direction of the jeeps, never looking back.

Dana looked down at the baby. "I would have tried to help you, also, little one. I would have done what Toni did. You are brave and your spirit will join that of your great forefathers. Rest, little calf, rest. My father will even the score for you and for Toni." and he followed his own kind.

Toni came to in the back of the dirty, worn jeep. She didn't open her eyes and she didn't cry out, but what she could hear were Oriental voices and that of Portuguese men. The road bumped and turned and she slipped down on the floor of the jeep. For now, she figured she was safe. She knew they thought she was Dana and she heard his name mentioned several times during the last few hours. As she was thinking this over, the jeep stopped. Arms slid under her, picking her up and two men carried her bodily to a house. Still she didn't make a sound. One man opened a door while the others threw her onto a stench-ridden bed, and then they locked the door behind them. The whole time they were talking, she couldn't understand a word. Why didn't they speak French? At least she'd have got the gist of that. A good question? Why didn't they? This had to be Sung and his men, not any rebels. Caulder had been right not to trust them.

Another question loomed. How long could she keep them fooled? Would Caulder come straight for her or would he take his son on to Yaoundé? She hoped the latter. It would be better that way. Dana would be safe and power would be restored. Then, Caulder could bring his army for her. Who was she kidding? She couldn't hold out that long... or could she? The room was dark, but through the torn and filthy curtains she could see by the shafts of light. She could also see huge beetles in the corners of the room and roaches on the walls. She huddled up into a ball and stared about her. Still she couldn't cry. Boys didn't cry. Dana would not cry. She tried to focus on that. Caulder would find her, she knew he would. But when?

Just then the door opened, creating light and Sung stood before her. He spoke to her. She had no clue as to what he said. He tried again, in English. This time she understood.

"Dana, or should I say, Your Highness," he was sarcastic, "I could kill you right now and you would be the end of the revolution. But I want your father also. By keeping you alive, and letting him know I have you, he will come for you. Then I will kill him and then you. His army is strong, but without a leader they will look to another and I am just that. I, myself, wish to take charge of this city. We will tell the people that you are sick and that you died of natural causes. They will believe me when I tell them that. A ten-year-old boy can easily die of malaria out here, especially when he has been in the jungle for days. Pity you just didn't die at birth. We were rid of your father... no correction, your mother's husband, courtesy of assassins. Couldn't believe our luck. But we didn't bank on you being the son of a mercenary and not a king! We could have dealt with that. Made no difference until Caulder came back to put you in power. The governor was our man. You hear me boy? Never mind! Hold him and roll up his sleeve," and Sung waved his arms at his men gesturing them to hold the captive.

Toni tried to struggle and they held her to the filthy, vomit-stained bed. The needle stung her arm. She still made no sound.

"Tough, like your father, huh? We'll see how tough you are." Sung was enjoying this. "This will give you pleasant dreams, or unpleasant! Depending on how you look at it."

She could see and hear him, but it was through a cloud. She could hear his laugh and see his face distorted in the light. Strange noises filled her head, and then she passed out. She had no clue how long she was in this state, but it was light when she woke. She felt sick and dizzy and couldn't quite understand where she was. Falling from the bed to the floor she saw the roaches, only this time they were huge, out of all proportion. She threw up where she sat and her bladder emptied itself. She had no control over anything she did. Focusing on the window, Toni could see bars. Some kind of prison? How long had she been out? She tried to make her brain function.

"Concentrate, Toni. Concentrate. That's what Caulder would tell you. You can do it." She gripped the side of the bed and pulled herself back up and fell onto the bed. "That's a start, girl. You made it back to bed." She laughed. "Daniel would be proud of you, getting back into bed. That's where he wants you," and she laughed again, a kind of hysterical sound. Her head ached and again the nausea swept over her. This time she controlled it. She'd never been around heroin and didn't know that's what was in the syringe. Sitting up, she saw water and food in the corner by the door. Someone had put it there while she was out. Sliding down on the ground, she went on her hands and knees to the door. Eating like a dog, she stuffed the food down. Most of it came straight back up. It was then she cried. She wasn't tough at all. She was scared she was going to die.

Jeep tracks were not hard to follow and Caulder had pushed his party to their limits. He'd carried his son on his back, but now it was time to rest. The men sat under trees while they ate, but Caulder had declined any food and he just sat staring into space.

Ben had never seen him like this. His boss was becoming a man possessed. His thought process was disturbed as Dana came to talk to him, and the boy slumped down beside him.

"Why won't papa speak to me?" asked Dana. "Did I do something to upset him?" and the child's eyes were filled with tears.

"No, Dana. It's not you." This time he had to explain to the boy. "When a man meets a very special woman, something happens between them. Your father met Toni and that happened to them. He loves her like he loves you, and he cares what is happening to her. You know Sung. You know what he can do. Just thank god it's not you he has."

Dana looked up at Ben. "In that case, I wish it was me," and the boy got up and walked away... a man.

It took them another day to reach Caulder's army. And another day of heroin for Toni. They kept her doped on purpose. Sung had no interest other than keeping the child alive. But this time, she didn't come round so easily. She was out for hours and this time one of Sung's twisted group went back to her room.

"You pretty, boy... Yeah, you pretty!" He undid Toni's jacket and then her shirt. She started to wake, but not quickly enough. Long scrawny fingers pulled at her T-shirt. "You no boy! You no Dana!" He wasn't interested in a woman. "Mr. Sung, Mr. Sung, boss! This is not Crown Prince!" and the man all but yelled the place down.

At the loud hollering, Sung rushed into the room. He didn't ask why the man was there... he didn't have to. "What, not the boy? Of course it's the boy! Let me see..." and he did see. It was certainly not the body of a boy nor was she all brown. He grabbed hold of her, pulling her up on the bed, leering at her with hate in his eyes. "Who are you? Where is Dana?" Again he yelled at her. "Who are you?"

She laughed. "Not Dana," and she spat in his face.

His hand came down and hit her hard across the mouth and then again for good measure.

"Mr. Sung, no. She cannot tell you if she dead." His man held Sung's arm back from hitting Toni again.

"You're right. But she was with his party. They dyed her skin to make us think she was Dana. Very clever of Mr. Caulder. By now he will be near his destination. Damn you! Who are you?" He rubbed at her skin and the oil began to fade. "You're a white woman, and therefore you're still valuable to me. You're his lover? Is that it? Answer me! I know he likes his women young... black or white!" He turned to another man and snatched the syringe he was holding. Sung held it by her face and he laughed, waving it in front of her, leering at her in a grotesque manner.

Toni was hurting and she was staring death in the face. Had she given them enough time? She hoped so, because she couldn't hold on any more. She cried out loud at Sung. "I'm his lover and he'll come for me... and kill you, you bastard!" and again she spat at him, jeering at him, taunting him with the fact she was Caulder's woman.

Sung wiped the saliva from his face and stuck her with the needle anyway. Then, slowly, he pulled the belt from his pants...

Chapter 6

By the time Daniel Caulder got anywhere near to Sung's home-made fortress, he'd gathered fifty or so men with him... some once loyal to the rebels and some always loyal to Caulder's cause. And right now, his money looked better. But first he had to fulfill his pledge to his son. His plan was going to take him speedily on to Yaoundé and come back for Toni. That should have been the plan! Daniel was sitting by the campfire watching the flames and thinking of Toni and their night together when the news came.

As Sam approached his boss, he coughed discreetly. "Mr. Caulder, there's a man wanting to see you. Says he has information about a girl. He wants..." Sam didn't finish.

"Bring him here, now!" Caulder jumped to his feet, stamping out a cigarette with bitter contempt as he did.

The scruffily-dressed native came to him shaking in the very boots he wore. "I have news, Mr. Boss, of a person that an Oriental man has captive. I need money, boss. Please, I risked my life to come here. Please?" The only thing he needed money for was his addiction. He groveled in the dirt by Caulder's feet hardly looking up at Daniel.

Caulder dug into his pants pocket and threw coins at the man's chest, and then, without warning, leaned down and hoisted the drug-ridden sot up by the shirt. "Tell me what you know, and you better be right!" His eyes narrowed as he spoke, and anger seethed from every pore.

"He has a girl in the house by the old church. People have heard her cry. They say she is still alive but he keeps her on heroin..." and this time he stammered, afraid that he might be in for a beating.

Caulder didn't want to hear any more. He let go of the shirt, dropping the man to his knees and turned away from him. "Sam, you deal with this wretch. Makes me sick to look at him," and Caulder knew it was a trap, but he started gathering his backpack and guns to him.

Ben had been watching the proceedings from a few feet away. "You going after her tonight?" he asked, shocked that Daniel was even thinking of doing so.

"What the hell do you think?" retorted Caulder with wild eyes staring at his number 2 man.

"I think you should go on to Yaoundé with Dana and let us go for Toni." Ben was totally serious.

Daniel stared at him. "Have you gone insane? Sung wants to trade. He wanted Dana and he doesn't have him... he has the girl. By now he'll have found out she's my lover. She's only human, and she will never stand up to him. If he's feeding her heroin... anything can happen. He wants one of this family in exchange. He knows he'll never get Dana and I'm sure as hell not letting him get his hands on another son," and Caulder reached for his rifle, slung it on his back and tucked another gun in his belt. In his boot he carried the sharpest blade known to mankind

It took a moment for Ben to realize what Caulder had said and he grabbed his boss by the arm. "What did you say? Another son?!"

Caulder looked down at his arm and Ben's hand on it. Ben released it immediately. It was then Caulder realized what he had said. He tried to change it.

He failed.

"You said, son. That's what you said. Is it true, is it?" Ben was angry, almost uncontrollably so. He yelled loudly, taking a step back from Daniel.

Caulder turned his back on him and carried on his preparation to leave the camp.

"Damn you, Mr. Caulder. Is it true? Am I your son? Is that why I'm as dark as you and have feelings for Dana? Is he my half-brother? Who is my mother? I don't understand any of this. And Toni? How does she figure into all this? That's why you wanted her to choose for herself… it all makes sense now." He was frantic and paced up and down trying to figure it out.

Sam appeared on cue. Caulder turned in his direction. "Explain to my son. I don't have time for this. I have better things to do."

"Sam knows, too?" exclaimed Ben. "How many other people know? Does your mistress know? Did you tell her that night when you had her against the wall?" Ben yelled.

Caulder turned around slowly with blood in his eyes and landed his fist square on Ben's jaw. He fell backwards, almost to the ground and blood gushed from his mouth.

"You listened? You were listening outside? What kind of sick bastard are you? You went too far, Ben. Leave Toni out of this." He leaned down and hissed at him. "If we made love ten times, it's none of your business. Jealous, are we? Or are you in love with her yourself? Too bad, **boy**! In that department, I can beat you… hands down!"

"Well, you sure have had enough practice!" Ben screamed at his father and stood up ready to do battle, clenched fists at the ready, in case Daniel hit him again.

Caulder was furious and it showed in his manner and stance.

"Stop it, both of you!" Sam leaped in between them. "This isn't helping anything. While you two are fighting, Toni is dying! Is that what you both want?" Sam stood in between them… his strong arms dividing them.

Caulder regained his composure first. "I'm going after her. Sam, you take Dana and keep him safe. You wait for my return, but if I'm not back in a day, go on to Yaoundé and put the boy back in his rightful place. The people know and trust you. Leave a good number of men here. If this is a trap, then they'll follow us, and I'll need backup. And you," he turned to Ben, "you stay here. Sam will tell you anything you need to know. I'm sorry you found out this way and no, my mistress, as you so crudely put it, does not know!" He took plenty of ammunition, a spare machine gun and he left his bloodied son, and walked away.

"He's going, just like that? Just leaving? He didn't even say goodbye to Dana." Ben exclaimed, pointing a finger after his new found father.

"He said goodbye to one son and look at the reaction he got. How can he say goodbye to another? He thinks equally of you both!" Sam still had his hand on Ben's chest.

"I don't understand any of this. I have only been part of his life for the last few years. I lived a nice peaceful existence with my parents... no, not my parents." He threw his hands up in the air. "I had anything I wanted..." He stopped. "Did blood money pay for all that?" He didn't want to know the answer.

"Yes, your father paid from the day you were born. You did live with your real mother. Mr. Caulder and she were very young when they conceived you. He was just getting into this business and was away most of the time in South America. Your mother had everything she needed, and so did you. He bought her the house and then along came a husband. No one else knows who you are. Just your parents and myself. Mr. Caulder and your mother were never in love. But he did right by her, and by you. He put you in the best schools he could find and stayed away from you on the condition that when you turned twenty, you came to work for him. That was the understanding. It was best for all concerned."

"For him, you mean! He was free of the responsibility of a child." Ben turned up an oil drum and sat down on it. He couldn't think straight. Even though this was a blur... it did make sense.

"Ben, why do you think he made you number 2 over me? Didn't you ever wonder? He loves you and Dana. Two sons, but from two very different lives. Sons he can never live with and can never be without!"

The last statement hit Ben hard. "And Toni? Is he really in love with her or is she another of his little indiscretions, another play toy?"

"Your father has only loved two women in his entire life. Dana's mother... and now, Toni. He will give his life for her if needs be."

"Then why did my father go on his own? He could take out the whole place with these men." He couldn't make sense of that one. Ben looked around at the army of soldiers.

"Because, that's just what Sung wants. He would kill her before Caulder ever gets close. He wants your father and anyone connected to him. Sung obviously intends to take power in Yaoundé. Mr. Caulder always wondered if that was the case. Seems to me he guessed right. What I don't understand is how he knew for sure about Dana. There are only so many people who know he's Caulder's flesh and blood, unless he just wants to get rid of the heir." He paused, thinking. "No that doesn't make sense. He knows, but how? Someone told him. You and I knew, the people at the mansion… no, not them. Too obvious. Someone back in the city, but who? Your father is walking right into a trap!"

Caulder took one other with him, the Brazilian, who joined him on the outskirts of the camp. The two men had formed a strange kind of alliance, with Andre having no time for men that betrayed their own, and Sung had done just that.

It took them a few of hours to reach the place. A small village with a church, just like the native said. Both men crouched in the bushes, watching the movements from in and out of the house. Then Caulder heard her cry. A long and plaintive tone. He knew what Sung was doing to her. He knew then that Sung was about to rape her or maybe already had. They had to get her and now, and Andre waited for his boss's command, watching Daniel's face, seeing the anger inside of him. They closed in on the shanties waiting for a chance.

Inside the house, Toni lay on the bed with her hands tied to the bedposts. The needle hurt her so badly now. Constant retching had left a mark on her throat and her bed stank of urine. She'd eaten nothing since the first day of captivity and her bones craved meat. Her eyes were closed and she lay in some kind of sedated state. She had no idea what day it was or where she was. When she'd tried to focus, everything was blurred. Most of her clothes were gone, and a blanket covered her body. Sung had beaten her, just enough. Caulder wouldn't swap for damaged goods and now that he was sure his messenger had succeeded, it was time to take what Caulder wanted back the most. Sung looked up at the windows and the shafts of early morning light, knowing that Caulder would come.

Light was seeping through the dense jungle, and Daniel motioned to his man to move around back. He gestured with his knife what he wanted him to do, and sheathed the knife back in his boot.

It was then Caulder walked straight up to the door, hands held above his head. Sung's guards rushed to him and leveled rifles at his head. Daniel never flinched, his eyes straight ahead.

"Mr. Sung, Mr. Sung…" yelled the guards in unison, and Mr. Sung appeared. Bald and fat, Sung was even more repulsive than Daniel had seen him. And with that turned-up smile, he was totally unbearable.

"So, you came, Mr. Caulder. My courier did well. Did you hear your woman? She is your woman, is she not? And she is good. But then you know that! She must mean a lot to you. I wanted the prince. I know you want to put him in power. He's also your son, is he not, Mr. Caulder? Even so, he is entitled to the crown. By the look on your face, you are wondering how I knew. That you will never know. You are good, Mr. Caulder, very good. But me, well I am ahead of you. But getting back to your woman, I know you want to see her. Come, let's go! I see you have no weapons! Smart, Mr. Caulder, very smart." The fat little man led Daniel inside the hut.

Caulder never said a word. He tried not to give anything away, and followed Sung into the house and to the room where Toni lay where the stench hit him full on. Sung moved to the bed, pulled back the blanket and Daniel could see Toni had belt marks across her body. Sung had beaten her… badly. It was worse than Caulder imagined. She hardly had any clothes and it was obvious that Sung had or was about to take her. Toni was barely conscious and Daniel watched her, his blood boiling. Those once bubbly eyes lay in hollow sockets, and he could clearly see the needle marks in her arms.

Slowly lowering his hands, he leaned down on the bed. "Toni, can you hear me? It's Daniel. Wake up." He turned his head towards Sung. "Untie her! I want to see her properly and I want her conscious before I give myself up to your men." He was calm… too calm.

"Bit late for that, Mr. Caulder. Think I have you both, no?" Sung was over confident and had already sent his men to the back of the room.

"No… You don't! You never will!" replied the mercenary and stood tall waiting for the next move.

On his way in the back entrance, the big, powerful Brazilian took out several men, his way. Now, he stood by the door, rifle in his hand, and his blood red knife at his side. Caulder's timely arrival at the front door had been distraction enough for Sung's army, and Sung, himself, had been careless in the delight of capturing Daniel Caulder.

"Untie her, Sung, and then you will take us out of here," stated Caulder.

"Don't be ridiculous, I..." It was then he turned and saw the man by the door. A big burly man with blood red hands and blade. Sung had no choice but to proceed to do as he was asked and turned his head back towards the bed. Next thing he felt was Caulder's blade at his throat, a knife that appeared from nowhere.

"Now... you are going to take us out of here, either dead or alive. Makes no difference to me. Dead men do walk!" and Caulder showed no expression on his face.

"How far do you think you'll get, Mr. Caulder? You'll have to carry the girl to your transportation and get back to your army. It's a joke, you are making?" laughed Sung mockingly.

"No joke! As much as I hate to let you touch her again, you're going to carry her. Now, let's go! No tricks! Pick her up... now," he whispered right next to the repulsive man's ear.

Sung slid his arms under her and Daniel cringed as he watched him touch her skin. Toni's body stayed limp in Sung's arms, her chest hardly rising with life, and the blanket falling from her body.

"Let's go!" Still Caulder was calm. Inside, he wanted to kill Sung, but now was not the time or the place. But it would come... Hell yes... it would come.

Andre closed in tight behind Caulder, protecting his back. Sung and the girl went out first.

"Tell them to stay back. Tell them!" Daniel demanded. "And no tricks. My friend here can understand you." Caulder held the knife between Sung's shoulder blades to spur him on.

Sung yelled to his men to stay away, and a dozen or so rebels backed away and stayed there. He carried the girl into the fresh air and Caulder made Sung walk to where they'd left the jeep. Sung's eyes darted everywhere in the hopes of escape, but still he walked and still he carried Toni, a lightweight in his arms.

They reached the jeep and Daniel barked orders. "Put her in the back seat, and then get in the front and drive!" Caulder knew Sung's men were closing in fast, and like Sung, he knew that a body was no good to him. "Drive!" and he tossed him the keys, seating himself next to Toni, with Andre on the other side of her.

"What?" the Oriental asked.

"Drive, you bastard, before I slit your rotten throat right now! Oh, and Sung, when we get back to my camp, I will not be responsible for my actions… especially if I find out you raped her." Caulder's eyes narrowed as he spoke, and his voice raised an octave.

The little man twitched. He knew of Caulder's prowess with a knife so he drove, like someone possessed. But he also knew he couldn't let himself be taken by Daniel Caulder and his army.

Toni leaned against Daniel, her body half-clothed in Dana's pants and a torn vest that covered little more than the imagination. Daniel removed his own shirt and pulled it around her body, causing her to murmur his name.

"I'm here, Toni. My god, what did he do to you!" Daniel attempted to pull her arm through the sleeve and clearly saw the needle marks. Looking up at Sung he asked, "How much did you give her, you son-of-a-bitch? Was it clean cut? Was it? Or did you add something to it? Which? Answer me!" and he stuck the knife in Sung's shoulder right where he knew it would hurt the most.

The jeep swayed. "Clean! It was clean," he yelled. Sung kept control of the wheel as blood seeped through his jacket. His men were right behind them, some still on foot, but most in trucks and jeeps that were closing in fast.

"Faster, drive faster, unless you want to die right now!" demanded Caulder.

Andre pulled a machine gun into place on the back of the jeep and fired several rounds into the ensuing hordes. They dropped like flies, their blood turning green grass to red. He hit gas tanks, tires and anything that moved behind them sending chaos through the ranks. The rest of the men fell back into the trees, hiding and biding their time to regroup wondering how one man could wreak such havoc.

Caulder glanced sideward at Toni. She had slipped down in the seat. "Toni, for god's sake wake up!" She dropped forward and Caulder had no idea if she was dead or alive. He grabbed her shoulders and shook her, violently, forgetting his own strength. "Toni!"

It was all the distraction Sung needed. He slowed the jeep down to a moderate pace, and then, leaving the wheel, he jumped, knowing Caulder would not give chase. The car immediately veered off course and towards the trees and Daniel climbed over to the front seat, grabbing the wheel as he did. The car swerved, and Caulder turned the wheel violently this way and that till he had it under control. They made it through the trees and back to the road. Sung was free... for now!

The girl lay on the seat and Andre held her to him, cradling her in his arms. Caulder drove like a mad man, not stopping until they reached his camp. He brought the jeep to an abrupt halt; not even waiting to turn the engine off. Daniel jumped out into the heat and raised his arms to take Toni from his friend. There was a look between the two men, and a kind of understanding. Caulder nodded his head.

"Help me with her, she's hardly breathing. God damn it, Sam, Ben, get the hell over here, now!" Caulder was screaming at anyone that listened, his face streaming with sweat and his arms encircling his woman.

They laid her on blankets and covered her broken body with more. Her lips were purple, and there were no signs of life. Sam held a lamp over her and they could all see the state she was in.

"Come on, girl." Sam pulled her eyelids open and shone a torch in them. He rolled her sleeves up. "Been given a few days' worth! Was it clean cut?" he asked of Daniel.

"Yeah, as far as I know," replied her lover and sat cross-legged on the ground next to her, sweat pouring down his body.

Ben watched in horror. Sam, he somehow expected to know about drugs, but his father... Is that what Vietnam taught you? Then he'd learned so much in the last few hours, why should anything surprise him. Dana stood by watching intently, not wanting Toni to die. Caulder saw him.

"Get my son away from here. He doesn't need to witness this." Caulder did a double take. Both of them stood there. "Ben, take Dana, now," and Daniel turned back to the situation. He watched as Sam pulled something from his backpack. "What are you giving her?" He grabbed Sam's arm to stop him before he injected Toni.

"Something to jolt her out of it. To wake her up. You know what it is. You and I've used it to get us through missions. Don't you trust me?" Sam knew what he was doing.

"Yeah, I trust you. Will she survive that?" And Daniel pointed to the needle.

"Don't know, boss. I do know that if we don't give it her… she'll die." He waited for his boss's reply.

Aware his sons had not moved an inch, Caulder replied. "Go ahead."

Dana cringed as he watched the needle go in. When he saw her body twitch, Dana turned away, almost throwing up on himself. Toni did throw up and tried to fight it, her body not able to take any more.

"Sam, what's wrong with her?" Caulder was frantic. He held her arms and Sam held her legs, their arms stretched across her pinning her to the ground.

"Bad reaction. Don't let her choke! Clean her mouth out and hold her. She's not used to so many drugs." Sam looked around. "Ben, get over here and help your father." Sam had other things to do. He needed to get water into her. Sweat poured off Toni, and she shook on the blankets, writhing as if possessed.

Ben sat on the ground next to Caulder and held Toni upright, supporting her thin frame against him. Dana stood with mouth open. Had he heard correctly? Was Ben also his father's son?

Toni had to survive the night. That was the crucial part. If she could do that, then she would recover. Caulder sat down next to her and never left her side, but he was tired beyond belief. Slowly his eyelids closed and he almost fell onto her with Sam catching him before he hit the ground.

"Take over for him, Ben. Your father needs sleep. If not for him, do it for Toni." And Sam pulled a blanket over Caulder's body and propped another one under his head. He lay there then out to the world.

Toni was so pale in the firelight, so delicate and fragile. How had any of this happened? Ben wondered how he could be angry with this man lying beside him. Caulder had risked his life for this girl that lay there. Ben knew he would have done the same.

And then he cried.

As dawn broke and the sun rose in the West African skies, Toni came to. Gasping for air, the noise woke Caulder. Ben sat her upright and it stopped as fast as it had started. Caulder looked deep into Ben's eyes, as Ben held his woman.

"Thank you. I didn't mean to sleep, but I was so tired... getting old, I guess..." and he pushed his hair out of his face, and his hands rubbed his eyes.

"You don't have to apologize to me... Mr. Caulder. I'm glad to do this for Toni. After all, as you so rightly guessed, I do love her." Not wanting her to hear, Ben lowered his tone. "But she's in love with you, Sir... not me."

"Ben, I'm sorry about all this. I wanted to tell you months ago..." Daniel's speech was interrupted.

"Daniel?" a small voice whispered faintly, but calling his name.

"I'm right here, Toni." And he took Toni from his son's arms and pulled her to him.

Flopping against him, she cried, "I told them, Daniel, I told them! I couldn't hold on any longer. Am I going to die? Am I?" her body still shook and her hair was damp and matted. Bruises dotted her face and more serious marks adorned her body.

He clung to her. "No, honey! I won't let you." Daniel paused. "Toni... I have to ask you this... did Sung rape you?"

She looked her lover in the face and shook her head. Daniel breathed a heavy sigh of relief, and gently held her to him trying to reassure her that all would be well.

Ben stood up, aware he was intruding.

"Ben," Caulder called, "thank you for looking after her." His eyes were moist as he looked at this man, one he could now openly call son.

"That's okay... Daniel." That's as close as he could come right now... maybe ever and he walked away.

Hours later they wrapped Toni in dry blankets and put her in the truck. In Yaoundé, they would find her a doctor. Nothing fancy, but a doctor, none the less, and then they would come back for Sung.

As Dana rode with Ben in another jeep, the boy sat looking at the dark-haired man next to him. "Ben, are you really my brother?" asked the prince.

"Seems like… a new experience for both of us. Maybe, when we get to Yaoundé, our father will talk to both of us. But right now he has more important things on his mind. Perhaps it's not so bad. At least I get a prince for a brother!" He joked about the situation, but underneath his heart was heavy. He turned away and looked at the landscape… one he would come to hate.

Chapter 7

Caulder put his army on full alert. Sentries guarded the jeep carrying both of Caulder's sons, and Sam rode with Daniel and the girl. News had spread quickly through the ranks that Ben was the new found son. The whole party was not far away from the city, but they still had to get there. Caulder had a feeling that Sung would try something. What... he did not know... but something.

His feeling was right.

Even though Caulder's men were superior to Sung's, the repulsive little man had an advantage. He spent more time around the jungles of Africa while Caulder had spent half his time living the lavish life in L.A, and in a playboy style to boot.

While Toni lay in the truck swathed in blankets, Sam watched over her as Caulder rested in the back, rifle in hand, watching and waiting for trouble. His eyes scanned the horizon and his mind wandered. Would Sung get to them before Yaoundé? Sung could not afford to let Caulder reach his destination. The power of the throne would be Dana's, and rightfully so.

They journeyed on, twisting and turning through the trees. Following paths not trodden for sometime. All seemed quiet... too quiet. Caulder knew that Sung could not give up even with a bedraggled army, and it would still take them a few more hours to get there. Sung could radio ahead to his troops whom Caulder felt sure still surround the city.

On the horizon, Caulder had seen lights. They were many miles ahead, but still they shone out as dusk once more settled over Cameroon. A good day's journey and they would be home.

Toni moaned in her sleep and brought Caulder back to reality. He turned towards her and Sam, looking to see what was wrong.

"She okay," he yelled back to Sam.

"Yeah, just restless. Drugs are still reacting in her system. She needs the hospital badly! Needs to be checked out. Her color is a little too flushed for my liking." He felt her pulse which was rapid. "She's getting a fever. Maybe one of those welts is infected. You want to check her over?"

"Yeah," and he laid down his rifle, moving closer to the pair.

Sam moved back into the truck out of his boss' way, and picked up his rifle just in case.

Caulder pulled the blankets from her body and Sam watched the reaction on his boss' face. He saw the anger... an anger that would only result in one ending.

Caulder removed his shirt from Toni's body. He checked her stomach and her upper body. Nothing out of the ordinary. When he turned her on her side, she yelled out in pain. Gently he rolled her back and looked at her side. The welt was red and inflamed where dirt had managed to cling to the seeping wound, and blood and guts oozed from it.

"Toni, wake up! Come on, girl. You have to wake up!" He knew that blood poisoning would soon set in. He tried again. "Toni, come on. Wake up, damn it." Daniel gently sat her upright and she leaned against him.

"Daniel," she muttered.

"I'm here, Toni. Your side is infected. There is pus from the welt mark. We're going to stop here for the night, and I want you to understand. I will take a knife and lance the poison. Can you hear me, Toni?" Daniel leaned even closer to her.

"Do you have too?" Her voice was far to faint.

"Yes, honey. I do."

Tears streamed down her face.

"Sam, tell them to stop the convoy."

"Yes, Mr. Caulder," and he moved in the truck and tapped the driver on the back. "Pull over." And then Sam jumped out of the back of the truck, stopped the rest of the procession from moving on, and then returned to his boss.

Toni cried into Caulder's arms. She was in terrible pain and he knew it. He had Sam heat up two knives over his cigarette lighter, while, after hearing the news, Ben and Dana hovered outside the truck.

"What is papa going to do, Ben?" the boy asked, looking into his brother's face.

"He has to get rid of the poison in Toni, so we must all stay here and wait for their truck. He will not leave you or her." Ben knew that to be true.

He had hardly finished the sentence when they heard her scream. A long and piercing sound that made the jungle come alive. Dana shivered at the sound and turned to Ben for comfort.

Caulder clasped his hand over her mouth. The wood he had given her to bite on was in half, and lay broken on the truck floor. She cried bitterly while Caulder held her down, her tears piercing his very soul. Sam sealed the wound for her and her screams broke through her lover's hand and ripped through the strongest of men… And then she passed out. Ben flinched and Dana cried silent tears, leaning on his new found brother.

If Sung's men had any doubt as to where the opposing army was, they didn't now.

Dana turned his head into Ben's chest and put his hands on his ears. "Why Toni? Why did any of this happen to her? Why did papa bring her?"

"That's beginning to be a good question, Dana! Our father is the only one that can answer that," and now hate was creeping into his heart for the man he now could call father. Ben moved Dana away from the truck, to wait somewhere else.

The group was too occupied to notice that sentries had begun to disappear. They were more concerned for their boss's woman and the terrible ordeal she was going through.

It was Andre that first became aware of the fact. Without becoming alarmed, he moved forward to where Ben was standing and whispered in his ear. Ben walked back to the truck, climbed inside, and the sight that greeted his eyes was one of unbelievable horror.

Toni lay on the blanket. Her breast was exposed and blood ran down her side. There was a smell of burnt flesh, and in both Sam and

Caulder hands were the knives responsible for the deed. If Ben had hated him before, now it was total.

Daniel looked up at Ben. "What the hell are you staring at? You want her to die?" Caulder yelled at his son.

"Of course not, but to do that?" Ben retorted his face screwed up in horror at the site.

Daniel waved the bloodied knife at his son. "This…or death? What would you have done?"

"Okay! You made your point. There is another problem outside. Andre thinks we are surrounded by Sung's men. Sentries have been disappearing for the last hour."

Caulder's eyes flashed at him. "You let them get that near? What the hell were you all doing? You stupid son-of-a-bitch! Sam, stay with her. Ben, out now! Get Andre and go around back of them. Come up from behind and take them out. You can manage that, can't you? Or is that beyond the realms of your brain capacity?"

"Mr. Caulder!" yelled Sam, starring at his boss, not believing what he had just heard.

Caulder regained some sort of dignity and control of his tongue. "Okay…okay! Just do it Ben! Get going. I'll take some men and go round the other way. You go left and I'll go right." He wiped the knife down his pants leg and followed Ben out of the truck

Outside it was dark as Caulder and his men dropped down and crawled though the undergrowth. He could hear boots crack branches in the dry earth. Then the boots came into view. Caulder motioned to his men to stand and take the opposing forces down. They rose up out of the long grasses and slit some Chinese throats just like it came naturally. Once more Caulder wiped the blade clean on his pants, realizing it was the same blade that he had just used on his lover. He dropped it to the ground as though it was on fire.

"Caulder," a voice boomed. "Behind you!" A grenade rolled along the ground and Caulder dived head first into the undergrowth. For some reason only known to god and man, the grenade did not explode. It was not Caulder's time to die.

He sat in the grass as he heard other grenades go off around the camp and could see fighting amongst the rival factions. Then his thoughts turned to Toni, remembering she had only Sam for protection. He ran back through the carnage, pushing Sung's and his own men out of his path. He reached the truck just in time to see scrawny Chinese hands holding his son by the throat. Without a thought for his own safety, he lunged at the man and pulled him from Dana. The boy dropped, choking to the earth, gasping for air. With his bare hands, Daniel Caulder broke the man's neck. All Dana heard was the crack.

"You okay, Dana?" and he leaned down next to his youngest son.

The boy nodded, still taking in gasps of air.

Caulder climbed into the truck. Toni lay huddled in Sam's arms where his strength was sheltering her with his body.

"Toni?" whispered Daniel. He was almost afraid she was dead.

"She's fine, we both are. And you?" Sam looked up into the mercenaries eyes.

He never answered, just leaned down on the floor and held Toni's hand and listened for her breathing.

It was over as quickly as it had begun. Caulder's men gathered up the defeated army and paraded them in front of the cloth on the truck.

"Hey, Mr. Caulder," yelled Ben. "What do you want us to do with them?"

Caulder stepped out of the truck and into the night air. "Shoot the bastards! All of them!"

Yaoundé was not exactly a thriving metropolis, but it was the capitol, and there was a hospital and driving through the streets was easy now as Caulder's army escorted them in. He returned like some conquering hero. Ben was more than impressed while Dana was overwhelmed at the response he, himself, received. The return was only overshadowed by Toni's condition.

The city's people ran to the jeeps and clamored for the boy's attention. Dignified, and in total control, Dana greeted his followers. Ben watched with admiration at this boy... a child king, a brother, and one to be proud of. He watched as they stopped at the hospital gates and he saw his father's jeep turn in. Then the procession continued on to the presidential palace and the royal home of Dana.

Ben had never been to Cameroon before; many missions with Caulder, but never here. Now he knew why. Splendid for its location, Dana fit right into his surroundings, a natural born comfort with his life style. Sam led the boy and the guards up the white-walled stairs to the balcony, and away from the crowds. Half way up, Dana stopped and spoke. "I want my brother with me."

Sam smiled. "Anything you say, Your Highness."

Ben climbed the stairs and noted the paintings on the walls. They were familiar to him from his father's home in Los Angeles. He wondered where they had gone and now he knew.

Both sons had one regret… that their father was not with them.

Caulder stood back in the room while the doctor examined Toni. She lay there half awake and trying to focus. She was filthy dirty. Daniel wanted so badly to scrub her clean of all this mess, but nothing would ever take away what he'd let happen to her. He had some decisions to make in the next few days. He knew he had to stay awhile with Dana, but as soon as she was fit, the girl should be flown out. He would contact her uncle and get him to pick her up. Sung was still free; and there was no way she could go back the way they came. But somehow he would get her out of there before the rainy season set in. Caulder had control of the city for now. He sat down on the stool by the window and looked out. Here, was his one son's home. Los Angeles was his other son's, and right now that seemed a million miles away.

The doctor was talking. "She's dehydrated… starving, well, I don't have to tell you. She needs a few days rest, food and lots of liquids. A little more heroin and she wouldn't have made it. See her eyes and her mouth? That's a sign of how close she came. You did well with the welt infection, Mr. Caulder. We'll do some tests to make sure that there is no more infection. There's something else, though. Notice the way she's shaking? Not all from the heroin. Something else was injected into her. Did you give her anything?" The doctor was serious. He knew that there was a substance in her that he didn't know about.

Caulder stood up and moved to the bed. "We gave her an upper to bring her out of it. Is it that?" He looked at Toni's color.

"Probably. Is she allergic to anything? I see a bite on her. I'll just run those tests on her. You can stay if you want. If she's half conscious she may need a friendly face." The doc carried on about his business.

Caulder wasn't sure about how friendly Toni would consider his face. All he'd brought her was grief. "Can I wash her a little?" He felt so bad for her.

"The nurse will do that. Just sit and hold her hands. She needs reassurance right now."

Daniel looked again at the marks on her. Sung would pay... with his life. When he caught him, Caulder would cut out his black heart!

In the depths of despair, Toni could see Daniel. She wanted him to hold her and make love to her. It was all that had kept her going in the last few days. She felt water on her body, and she winced when they touched the belt marks. She was hungry, yet she wasn't. Wanted water, but could not drink. She ached inside, a deep penetrating ache that wouldn't go away. She remembered the syringes and she remembered Sung's words. He'd wanted her to die. She could hear the doctor, and she could see her lover. Down inside of her she knew how close she had come to death. She watched the look on Caulder's face. Gradually she came around... enough to speak to him. But words would not come.

Daniel knelt down beside her, tears in his eyes. "Sam was right. You are brilliant, and beautiful, and I love you so much. I never thought I would love again. You bought us the time we needed. Doesn't matter about the last encounter. We beat those bastards, Toni."

Tears streamed from her eyes. They were words she would come to quote and words he would regret he ever said.

Caulder stayed with her through the next two days, sleeping by her bed in a hard whicker chair with a blanket wrapped round him. The tests came back negative. Caulder knew that Sam would care for his sons while he was gone. He also knew that he had to face Ben sometime, and that time was approaching quicker than he anticipated.

When she finally woke up, the soft morning light trickled through the windows of the white clinical room. Caulder sat next to her on the hard chair, and he still he slept. His arms were across her and the bed. She noticed her arms were no longer black and once more she was her tanned color. She reached her fingers out and touched his hair awaking him as she did.

"Hi," and he brushed the hair from her eyes with his free hand.

"Hi, yourself," she whispered. At least this time words managed to break free from her brain.

"How do you feel?" he asked, showing total concern for her.

"Strange, like I had a bad dream. It was a dream, right?" She was confused and she treid to make her brain think straight.

"No, honey. It was real enough. Could you eat something? I could get you..." He stroked her hair and let his fingers linger there.

"No. Just stay with me, Daniel. I'm brilliant, remember. Brilliant people don't need food."

"You heard that? What else did you hear?" He hoped she hadn't heard the rest, not that he regretted it, just that it wasn't the best time for her to hear it.

"Nothing," she lied. "Daniel, where are we?" She looked around the room. "Is this a hospital?"

"We're in Yaoundé. We're safe. So are Ben and Dana. Dana is in the presidential palace. Ben is with him. Toni, there's something I have to tell you about Ben." He held both hands on her shoulders and gently kissed her. "Ben is my..."

And the door swung open breaking the moment.

"Visitors for you, Mr. Caulder," announced the doctor, and stood back to let them in.

Dana burst through the doors. "Papa, we missed you! And you too, Toni," he added and ran to his father and hugged him.

"Dana, it's so good to see you." Daniel hugged the young boy to him, not wanting to let him go in case he should disappear. "Go gentle around Toni. She's still weak." Caulder was overjoyed to see his son and let him go to Toni. He glanced back to the door.

Ben stood silhouetted in the archway. He walked across the room. "Daniel," and he put his hand out to Caulder.

"Ben, good to see you." The cordiality was still there.

"Toni, how are you? Dana wanted to come and see you," Ben said kind of slyly.

'Yeah, right,' thought Caulder. 'Dana did?' "Ben, I need to talk to you. Step outside with me for a moment," and Caulder stood up and opened the door. "Dana, stay with her."

In the lobby, Caulder leaned on the wall. He waited till there was no one else around. "So Dana wanted to see her… never mind that. I want you to do something for me. Soon, the rainy season will be here. You and I both know that I have to stay and keep Dana in power, for however long it takes. You, on the other hand, don't have to. I want you to take Toni back to Los Angeles. I'll get in touch with her uncle and…"

Ben moved back and gave Caulder a look that disturbed him.

"Whoa, slow down here." He raised his hands. "You want what? To send her back? Do you really think she's going to leave you here and go back with me? Did the sun get to you? Or have you been at the heroin?" Ben was astounded at the suggestion.

"You love her, don't you?" asked his father, a frown on his face.

Ben nodded.

"Then get her out of here! It's only a matter of time before the confrontation with Sung himself, and this time I intend to kill him. The rebels around here will present no problem now. Once Sung is dead, I can leave Sam here with Dana…"

"Stop, right there… you have no intention of coming back, do you? You just want her out of the way, like you did with my mother! That's it, isn't it? God… and I was coming here to make my peace with you." Ben paced up and down the hallway. "You haven't changed from the mercenary you are! You'll always be what you are. A cold-blooded killer and a man who uses young women for his own needs…"

Caulder grabbed his son and pushed him against the hard, cold walls, pinning him by his shoulders. "Did you ever think I may be doing it to save her life? Did you?" Caulder was angry. "Think on it awhile. I don't care what you think of me. But give me your word that you'll take her out of here when I ask you to!" He stared into the other man's face.

"I'll take her, just to get her away from you. What are you going to do? Make love to her a few more times for your own pleasure?

Then when you've had enough, send her away? You're not my father, and you never will be!" he yelled. Ben pulled himself free and walked away down the hall and out the door.

Caulder watched the last threads of family ties walk away into the shadows. He had done what he set out to do. He was severing ties, and there was one more left to go. This one would be harder. Was his son right? Was he a user of women? He walked to the windows and looked out. Out there was freedom, for him and Dana. But it had a big price tag. He had to give up this girl, and he couldn't let her go, just yet. He did need to make love to her a few more times. Then when the days got rough, he would have someone to remember... to have and to hold, in his dreams. Even a cold-blooded killer could have dreams.

Even Daniel Caulder.

He composed himself and walked back into the room. In front of him was his future and behind him lay his past. His last obligation to her was to get her out of this situation. He had got her into it, and the whole thing should never have happened. He knew that now... and now was too late. If she had died... he would have lost the will to go on and he knew that. Never before had he felt this way... and it frightened him. A voice disturbed his thoughts.

"Papa, can I stay with Toni a little longer?" The child looked at him.

"Sure, why not." There wouldn't be many more times with her.

Toni saw the expression on Caulder's face. He was lost in thought. He was dreaming of what might have been and of what the future may have held... for all of them.

Chapter 8

It took Toni a few days to come round to her normal state. Finally she was ready to leave the hospital and Daniel was there to collect her.

"You want to go over and see the palace? I'll take you there in the jeep. I have one of the suites, and we can be on our own for a little while." He waited to see her reaction, wanted to see if she'd changed her mind about him, feeling he couldn't blame her if she had.

Toni blushed. "I'd love that, being on our own, I mean. Doctor says I'm fit and healthy again, except for these marks. Maybe you won't want to see me like this?" and she pulled the hospital gown round her body.

"Fit and healthy for what, honey? And why would I not want to see your body?" he teased. Daniel sat in the white, wicker chair and watched her sitting on the edge of the bed. Her legs hung over the side and the nightgown was huge on her.

"For the assignment I came here to do... what do you think, Daniel? To make love with you, if you still want me," she asked coyly, dipping her eyes at him.

"Toni, I was wondering about the assignment. What will you say about me?" he asked nonchalantly, pretending not to have heard the statement she made as his fingers toiled at his shirt buttons.

"I don't know yet. It'll be hard to write about this... and some of it I can never tell," she uttered and dropped her eyes even further.

"Such as what?" He watched her with amusement.

"The part that I think you have in mind for tonight."

"Did I say anything that upset you? I just thought you would like to spend some time together." His expression changed.

"Oh, I thought you…" She was embarrassed.

She made his task all the more difficult. Now was not the time. He couldn't let her go, not just yet. He needed the warmth of her body next to his and to feel her in his arms. Caulder couldn't even remember loving Dana's mother like this. Toni had such grit and determination. She had that and everything else rolled into one woman. She'd been willing to give her life for his son; a debt he could never repay. And all he had done was put her through intolerable pain and take away her virginity.

Daniel got up from his seating and encircled her in his arms. "Toni, of course I want to make love to you. I have a surprise for you at the palace. It's not the Ritz, but I think you'll like it." He brushed her face with his fingers. "You know, I remember a certain young woman telling me that she had no intention of letting me take her and look now! You're the one making advances to me," he joked, stroking her face with scared fingers.

"I did no such thing, did I?" She thought a moment. "Daniel, what will you do when this is all over?" Her eyes searched his face.

She had caught him off guard… Something that never happened to Caulder. He could not answer her… not truthfully. For him it wouldn't be over for a long time to come. He turned away from her gaze. "Don't know," he murmured. And changed the subject. "You just going to stand there, or do you want to go? We can talk some more later." He had to think up some good answers for her and he would never think of the right one. He only knew what he had to do, and what he had told Ben still stood. Now even more.

Toni knew he was avoiding the issue. She knew deep down, that this could not last… as much as she wanted it to. She now knew who and what Caulder was.

As she dressed in a fresh, white linen top and pants that Caulder had brought her, he watched her. He never took his eyes off her. She had only one thing left of her own… and that was the jacket. All she had to do was find it… that and her camera.

She knew he was watching her dress. The top was tight and buttoned up the back and the pants were loose and hung on her. She had lost too much weight in the last few days and with the heroin leaving its mark, still didn't want food. She brushed her hair. It still stood in tufts.

Toni was definitely all woman… and tonight Daniel intended to taste that womanhood again, and his pulse raced at the prospect. "You ready?"

"I don't have any make-up to wear. Isn't there somewhere I can buy some?" she asked innocently.

"This is Cameroon, not downtown Los Angeles! Why do you need make-up? You've a tan, you have beautiful eyes, and what else do you need? And, tonight, I'm the only one you have to impress. But if it bothers you so much, we can stop by the market and you can buy some things. They have jewelry and clothes, and you will need a dress for Saturday. There's to be a function when Dana takes his rightful place at the head of his country. Then we'll see about going back to L.A.," he lied. Lying came naturally to a womanizing mercenary.

She left the hospital, walking on her own strength, determined to let him see she could; and outside, the air was rich and warm. Caulder had one man with him to drive the jeep… Andre. Toni wondered where Ben was.

As they traveled through the streets, Toni watched the people with Caulder. He was like some sort of blessing to them. They practically fell at the car and when they tried to walk through the town square, it became impossible. Right now, Toni wished she had her camera. This was no terrorist or mercenary. It was then a title came to her for her article. 'DANIEL CAULDER PUT THE MEANING OF MERCY IN MERCENARY'. He was more like a saint to these people. The thought amused her.

"Something funny?" he asked, seeing her expression.

"No, actually kind of sad!" and Toni smiled at him, a rich and full smile.

They found jewelry, and Caulder picked a white silk dress for her to wear. It was beautiful and had the most exquisite lace and pearls on it that Toni had ever seen. Very old and delicate, the dress had once belonged to a princess. She wished that Caulder had never thrown away her very much-needed mascara. There was nothing to be found like that where they walked. But Daniel did find her something. He found a ring for her. It was silver and had little markings on the side. He knew what they meant. She didn't. Inside was inscribed the African word for 'love'.

Finally they arrived at the palatial palace. Inside, it was cool and airy. Toni was looking at Caulder's army. They were well dressed in African colors—not what she had expected—and stood at attention as their boss walked through to the great room. She glanced back at them. Gold and red silks adorned their bodies, and they carried the finest guns that money would allow. They were very different from the soldiers outside the palace. These guys were handpicked purposely by Daniel Caulder.

They were greeted by Sam and one very excited young man.

"Papa, Toni... I am so pleased to see you." He hugged Toni to him not caring who saw him.

Caulder felt a lump in his throat. Even his son would miss her. Was he making a mistake? What if she stayed? What if Sung caught her? When Sung was out of the way, he could fetch her back. So many questions... he still came up with the same answer... she had to go back, and soon, before he changed his mind. This was no life for a city girl.

Toni looked around. "Where's Ben?" There didn't seem to be any sign of him.

"Hasn't been back since..." Sam stopped short, as he saw the look on his boss's face.

"Since what?" Toni innocently asked.

"Since we came back to live here. He prefers the great outdoors!" Caulder answered.

"I can't understand anyone not wanting to live here. It's beautiful." Trophies lined the mantels and animal skins lay across the sofas. A huge oak table was the centerpiece of the room and rugs lay sprawled on the floor. "So what's my surprise?" she asked excitedly, and sat down on the sofa.

"We eat first, and then you get the surprise. Sam, have a servant put her things in my rooms." Daniel handed him everything except the ring.

"Not hungry." She pouted at him pulling her legs up under her.

"Don't eat, don't get your surprise. Simple as that," Caulder retorted. He stood tall in front of her almost exercising his power.

"That's not fair. You're not my father..." She stopped.

Caulder turned and went to fix himself a drink. Whiskey that went down in one go.

She jumped up. "Daniel, I didn't mean anything by that," she tried desperately to smooth it over.

"Maybe not, but it's something to keep in mind, isn't it," and he swallowed the glass of golden nectar down in one go and poured himself another.

"No, but you're my father! And I would like you to dine with me and for Toni to join us." Dana was so quiet and reserved and very good at keeping the peace. He'd watched the whole of the proceedings.

Toni spoke first. "Then, Your Highness, we will do just that."

By the time dinner had arrived, and they were seated in the great room, the atmosphere relaxed a little, mainly due to Dana, and to his father's liking of alcohol. The table was set for four and the spaces left only created a bigger and noticeable void at the table. Toni ate, just out of sheer determination to make it through the rest of the evening in Caulder's company. She had to admit the food was good, but she wasn't used to such alien flavors... Too much spice.

"Did I eat enough for your liking, Mr. Caulder?" Toni mimicked him.

"Yeah, guess so. Some wine?" he asked.

"Why not?" Toni's reply came back very fast. They were playing games with each other.

Daniel started to pour from the bottle.

"Boss, no. She can't have wine... not just yet!" Sam interrupted.

Caulder realized his mistake. It brought him to reality. "Toni, I'm sorry..." He dropped the surliness. "Want your surprise now?"

"Been waiting all evening," she replied licking the last piece of flavored meat from her fingers.

He leaned across the table and whispered low. "So, have I, young lady. So, have I." And he winked at her as he stood up from the table and took her hand in his leading her away from the others.

They left the company of the rest of the party and retired up the stairs. At the top, Caulder stopped her and picked her up in his arms. "Now, close your eyes."

"What?" Toni asked, as her arms circled his neck.

"Not again! Close your eyes, damn it. Do you always have to question things? Just do as you're told for once in your life." He pushed the door open with his foot and carried her into the room. "Now, you can open them."

She did as she was asked. Still in his arms, she looked around. Candles lit the room, a ceiling fan spun overhead, the room was decked in flowers, and the bed was all in white… not silk as she wanted, but white linen. He let her down on the rugs, white, thick piled rugs that cushioned her feet. She stared at the setting, realizing he had done this for her. The dress they bought in the market hung from the old-fashioned dresser.

Caulder dug into his pocket. "For you," and he took hold of her left hand. On her third finger he placed the ring. Then he leaned forward and slowly undid the buttons on the back of her blouse. He slid it down her shoulders and it fell to the floor. As it did, he kissed her lips, and she could smell alcohol on his breath. It only enhanced her feeling for him. His hands found the tie on her pants and the linens dropped to her feet. She stepped out of them. Her fingers undid his white flannel shirt, and he pulled it off him. Scooping her up in his arms, he laid her on the bed and had no time to remove the rest of his clothes. His need for her was great and the thought of losing her overpowering.

She understood his urgency for her. She had the same feelings for him and clung desperately to him. The second time, she managed to push the rest of his clothes from his body. She wanted to see all of him, as he did her.

Caressing her body, he touched one of the belt marks, and she cried out.

"Toni, I'm sorry. I'm trying not to hurt you…" He backed off.

"You didn't, not in that way. Your hand caught me on my ribs. The belt mark still hurts."

He rose up. "God damn, that bastard. I swear I'll kill that son-of-a-bitch!"

She tried to ease the tension. "Daniel, come on. Don't let it spoil what you have done. It's so beautiful. I dreamt of a night like this. It's all that kept me going… thinking of this time with you." She pulled him back down onto her body.

Daniel looked into her eyes. He wanted only this woman for the rest of his life, and he knew that couldn't be. But he did have her now, and her undivided attention. He would deal with Sung later… his way. As if he had mentioned Satan's name, lightning flashed across the windows. Thunder rent the air, and the candles flickered from the temperate winds. There was no rain… Only a lightning storm.

She was startled, momentarily, and then became intoxicated by the power of the storm. It was as though it were conducting itself to Caulder's tune. In the flashing light, she could see him. A man she could never forget, dark and vibrant… her lover, tanned and glistening with sweat from their lovemaking.

The storm aroused senses in her she never knew she had. She'd left no inch of his body untouched. She wanted to know every crease and every curve that he had. Her fingers etched a shape on his chest and drew on down to his stomach. She had nothing else to compare his manhood to, but as she clasped her hands around it, she felt the pulsating vibrancy of his power. A power he used very well. She slid down under him and replaced her fingers with her mouth. He arched his back and let out a sigh of satisfaction.

He whispered her name.

And she thought she heard him tell her again that he loved her.

Tears rolled down her checks. Would he remember what he'd said tomorrow? It didn't matter. All that mattered was tonight.

He turned on his back and pulled her on top of him. She lay there and his arms circled her body. He lifted her up with his body, his erection knowing no bounds. He held her there, her body shaking with passion.

The storm passed, and Toni dozed in the morning light. She turned in the bed and felt for Caulder. There was a cold indentation where he had been. She panicked. She looked for something to cover her body and found one of Caulder's shirts. She slipped into it, and the flannel was huge. She ran from the room and down the stairs, with a bad feeling inside her. Why would he leave her so early… she knew why! She passed the guards on the stairs. They stared at her, but she was Caulder's woman, and they dared not stop her. She burst into the great room where Sam and Dana stood.

"Where's Daniel? Where is he? Tell me! He's gone after Sung, hasn't he?" She was hysterical. "Sam, tell me, has he?"

How could he lie to her? "He didn't tell me where he was going, just said he would be back by dark and that you were to stay in his rooms."

She didn't believe him and it showed on her face. "You're lying, I know you are. Where's Ben? He'll tell me the truth. Where can I find him?" She pulled the shirt tightly around her hiding her body from them.

But Sam could see the welts on her thighs from the beating, and he saw the marks on her neck. His room was next to Caulder's, and he'd heard.

Dana approached her. "Toni, I will stay with you till papa returns. You can help me prepare for tomorrow. I have to make a speech…"

She looked at him. Whatever she said, no one was going to tell her the truth. Then, she saw Sam's gun on the table. She grabbed it. "Tell me, damn it! Where did he go?" She held it steady.

Still no reply, just a look of apprehension on Sam's face.

She pointed the gun at the mantel. Aiming at one of Caulder's trophies, she pulled the trigger. "Now, where is he?" and she hit her target.

"Gone after Sung!" It was Ben's voice as he entered from the open door.

She turned, and as she did, Ben grabbed the gun. Sam moved forward, and Toni collapsed in his arms.

"Why the hell did you tell her? Your father won't be a happy man." Sam held her to him, protecting her.

"Father, what father! She has a right to know what kind of man she's sleeping with."

"She knows, Ben. She knows far better than you who she's laying with. This is why I didn't want the boss to tell you. Knew this was how you'd react. This child here has more sense than you! She's not over the heroin yet, couldn't you see that? She was wild. Get out of my way, but remember the promise you made your father. If you don't keep it, I'll be waiting... for you! Dana, come with me," and he carried Toni back to Caulder's rooms.

Ben slumped down on the couch. So Sam knew what the plan was. Did everyone know before him? He didn't know Caulder at all, and now he was realizing that fact. He waited an hour and then he left. He'd come back here to this mess in his own good time.

This time a guard was posted at her door. Toni sat on the bed and looked through the mirror. She was a wreck. Was this how she repaid Caulder? She could at least wash and put on a fresh gown.

Bathed and dressed, in cotton slipover robe, she waited. She helped Dana with his speech, and she talked small talk with Sam, but all the time her eyes were on the door. It seemed like forever.

"Toni, I'm hungry. Can we go down and eat?" A ten-year-old was hard to refuse.

She gave in. "Okay. I will eat with you. I'm feeling just a little hungry myself," she lied, but once again she'd had a good teacher.

Sam took that as a good sign and he ushered his little party down the stairs.

As they sat eating at the table in the great room, just Sam, Dana, and Toni, the door opened and Caulder appeared. He threw his gun down hard on the table. Toni pushed her chair back, rushed to him, clung to him, and he held her in his arms.

"Did you find him?" asked Sam afraid of the answer.

Caulder cut his eyes to Toni.

"She knows. Ben told her!" replied Sam, who had dropped his chicken breast he was eating to the plate.

"He's been here?" A frown spread across his face.

Sam nodded and licked the ends of his fingers. He'd noted that Toni hadn't eaten a thing, just pushed the food round the plate

"No, I didn't find him, not yet. He covered his tracks well. Tomorrow is another day," he commented and looked down at Toni. He could smell the fresh fragrance of the soaps and oils and could feel her body through the robe... and he wanted her.

Sam could see the look in Caulder's eyes. "Dana, think it's time for bed. You have one huge day ahead of you tomorrow."

"Papa, I hope you find him for all our sakes." As he left the room, his father answered him.

"Goodnight, my son. Tomorrow we will all be here for you. Tomorrow we will put aside anything else, and it will be your day." Caulder hoped he was telling him the truth.

Toni wanted to ask Caulder why he left her, but she could not break the spell. He led her up the stairs, not to the bed, but to the nearest couch and threw the cushions down on the seats. Gently, he let her gown drop to her waist, and he kissed her. Slowly, his mouth moved down her body. In her head she could hear music... music of the passion he had for her. Tonight, she was all his, to have and to hold from this day forward... for the rest of her life.

And Caulder felt the same.

They woke at dawn. Sun streamed through his bedroom windows. This time Caulder was still beside her. She watched him sleeping and remembered back to the night. She smiled. Her eyes caught the dress hanging on the door. Today, she would wear this. Today, Dana would be a boy king. Then they could get on with the rest of their lives. This was her dream. For Toni, sometimes dreams did come true. For Daniel Caulder, would they ever?

The proceedings began at four. Crowds had been gathering in the streets for hours. As they did, dark storm clouds loomed overhead. If the rains came early, it would be unusual. But everything about this escapade had been unusual.

They ate lunch in the great room, more seasoned meats, followed by wine, and Toni found it difficult to concentrate on either. Every time she looked at a couch, it reminded her of last night.

Caulder was amused by her. He was not amused by the shot she'd taken at his trophy. He was, however, impressed by her aim, but he made no mention of it.

When she returned to his room to change, she went alone. It was custom for the men to be dressed for formal occasions. She found a package on the dresser and on the chair lay her camera and jacket. She opened the package. A card said, 'Toni, you wanted this!' Inside was her mascara. Caulder had kept it all this time. Inside the lining of the jacket lay the film. He had to know it was there. Why didn't he take it?

She bathed and changed into the silk dress which clung to her body. She added pearls for her neck and bracelets for her wrists. She donned her faithful mascara, and pinched her suntan cheeks. Her hair had experienced some restraining with pretty combs. Standing in front of the mirror, Toni looked hard at herself. She wasn't the same girl. She'd left that person in Los Angeles. Except for her short hair, she had become a woman, and right now, felt a little overdressed.

Quietly, the door behind her opened. Toni turned to look. In the archway stood father and son. The boy was dressed in red and gold silks and his hair shone in the light. Her gaze turned to Caulder. He wore a black African silk suit. If money ever talked, it was shouting from the rooftops. He was unbelievable… And her heart missed a beat. Never had he looked so magnificent… and he knew it.

He stared at her. "You're beautiful, Toni," and his eyes traced lines on her body.

"You…," and she averted her gaze, "and you, Dana, are pretty impressive. Have you seen yourselves?"

"Papa looks wonderful doesn't he?" Dana was doing his best to bring these two people together.

"Ah, ha," was all she could muster and she moved towards him as if in slow motion.

Caulder offered her his arm… and on it he wore his heart. Toni took them both.

"Papa, is my brother going to be here?" An innocent question from the boy king.

"I don't think so, Dana. I'm sorry. I wanted him to be here for many reasons," and he glanced at Toni.

She hesitated. Had she heard him right? "You have a brother? A real brother?" She looked from Dana to Caulder.

Now was not the planned time… but it was as good a time as any. "Ben is my son!" Caulder changed the subject. "Now, let's get down to the thing we came all this way to do. Dana's people are waiting. You and I will talk later." He escorted them down the stairs.

"You're so right we will! Any more surprises that you forgot to mention? More sons that just may pop up?" She was angry, and it did not become the time or place.

He had a tight grip of her arm. "Stop it, right now! There's no more, not yet, unless you're pregnant! Like I said, we'll talk later, in private. Remember, Toni, you're my lover… you don't own me." He gave her no chance to answer. His grip on her arm tightened until he hurt her and he led both his son and his lover down the stairs.

In the great room, the servants hustled and bustled. Dignitaries were arriving, also leaders of the African nations, and Caulder's army was in very obvious view.

"I'll be back. I forgot my camera," and she broke free from Daniel's grasp. She had to get away. This was all too much to take in.

Daniel stared at her… somewhat displeased at her behavior. Toni rushed up the stairs and into the bedroom. Grabbing the camera, she loaded her other film and tried to collect her thoughts together. She failed. Totally confused, she started back down the stairs.

On the way down, she saw a shadow lurking and she drew back against the wall almost afraid.

"I'm sorry, Toni. I didn't mean to startle you." It was Ben, hiding there in the half-light.

"You frightened me. Are you coming to the party? You should get dressed, if you are." She looked at his clothes, stained and dirty from the trip. He hadn't even bothered to shave

He looked at her with want in his eyes. "Did my father tell you yet? About me?"

"Yes, about ten minutes ago. I asked him if he had any more sons that I didn't know about. None of this is in his dossier. How did he manage to keep things so quiet?" She frowned and took another step down the stairs.

"Caulder has his ways. He will always have ways of getting what he wants. Toni, you really love him, don't you?" Why the hell was he asking her that question?

"You already know the answer. Ben, what's going on? Why aren't you with your family? Dana was asking for you. Do you hate Daniel that much just because he didn't tell you?" She was still trying to figure it out.

"Toni," and he put his hands on her arms and held her, almost pleading with her. "There's a lot you don't know yet. Caulder's going to…"

"Caulder's going to what, Ben?" Daniel stood at the bottom of the stairs, Andre behind him… gun in his hand and ready for trouble.

Ben froze.

There was a cold dead look on his father's face. "Don't mess with what's already mine, Ben. Not if you want to stay alive." He threatened his own flesh and blood and the rift grew wider.

"Daniel, he's just talking to me. What's wrong in that?" She was amazed at his actions.

"Toni, get down here now. I said that you didn't own me, but I sure as hell own you." He played on the situation making it obvious in front of his son.

She walked down the stairs and as she passed him she whispered so only he heard. "No, you don't, Mr. Caulder. Only my heart." And she walked into the great room and left him standing.

Caulder stared at his son, a smug smile on his face. "Ben, get down here, also. I'm still your boss."

He did as he was asked. Caulder seized his arm and hissed in his ear. "Tonight, you will get her out of here. Tonight, you hear me. Remember what we agreed. And if you ever tell her the truth, I'll tell her that you knew all the time, and she'll hate you as much as she just began to hate me. By the time I have finished with her, she will be glad to go with you. But, listen well, Ben. You ever touch her as more than a friend, I will know. You hear me, boy? Do you understand?"

Caulder's grip was tight. "I hear you, you bastard!"

"No, son, that's you!" and Caulder turned and walked back to join the party.

Caulder found her by the window. "This is what I do, Toni. Get used to it, or get out, now," and he walked away leaving her standing alone to watch Dana.

Dana gave his speech and Toni listened. Inside, her heart was breaking. She felt as though Caulder had given her an ultimatum. But why? Something was going on that she did not understand. She was a reporter, and lately she had fallen down on the job. Her thoughts were interrupted as Sam came up to her.

"Mr. Caulder wants you to join him… now." His tone was also cold and uncaring and for some reason he looked big and menacing to Toni right now.

"Can't he wait? I wanted to see Dana…"

"No. He said now," retorted Sam.

She didn't believe all this. Sam, too?

On the balcony, she had stood near to Dana. His eyes were bright and fiery and he waved at the crowds below. As darkness loomed, firecrackers echoed 'round the sky and drums beat in the distance. The capitol was on fire with happiness. Everyone was happy. Everyone? She watched the dancing in the streets and the merriment of the people. Everyone was happy tonight. Except her… and one more person.

Caulder had watched her from the doorway. He had to hold her one more time before he let her go. Inside the room the drums played and music was in the air. As she walked towards him he took her hands. "Dance with me." It wasn't a request.

"Is that an order? Mr. Caulder." She stared at this man she thought she knew.

"Yes. It is." He took her in his arms. It would be so easy to change his mind. But he'd listened to the reports tonight of Sung inside the capitol; he could not risk her staying any longer. He'd get her back… one day. Yesterday, he'd called Bryan Sinclair and told him where he'd find his niece. He knew Bryan had taken the next flight out of Los Angeles.

Daniel inhaled her fragrance one more time, and he pressed her body to his. Both felt the desire in their bodies. He held her tightly to him, her hand in his and his other hand on her back. Almost nervously, she clung to his waist. Music swirled in her head, and she looked up into his eyes, eyes that gave nothing away. She could hear the strains of the tunes, she could feel him against her and she never wanted this moment to end. The music stopped, and life as they both knew it changed.

"Come with me." He took her by the hand and led her outside to the gardens oblivious to the proceedings around him and then he stopped. Towering over her, he began. "Toni...your uncle's on his way to collect you from Belem. A plane will take you there!"

She stared at him looking into his eyes. "I don't believe you. This is some kind of joke. All this evening is. This morning we were making love, and now you want me to go, just like that?" She didn't believe she was hearing this.

Sam appeared at his side and handed Toni her jacket and the camera. "Believe these are yours?"

"Are you all in on this? Am I going mad? Tell me I'm going crazy. Daniel, stop this now. The joke's over," she frantically yelled at him.

"No joke, Toni. I don't want you around anymore. Dana is in power, and that's what we all came for." It was a good thing it had grown dark. If Toni could have seen clearly in his eyes, she would have known. "We had fun, but that's it. Go back to your uncle. You're a city girl and always will be. Oh, and Toni, did you really think you could satisfy a man like me? A twenty-four-year-old virgin," he laughed at her, and it hit her where it hurt the most.

"Daniel, stop it! If you don't want me, please don't humiliate me." She started to cry and as she did, so did the heavens.

Now, time was of the essence. Immediately, the rain soaked her dress. It clung to her, and he could clearly see her body, one he loved so much.

Sam looked at his boss. He knew what Caulder was thinking. "No, boss. She has to go!"

In the pouring rain, Toni stood clutching her belongings. "Caulder, I love you. Please, Daniel, don't send me away." She moved forward and slipped on the ground and sank to her knees. "Daniel, please?" She slumped in the mud. A degraded girl in the land of fire...and ice!

Caulder reached down for her. "Have you no pride, Ms. Sinclair? Is this what you do when someone dumps you? Understand me. I never loved you. I used you for my own pleasure. You were a virgin, and I'd never had one before," he lied. "You were a challenge to me. Do you get the picture now?" He'd pulled her to her feet.

She understood only too well. She stared him in the face and then pulled the ring from her finger. She held it high in the air, and then slowly let it fall into the softening ground. "I hate you, Daniel Caulder. I hate you! You took everything I treasured. God, how I hate you! May you rot in your own hell."

Lightening struck him deeply in his heart.

But he had succeeded.

On cue, Ben appeared.

She turned to him. "Take me away, Ben. Just get me away from this bastard. Now I know why you hate your father," and she cried bitterly.

Ben put his arms around her and led her away. She never looked back, and neither did Ben.

A fallen angel, that's what she reminded Caulder of. He almost gave in and stepped forward to get her. Sam caught him by the arm. "No, Mr. Caulder. Let her go," he whispered.

"But look what I did to her," Daniel murmured, his eyes full of despair.

"I saw what you did. You gave her back her life."

Caulder leaned down to the sodden earth and picked up the ring, holding it to him. He had never loved so much. Tonight not only had he lost her, but also his son. Now, he had only one thing to live for… and that was to kill.

And Sung watched from the shadows.

Chapter 9

Totally unaware of Sung in the palace grounds, Caulder walked back into the building. He was soaked to the skin, his clothes skintight to him, and he was totally unaware of the man in the shadows.

Sung debated going after the girl... or going for gold. He decided on gold, and Dana. Only Caulder stood in his way. He'd wait until Daniel retired for the night and then make his move. In Caulder's present state of mind, to get to Dana would be easier, or so he assumed.

Finally, the evening ended. Dana had exceeded everyone's expectations, but now he sought his father's company. He looked for him and was at first not able to reach him. He did, however, find Sam.

"Sam, where is papa? I cannot find him or Toni. Where should I try now?" The young boy looked up to the so much bigger man.

Sam took Dana to one side. "Your father is in his room and Toni," he took a deep breath... "she is gone."

He was surprised. "What do you mean, gone? To where? Back to the hospital? Is she sick?" He had no idea of what had happened.

"She's gone back to her uncle. Your father thought it best. Sung is very near... and the threat still looms for her. Now, he only has to worry about you. Best talk to him tomorrow; he'll be in a better frame of mind then." Sam turned away unable to continue.

"You mean, he's hurting... or is he drinking?"

Sam raised his eyebrows. Dana knew his father well. "Both, Dana, both."

"Can't you help my father?" the son asked.

"Not a good time to try." End of conversation.

In his room, Caulder was devastated. What had he done? He'd sent her away with a son he didn't trust, on a small plane to Belem. Toni hated the small planes! But then, she hated him. It would have been easier to knock her out and put her bodily on the damn plane. It would have been less hurtful for all concerned.

His clothes had dried on his body. Since then he had downed half a bottle of bourbon. Caulder held Toni's ring in his hand. It was the only thing he had left of her, except the memories. He tucked the ring inside his jacket. Lying down on the bed, he lay looking at the ceiling fan spinning round. The smell of flowers filled his nostrils, and her perfume lingered on the sheets. This was his hell. Two more glasses of bourbon, and he didn't care much what happened. He lay there in his own misery... but sleep would not come.

The house was quiet now. The guards on half alert sensed no trouble. And that's how Sung made his way up the back stairs. He figured Dana would be protected, and he guessed that his first victim would not.

Caulder had no guard. He'd never needed one, until tonight. But someone was watching over him... Andre. He saw his boss take a bottle up the stairs, so he took a cot in the next room... just in case he was needed.

The door handle turned in Caulder's room. Sung slipped inside and left his own bodyguard outside. His first mistake. He saw the bottle lying on the bed, and he could see Caulder's closed eyes. Sung had planned to make it a slow and deliberate death. He'd lost face in this country and no man wanted that... especially a leader of men.

Rounding the king-sized bed, he looked down at Daniel Caulder, a man who was everything he was not. Sung pulled the syringe from his pocket, one filled with heroin... it would take time for Caulder to die. He moved closer with the needle... and Daniel opened his eyes. For someone with that much alcohol in him, he was fast. He rose up from the bed and grabbed Sung's arm. The fat little man yelped in pain and dropped the syringe on the floor.

Sung's bodyguard heard his scream, but someone else was quicker. This fight was between the two of them… to the death. Caulder's drinking hindered him just a little. It only stood to make the two men equal.

"You want my son, Mr. Sung? Over my dead body." He pushed Sung up against the wall, but Daniel was having a hard job focusing properly, and blinked his eyes furiously.

Sung brought his free hand up and caught Caulder in the stomach. It winded him. For a second, he stumbled. It gave Sung the chance to draw a knife from his belt and he slashed at his foe. The blade caught Caulder across his left arm and chest, and blood gushed through his silk shirt. Clutching his hand to his chest, the blood oozed through his fingers. He uttered no words of pain, and stared ahead at Sung, which frightened the other man.

But it sobered Caulder… very quickly. He stared into Sung's face. "This is for Toni." He grabbed Sung by the neck and hit the man's head against the wall. Sung dropped the knife and hung from Caulder's bloody grasp. "Now, let's see if you have any balls!"

Sung screamed. His man was no help to him now. The door opened and behind them stood Andre with a body in his grasp.

Caulder yelled at him. "Do you have balls, Sung? Let's find out!" and grabbing Sung's own knife, slit the Chinaman's pants wide open.

Caulder looked down and with one flash of the blade he removed Sung's testicles. "No, guess you don't!"

His victim screamed in pain and was blacking out.

"Oh, no, my friend. That would be too easy," and he threw a vase of water on his opponents face.

Regaining semi-consciousness, Sung focused in on the syringe that Caulder had grabbed and now held before his eyes.

"An eye for an eye, Mr. Sung. I warned you a long time ago not to cross me. And you played both sides and slept with the enemy. Who was it Sung? Who betrayed me?" He ignored the blood running down his chest, and he knew he was wasting his time by asking the question.

Sung was screaming loud enough to wake the dead. "Caulder, no. That's a lethal dose!"

"Yeah, the one meant for me. How much did you give the girl? How much? This much?" and he plunged the needle into Sung's nose. "More, you gave her more, that what you said? Okay, then more you shall have, until it's all gone! Now we'll watch you die… a slow and painful death." Caulder was merciless.

Now the whole building was awake and Sam came rushing into the room half clothed from changing his attire from the rain.

"Daniel, for god's sake, that's enough! He's dying just like you wanted. Let it go, boss. You have what you wanted." Sam heard what was happening and came running… and he grabbed his boss's arms.

The hate in Caulder overwhelmed him. "You're right, Sam. It is enough!" And he dropped the syringe, took the knife from where it lay and cut Sung's heart from his body, dropping him to the floor. "Now, it's over," and Caulder slumped down on the floor beside his victim.

Sam leaned over him. "Boss," and blood gushed from Caulder's chest. Sam pulled the shirt open. It was bad and he knew it. How Caulder had finished the job, he never knew.

"I kept my promise to her, Sam. Did her plane take off safely?" Daniel spoke with quietness.

"Yeah, boss. They're on their way to Douala. A jet is waiting to take her back to Belem, and Dana is safe now that Sung is dead." Sam tried to stem the flow of blood.

"Good. That's good, because you know what, Sam? I may not make it this time," and he passed out.

Dana stood quietly in the doorway. He stared at the white room, now stained blood red. Quietly, he moved to his father. "Is he…"

"No, he's not. I think… well, doesn't matter what I think. Let's get him into another room." Sam motioned Andre to help carry Caulder. He was dead weight as they moved him.

And there Dana's father lay for what seemed like an eternity to him. He and Sam watched Caulder's pain, not just physical but mental. The top half of his body was swathed in bandages and how he clung to life, no one knew. The knife had struck him deeper than was realized, and had divided his heart in two. As soon as they could, they'd fly him out of there, and away from the pressure he had been under.

Toni sat in the small plane with Ben and the pilot. She clutched her jacket in her hands and could feel the films in the lining. Now she had two films to portray the last three weeks. Two films and one broken heart, not bad for a prospective Times top reporter. She shook with the cold and dampness from her clothes.

Ben gingerly put his arms around her and she fell against him. Looking into his face, she asked, "Why, Ben? Why did he humiliate me like that? I really thought he cared. He told me he loved me... I believed him. You know, that's really funny, I really did believe him," and she started to laugh. "It's funny, Ben, like you, I trusted him. What fools we were, you and I. He can go rot in hell for all I care. He can share his bed with any whore he cares to."

"You don't mean that, Toni," he cradled her wet, muddy body to him.

"Yes, I do," she stammered. "No, I don't, Ben. I wish to god I did." She cried softly.

Ben nestled into her hair and held her while she cried. He held her in his arms for all the wrong reasons. He'd tried to understand his father's attitude towards the girl, and maybe now he was beginning to. She couldn't take anymore. She was cracking. If Sung had ever found her again, she would not have survived. The only way was to let her go back... just like Caulder had done.

Toni cried all the way to Douala. Ben pulled her jacket from her hands and stretched it around her back. The dress was ruined and clung to her body. He felt more than sorry for her. He felt her pain.

The small plane touched down without incident, and they disembarked. One girl, one man, two passports and a camera, and that was it. They boarded the next flight, together. He would take her on to Belem and then make a decision about his future. For now, all he could do was to keep her company.

Toni sat by the window in the jet. It was still part of Caulder's fleet, and she hated the thought of being on it. Anything that belonged to Caulder, she hated. She was tired and cold. Her dress was drying on her. She slipped out of her shoes and sat barefoot on the seat, the jacket her only protection. Ben found her a blanket and he wrapped it around her.

"Try and get some sleep. I know that's not easy for you, but try anyway. Here, rest against me. I make a good pillow," he suggested.

She looked at him like he was insane, and then looked away and snuggled down into her blanket. He was Caulder's son and right now she wanted nothing to do with any Caulder. She stared at the blackness outside and felt the same blackness in her heart. They were flying to Belem and going backwards in time. How she wished that were true. Why could it not have been last night with her once more in Caulder's arms? Tears streamed down her face and the pain inside would not go away. The beads on the dress brushed against her legs, and all they did was remind her of him. At last she dozed, a fitful sleep with dreams of her lover. She could see him on the lawn sending her away, and she could hear his voice... and yet she couldn't. It was as though he was disappearing from her, fading into the background. Little could she know that at that moment Caulder was fighting for his life. And yet somehow... She woke with a start and yelled out loud. "Daniel!"

"No, Toni. It's Ben. Daniel's safe. And so are you. I'm here for as long as you need me. Your uncle will be waiting and soon..." He didn't finish.

"No, he's not safe! Something has happened to him! Call someone. Find out. I know something has happened!" She panicked.

"And what if it has, Toni? Will you want to go back to him?" he asked.

"How can I? He doesn't want me." Her eyes held such pain. "No, Ben, I won't ever go back. But make the call. He's your father for god's sake!"

He made the call from the cockpit, and he listened to Sam. Then he hung up the line. The connection had not been good from the plane. He walked back down the plane to her and looked towards Toni. Had their relationship been that close? Now he knew for sure why his father had sent her away. Should he tell her the truth?

"Toni, he's..." he took a deep breath.

"Don't say it… please don't tell me." There was total despair on her face.

"He's not dead, if that's what you are thinking. Sung was in the grounds the whole time. He went to Caulder's room and… well, Sung is dead. Dana is safe, but my father… he isn't so good. They're flying him out, I don't know where. I couldn't understand everything that Sam was saying. We'll call from the ground in Belem. Another hour and we should be down. Toni? You okay? You want to go back?"

But Toni figured she would never be okay again. She'd lost him twice over in one night. "No. I need the bathroom." She went down the plane and into the lavatory. Looking in the mirror, she felt sick with fear and pain. Then she threw up.

When they landed in Belem, it was dark when they walked from the plane to the airport lounge. A barefoot girl in a long white dress, clutching muddy shoes and sporting a dark windbreaker was a strange sight. She hadn't eaten for hours and her pallor was sickly.

It was there that Bryan caught sight of her. He gasped. What had she gone through? He saw the dark haired man with her, but it wasn't the Caulder he knew. He was too young, but still he had his arm around his niece. Bryan rushed forward to greet her and put his hands out to her.

"Toni, my god, what has happened to you? Look at you!" He took hold of her arms and then he looked at Ben. "And who might you be?"

"I'm Ben Caulder, Daniel's son." At last he had said his name, but he said it with shame in his voice.

Bryan replied, "Are you responsible for this?" and he looked to Toni.

"No, sir… that can only be attributed to my father."

Toni opened her mouth to speak. But she couldn't think what to say to her uncle. At least he didn't say… I told you so. Instead she turned to Ben. "Please go and make another call. I have to know before we leave here."

"I'll be back," and he left her there.

"Know what, Toni?" Bryan took it gently.

"Know if he's still alive. I have to know… you don't understand." She blurted the sentences out. "What are you looking at me like that for?" Then she remembered how she looked and pulled the jacket around her. "Is there somewhere I can get some clothes? A store or something in the airport?"

"We'll find some jeans and shoes for you to wear. Is he really Caulder's son?" Bryan asked.

"One of them," she retorted way too quickly.

"One of them!? How many has he got?" Sinclair replied.

"Two that I know about. One's a ten-year-old now in complete control of Yaoundé. He's a prince." She hesitated and watched his expression. "You looked surprised. Not as surprised as I was to find all this out and certainly not as shocked as Ben. He didn't even know that Caulder was his father. I have two rolls of film in here," and she fumbled in the lining. "Wait till you see these pictures and the story I have. Will shock a lot of people, make me a top reporter, you'll be so proud of me… I know you will." Her voice became louder, almost hysterical. All the time she was watching for Ben to return. What was taking him so long? Then she saw him coming back through the crowds. He held a bundle in his hands.

"For you," and he handed her a pair of men's jeans, a T-shirt and sneakers. "Go put them on, before you get really sick."

"Where did you get them? And did you make the call?" She knew he was avoiding the issue.

"Yeah, I made the call. They put him on a plane bound for an unknown destination. He wanted to get away from there and take some of the heat away from Dana. But he's alive, Toni. That what you wanted to know? My father is still alive."

Bryan saw the looks that passed between them as if they shared some dark secret that only the two of them understood. He saw her take the clothes from Ben and turn for the bathroom. But he also heard the word's 'still alive'.

"Toni," Ben shouted. "Please come back to us."

She smiled and nodded her head.

Sinclair turned to Ben. "So, you are his son? And what is my niece to you?" Bryan was blunt. "It's obvious to any fool that you're in love with her."

"And you are no fool, Mr. Sinclair. I'm in love with her. But to her I'm just a friend. It's my father she's in love with." He was almost ashamed to admit the fact, and he hung his head.

"What, what did you say? With Daniel Caulder? How could she be? She's only known him a little over three weeks. How could they get that close? I know Caulder has a reputation and I warned Toni to stay clear. Were they..." He was afraid to ask.

"Lovers? Yes, very much so. I'm sorry to admit that my father did that to your niece. But, I have to tell you something. Even after all that has happened, and I am sure Toni will tell you, I know deep down that he loved her."

"Loved? Is there something else you didn't tell her? What other news is there from Cameroon?" As he spoke he followed Ben's gaze up to the T.V. screen that perched on the wall in the airport building. He didn't understand the language, but he knew what pictures they were flashing. Pictures of a man... a man he knew well.

Ben was watching intently. And he understood what they said. A plane was missing over the jungle north of Yaoundé. They saw Caulder's face and they both turned and saw Toni coming towards them. She didn't see the screen.

She approached Ben first. "Back to being a boy again. Where did you steal these from? Some poor janitor passing by?" and she saw the look on their faces.

"Toni, there's something else. I lied. They say that a plane went down over the jungle. It may be Caulder's. He may be alive or he may not. At this point, no one knows," and he looked up at the screen.

Toni saw the pictures. She didn't cry. She didn't do anything except walk away without looking back.

"She's been through too much, Mr. Sinclair, and I don't know how much more she can take. She can't go back for him. Maybe we should let her think he's still alive, for now. We have to let her come to terms with this in her own way. He's doing this for her. If it's okay with you, I'm coming back to L.A on your flight. They had a spare seat... I have to go back to my father's home and see to his affairs. Mr. Sinclair," he hesitated, "you can help me find out if he really is dead.

You and I both know that Daniel Caulder is good at what he does. And right now, he may be doing what he does best... being the mercenary that he is." And Ben looked straight at Bryan.

Toni walked through the airport oblivious to her surroundings. The jeans hung on her, and she rolled up the pants legs. She pulled the jacket tight and the films hit her ribs. They were all she had left of Daniel. The fact hit her hard. She sat down on one of the seats and stared at the floor. In one month, her life had changed so much. Then... she cried.

Her uncle came up beside her and sat down on the hard empty seat.

"Honey, come on. Let's go home." He collected her in his arms. "Please don't cry, Toni. Ben told me that you and Caulder were..."

"Were what? Lovers? Does that shock you? A man so much older than me? 'Were' is the operable word, isn't it? And he made a fool of me. Did Ben tell you that, also? Did he tell you about the heroin and the rest of the trip? Did he? By the look on your face, I guess he did. Get him to tell you sometime or you can read about it in the Times." She was striking back the only way she knew how and at the only other person she had ever really loved. "Ben knows everything. He was there, just like I was. And I wish to god that I had taken your advice and left when you said. But I didn't, and like the naive fool I am, I fell in love with Daniel Caulder."

Ben joined them. He stood there, silent.

"Isn't that right, Ben? Daniel made a fool of me. He didn't really love me at all. You heard him say that, didn't you? And it's true, right?"

"Toni, you know it's not. My... father was in love with you. He threatened me if ever I told you. He sent you away on purpose. All those things he said back in the grounds... none of it was true. I was told to get you out at any cost... and that was the price. He knew what was going to happen. That's how much he loved you. He wanted you to be free and he made me leave with you. And it took all this to make me realize just how much he loved us both."

Toni looked up into Ben's face and she could almost see Caulder standing there. She put her hand out to Ben and he took it and helped her up. Her uncle let go... not so much let go... he had lost her.

"I'm coming back with you, Toni. When you want we can go and get your things from the house. Let's go, Toni. Let's go home." Ben was taking over where his father had left off.

As they boarded the flight for the city, Toni was silent. This was a far cry from the trip out. No private planes, no stops anywhere, regular airlines with regular people on board. That was the point. It was all too regular. She had tasted life on the dark side and now her own life would never be the same. She sat in between her uncle and Ben, and stared at the seat in front of her like it would disappear. When the plane lifted off the ground, she was promptly sick, fortunately into the sick bag.

Recovering, she murmured. "I'm fine, really. Happens all the time, me throwing up over Ben and then passing out on Daniel…" She stopped speaking, slipped off her jacket and laid it on her legs.

Bryan couldn't help but see her arm and the needle marks on her. He stared in horror. "Was that Caulder, too? Did he do that also?" he said angrily.

"No, Mr. Sinclair. That was a man by the name of Sung… and my father cut his heart out. He kept his promise to Toni."

She didn't flinch, when he said the words. She would expect it from Daniel. What she hadn't expected was the way he sent her back.

But her uncle did. Neither of them noticed with more than enough on their minds.

"Better get a checkup when you get back, Toni. It's probably the after effect of the heroin. But better take no chances." Ben hesitated. "When you're ready, you can come by the house and pick up your things. I'll come by and give you a ride over if you like."

Bryan watched with interest. If the son was this possessive, no wonder Toni had fallen for the father. She had changed so much that he thought he would never really know her again… and he knew he had lost her to this family.

The flight was long, very long. They dozed periodically. Toni lay back in her seat, and her dreams were fitful. She thought she heard Caulder calling her. She could feel his hand on her arm. His touch was light, but there was no chemistry between them.

"Toni, wake up. The meal is being served and you have to eat." It was Ben's voice. That's why she felt nothing. Wrong Caulder.

She ate, and then she asked Ben a question. "When we get back home, I'd like to come back to the house with you, tonight. I want to see the rooms again. I want to see Daniel's room. I never saw it… please?"

"Of course, whatever you want." He was surprised and glanced across to Bryan.

"Are you sure you want to do that?" Sinclair asked his niece.

"Very sure." Her mind was set.

They landed at the airport in a dark drizzle. Toni was chilled in the cool, damp air. In the afternoon light, they walked from the airport and into the waiting limo. It sped through the streets and suddenly the whole place seemed alien to her. She realized that this wasn't where she wanted to be. Caulder had shown her a whole new world. A magical world… one of love and one of hate.

"Mr. Sinclair, would you like to come with us to the house?" And then he whispered to him so Toni would not hear. "Think we need to talk."

She looked out of the limo windows and never heard him speak. She'd made her mind up what she was going to do. Write the story, make it good, really good and then take off back to the jungles of Africa to find her man. She owed him that.

When they entered the mansion gates Bryan realized just how powerful Caulder was. Security was everywhere as though they were waiting for their boss to return. They were escorted from the limo by two burly gun toting men and into the house. Toni never hesitated. She climbed the stairs and stepped into Daniel Caulder's room… closed the door… and then let her feelings go.

Downstairs, Ben poured Bryan a drink. He moved round the house like suddenly he owned it. "Don't think too badly of my father. I still hate him for finding out the way I did. I hate him for not telling me I was his son. But on the plane I began to realize why he had sent us out, Toni and I. He knew Sung would come back for him and

Dana. He was doing what most fathers would do. You, of all people, should know that. You've been like her father." It was then the phone rang. "Excuse me a moment." He took the call.

"Ben... Caulder. Sam, is that you? No, I'm not. Give me a minute," and he turned and walked to the window. "Okay, I am now. Where's my father? Why weren't you with him?" he demanded an explanation as to why he wasn't.

Bryan could only hear one side of the conversation. Obviously about Caulder. He removed his jacket. It was warm inside the house.

"Are you sure? Did they find the wreckage? Why the hell were there only two of them on board? He should have had a dozen men with him. Yeah, she's here in the house, so is her uncle. Devastated? Of course she is! I had to tell Toni for her sanity's sake. She knows he did it for her. Keep searching for him, we cannot give up now. Do you want us to fly back? We can do that? Okay, tell Dana I love him. No, tell Dana we love him," and he hung up the line.

"Did they find him?" asked Sinclair, relaxing back on the sofa, drink in hand.

"No, Mr. Sinclair. Just the wreckage. Sam, his bodyguard was not with him, just his Brazilian man, Andre. They didn't find either of them. Just the burnt out shell of the plane. Like I said before, my father is very good at what he does. Very good!"

And Bryan Sinclair wondered exactly which side Ben was on.

Half an hour later Toni came back down the stairs. She had showered and dressed in some of her own clothes. "Ben, do you mind if I stay here tonight? I know I shouldn't ask that, but..."

"Of course you can stay. Where do you want to sleep?" he asked tentatively.

"In Daniel's room... just for tonight. Tomorrow I will leave you in peace and go back to my own apartment and then," she turned to her uncle, "I'll go back to work. I have a story to write."

Sinclair was not surprised... not at anything she said. "Then, I will bid you both good night. Ben, look after her, okay? You may be Caulder's son, but somehow I trust you." He slipped his jacket on and headed for the door.

"On that, you have my word. My driver will take you back to your home. And, I'm going to try and persuade this young lady to stay on here just for a while longer." Ben walked Bryan down the lobby and out to the car. "Maybe, we'll find out between us, just what is going on. Mr. Sinclair… the conversation we had about my father. Can we keep that to ourselves? I know she will never love me, but at least this way I am near her and can watch out for her. And who knows what may happen? If Caulder is still alive, maybe he can get back here or they will find him…"

"I hope for her sake you find him. I have never seen my niece like this. It'll be interesting to see what she puts in the story… and how she copes if he comes back. Answer me truthfully, Ben. Do you think your father's dead?"

"Honestly… no!" And he extended his hand to Bryan.

Bryan walked to the car. Caulder had better be, or he would have to face the music and answer to him for what he had done to Toni… him and one or two other people. He knew he had lost her to Daniel Caulder and he would never reclaim what he had lost… and neither would she.

Chapter 10

Bryan Sinclair made sure the film was developed quickly for his niece. He may not have the power that Caulder had, but he did have the contacts, and he intended to use them. He would find out where the mercenary was, if indeed he was still alive. And he really had no doubt that he was. He pulled the pictures from the packet. He quickly flicked through them until he came upon the ones from the palace. Here was Dana dressed in silks and basking in his new-found position in life, and there in the background stood Daniel Caulder.

Now, Bryan had a very up-to-date picture of the man. The black silks of Africa covered his body and his black hair was long and very obvious. The next picture showed Dana and Toni. Someone else had used her camera. Toni stood in the doorway and was obviously not aware the picture was taken. She was a beautiful woman. And the photo only emphasized the fact. And then there was one of the two of them. Caulder stood behind her, and his face revealed his feelings. A man in love, but also in despair. Bryan almost felt sorry about the situation. But he had led Toni into this mess, and when his contacts found him, he, too, would pay the price… the price of freedom.

Sinclair took the photographs around to the Caulder estate. The gate let him by on Ben's instructions. He drove up to the door, left his car in the capable hands of another gun-toting man, and was escorted into the library where he joined Ben and his niece. He noticed how at home she looked and recognized some of the plants from her apartment.

Ben rose from the leather chair. "Mr. Sinclair, how nice to see you again." He put his hand out to his guest.

Bryan returned the gesture. "Ben… Toni, how are you?"

"Fine." Dressed in grey sweats, she was quiet and sat on the sofa.

"I have something for you," and he handed her the packets of photos. He sat down next to her. For some reason the room looked even more lavish than the last time he had been there.

She was calm as she looked through them, until she came to the one of her and Caulder. There was a puzzled look on her face. "I didn't know this was being taken, or this one of me." She looked from one picture to the other. "I don't know who took them…"

"I did!"

They both looked at Ben.

"But you left after Daniel told you to…" Toni was curious.

"I came back and saw your camera lying there. Let's just say they're a keepsake." And he sat down in the chair, and crossed his legs.

"For whom, Ben?" retorted her uncle.

"One is for Toni… the other is for me. Toni knows how I feel about her. I think she has known all the time. And it has made us good friends, brought us closer together."

Bryan watched his niece. *'Yes, Ben, and that's all she is ever going to be to you. You're the wrong Caulder.'*

"I've nearly finished the story. Are you listening? I said…"

"Can't wait to read it. Toni, when are you going back to the apartment? I notice some of your plants are here. Planning on staying a while?" He wanted to know why Ben kept her there, aside from the obvious.

Ben spoke first. "I see you're one step ahead, Mr. Sinclair."

"You bet I am. What's the real reason Toni's still here?" Bryan stood up and leaned against the expensive leather sofa. "Come on, Ben. You know something that we don't."

Ben was concerned. Bryan was smarter than he gave him credit for. He rose from the chair and went to the desk. "This came from Cameroon. Apparently, my father wrote a letter the night of… well the last night. It has his name and Dana's seal. It's an official document."

She jumped up from the sofa. "Ben, you never told me you had anything from Cameroon. Why didn't you? Is Caulder really dead? I kept hoping they'd find him, or he would contact us. That's why I stayed, Uncle Bryan." She turned back to Ben, "But you knew otherwise since…?"

"This morning. That's all. I guess I kept hoping, too."

Bryan wondered if that was the real reason.

"I'll read it to you. Most of it's legal stuff just for myself and Dana. He and I get two thirds of the money, the cars, the jets… the family business, for want of a better description… but, Toni, he left you the house and everything in it, along with enough money to last you all your life. In short, you are a very wealthy young woman." He shuffled the papers around in good fashion.

Toni walked to the window. He could not have known; maybe he just hoped, as she did now. Next week she would be sure. She couldn't speak, couldn't tell them. Behind her there came a torrent of words.

"It's blood money! My niece won't have any part of it," yelled Bryan.

"It's the same way I was brought up." Ben came back at him. "And it does look like my father is dead. That should make you happy!"

Bryan stood straight and walked to Toni. "Let's go! You can't stay in this house. Come on, Toni, get your things together…"

"I can't leave, not now." Tears rolled down her face. "He really did love me, didn't he?" She took hold of the story that she had lying on the table and ripped it into shreds and held the photos precariously.

"Toni, what the hell are you doing? Even from the grave he's buying your silence? Can't you see that?" Bryan argued.

Through the tears she cried. "Maybe so. But I can never write the story that way. It was good, real good just like I promised you it would be, but it was written for all the wrong reasons. I wanted revenge. I wanted it because he let me go like he did. But I know why he did it, and I can't stop loving him. Doesn't anyone understand that?" she screamed. "I'll always be in love with him," and she stared out towards the pool. The first place she ever saw Caulder. Tears streamed down her face.

"Toni, don't say that. You're too young, honey. You have the rest of your life ahead of you. I know Caulder was your first real love and…" Bryan was trying to make her see sense.

"Lover? Say it. I don't care if he's had a thousand women. I'm not ashamed of the fact. He's the only man I want. I still don't believe he's dead. I never will." Toni was angry and unhappy all in one go. "If he left me his home, he left it for a reason and I'll be here when he returns." Her vision blurred by her own tears.

"Are you crazy, Toni? He's not coming back. He really is…" Sinclair pleaded.

"No, he's not, Uncle Bryan! There has to be a reason for all of this. He left me here for a purpose."

Bryan turned to Ben in desperation. "You try. You Caulder men seem to have more luck with this Sinclair woman. I can't reach her."

Ben put his arms out to her. "Toni, give me the photographs. We have to keep them of someone we both love. We'll put them in a frame on the mantle… you and my father."

Reluctantly, she handed them to him. "As long as you do just that. I'll say it one more time… Daniel is not dead! And here I intend to stay."

"Then you're not leaving with me?" asked her uncle.

"No. I'll be right here if you need me… in Daniel's rooms," and she wiped her face on her sleeve.

Bryan began to think his niece was losing it.

Ben thought differently. He knew how close the two had been. If anyone would know… she would. He also knew if Caulder came back now, Sinclair would be waiting for him. He figured by now that Bryan had contacts in high places, maybe even in government. It was different when Toni was on the assignment for him. It was like something from the past had caught up with the present. Now, was another situation. Not only was there animosity towards the mercenary but to the man who wronged his niece. Surely to god, Bryan could see what Caulder meant to her. Maybe that was the problem. Should he warn Sam that there was an enemy within?

That night when Bryan Sinclair left the residence, he was full of anger. Losing his niece was one thing but to a man like Caulder, was another. He wanted to kill him… and his son.

He didn't go home. Back in his office, he made telephone calls and called in some favors. His friends in the government would come in very useful. And from his pocket, he pulled the negative. By midnight, Daniel Caulder's picture was halfway round the world. The hate he felt for Caulder had finally surfaced.

The weeks dragged on for Toni. There was no fresh news. She gave up her apartment, moving everything she had to the Caulder household. She rewrote her story… twenty times, and still she could not print it. Each time it found its way to the trash bin.

Slowly, she spent less time at the office and her dreams of becoming a top reporter were shattered. Uncle and niece drifted further apart. On her last day there, she cleaned out her desk. Feeling the urge to throw up, she rushed down the lobby to the restroom. Bryan watched her from his office. When she emerged from the bathroom, he stepped into the corridor and confronted her.

"Does Ben know?" He stood in front of her, arms folded and blocked her way.

"Know what?" She tried to bluff her way out of the situation, and move past him.

"You know damn well what! This is the person that raised you you're talking to. Know you're pregnant? Which Caulder does the bastard belong to, Toni? Is it Daniel's or Ben's?"

She had never heard her uncle speak like this. She raised her hand and hit him across his face. He never flinched.

"How dare you speak to me like that. I thought you knew me better. Obviously not." She turned to go.

He caught her by the arm. "But you are pregnant, Toni? You can't deny that. He hoped, didn't he? That's why he left the house to you. Daniel Caulder hoped you'd be pregnant. Smart man! He tried hard enough. But, Toni, remember this… when he finds out, and believe me he will, he'll come back for you and his child. And I'll be waiting; me and the right side of the law!"

She faced him, her eyes wild and disbelieving. "You're the one who sent me on this assignment. You told me to go for it. Well, I did! And even if I'm pregnant, which you don't know for sure, nor who the father is, he will never let himself be caught by the likes of you and your friends. He's not some sort of common criminal. He's a man that the people in Cameroon love, including me." And it was said.

She turned in a blur of tears and walked out of her Times office for the last time. Toni did not know what she had said. But she had just given away his exact location!

When she returned home that night, Toni had news for Ben and the biggest favor she would ever ask him. She waited till dinner was concluding and then made her announcement. She sat back in her chair.

Plunging straight in, "Ben, how much do you love me?"

He was taken off guard. "Did I hear you right?"

"Yes."

"You know the answer to that. Why, what's wrong? Is it something to do with your uncle?" He leaned back in the chair and crossed his legs. This was interesting.

"Kind of." She fidgeted in her seat, then stood up and moved to the window. She looked at the floodlit pool. "Would you marry me?" She didn't look at him.

He almost fell from the chair. "What? What did you say? Would I marry you?"

"You heard me! Yes or no. Plain and simple."

"Plain and simple? I don't think so! What the hell do you mean? You have everything you want here. My father left you everything you... Oh, my god!" He realized he'd left her everything, literally.

She looked down at the floor. Scared and in a turmoil, Toni could think of no other way out. Her uncle had promised that Caulder would come back for his child and he would be waiting. And Toni knew he meant it.

Ben joined her at the window and looked into her face. "Are you pregnant?"

Tears weld in her eyes, and she nodded her head.

"My god! When my father does it, he does it well."

She stared at him. She didn't believe he'd said that.

"No, I didn't mean that... I meant the mess he creates. Oh, god, Toni. If Caulder is alive and finds out, he'll come back for you and your uncle will have him picked up. I checked up on some things. Mr.

Sinclair has been talking with friends from the government. Apparently, right back from the days in Nam, your father had been a war correspondent. He wrote under a different name. He was after a story on some Chinese official even then. You know who that was. And you know who else was in Nam! Years later they all met up again. Caulder and Sam were there. I'm told Caulder caused an accident and your parents were killed. Your uncle blamed my father. So, to get back at Daniel, Bryan used you to get to him and get him in the trouble he's in now. The photo I took of you two turned up everywhere. Because you believe him to be alive, so does your uncle."

She wasn't hearing this. "Is all this true? How did you find this out?"

"Toni, I have my sources, also." He'd been told what to say and this was only part of the story.

She thought about it. "It makes sense, though. All of it does. Does Daniel know this? He must never find out that it's his child. If we married next week, no one would know. We can say the baby is premature. I'm sure you know the right doctors. Daniel can't come back here. Ben, be honest. You don't think he's dead, do you?" It all came out in one big blur of words.

He hesitated. "We'll get married this weekend…" He had given her his answer.

It was to be a quiet wedding. Not the one Toni wanted. She would be Mrs. Caulder, but the wrong one. All they had to do was keep the secret a few more days. For Toni it was a marriage in name only. She had Daniel's suite, and Ben had his own rooms. Ben had hoped that one day… but Ben also knew the charade they were both playing. He'd keep quite about the baby for his own reasons. Bryan Sinclair was asked to give her away and Toni wanted to see if he still held the grudge. She never received a reply and somehow that didn't surprise her. She knew that he still did. She knew her uncle well and knew he wanted his revenge. She'd try one more time… and then it would be over. She knew deep in her heart that if Caulder had caused the crash, it had to be an accident.

"Come in," Sinclair looked up from his computer. "What the hell are you doing here?"

"Is that anyway to greet your niece? I came to see if you would come to the wedding on Saturday. Will you come, please?" She almost begged him. Toni didn't want the relationship to end like this. Him hating her, and the man she loved.

He slammed the books down on his desk and she jumped. "You're joking, right? You marry into that family, and you are no niece of mine. Toni, when I gave you that assignment, I had my doubts you would see it through. But you did and more. When you were in Cameroon, Caulder called me to come get you. I could have forgiven you for becoming his lover. But to move into his house and now marry his son, have you lost your senses? You're living a shady lifestyle, money made from killing people. What have you become, Toni? I don't know you anymore." He returned to his work.

Toni had been in this office so many times before. Now, it was alien to her. The spacious room was filled with books and old newspaper cuttings. Then something caught her eye. On a board on the wall hung the photo of her and Caulder.

Bryan looked up and saw her.

"So, now you know. I've been looking for him for several weeks. He's good, Toni. Your lover is real good. You and I both know he's not dead. Oh, he made a will all right… a living will… because he knows he can never come back. He'd been skating on thin ice for sometime. He may be a hero in West Africa but not in this country, not after I convinced the government he was a terrorist and I had pictures to prove it. Your pictures. He's also wanted for killing a Chinese official. Amazing what you can make people believe. If you had checked in the envelopes you'd have found more than one negative missing. He took you, and your parents, from me Toni Sinclair, and made you a Caulder. And the Caulder's of this world aren't fit to walk the earth!"

"Have you finished? Is it all out now?" she yelled. "What gives you the right to be judge and jury? This is a personal issue for you. Doesn't it matter what I feel for him? Would you really just turn him over to the government… just like that? You know what he did in Africa. He killed Sung for me… you saw the needle marks and you knew what he did to me. Sung beat me and then he tried to rape me. If it hadn't been for Caulder… Wouldn't you have done the same?

And all he did was put his son in power. His own son! That doesn't make him a terrorist… why? Why did you do it? You sent me there as a decoy, someone to get back at him! He saved my life, and gave me something very precious…" She stopped. "It's time for me to leave. I can see I'm wasting my breath on you. I'm sorry you carry such a grudge. I know about the accident and how you blame him for my parent's death. I don't!"

Bryan stared at her.

"Ben and I will be married at the weekend and neither you, nor god, can stop us. And Daniel, if he is alive, I hope he's safe. But I think now that he may not be. So that should make you one happy person. Goodbye. You and I will not meet again!" She turned on her heel, walked through the doorway and closed the door behind her. She almost gave in and went back. But she'd had a good teacher. Caulder had taught her well.

On the Friday night, Ben took Toni out to dinner. He'd picked an expensive hotel, and it was his gift to his future wife. That's what he told her. Ben made all the correct overtures in public. That was the easy part. The next part would be a little more difficult. "Honey, there's a man here who wants to meet me. Shouldn't take long. Want to come with me?"

He needed the right answer.

"Why not. I can't sit here on my own. I feel like the whole world is watching. Ben, I have a question to ask you…"

"Ask me later, honey. We can't keep our clients waiting!" and he escorted her to the elevator. The hotel was plush. As the doors closed, Toni watched a cute little fountain functioning in the lobby. She saw the man in the raincoat and shades, and the one by the doors. They were being followed. But by which side?

"Which floor, sir," asked the voice.

"That's up to you," replied Ben.

Toni could not believe her ears. She didn't turn round. She whispered softly… "Sam!"

"Don't turn around," he murmured in a low voice. "When you get off the elevator, go down to room 612. I'll join you."

She started to turn to him.

"Do as I tell you, Miss Sinclair. Ben... take her hand, get her to the room, and walk her in the bedroom." He never looked up. Sometimes inside an elevator a camera lurked unseen. The porter's uniform was a good ruse.

Toni was shaking as she stepped out of the elevator and walked to the nominated room. The porter stepped in front of them and opened the door. The suite was huge. One meeting room, and off to the left, a spacious-looking bedroom.

Sam closed the door behind them. There were two men in the room... two armed guards and they weren't wearing shades and raincoats! She was looking round the palatial room when Ben took her hand, and led her through to the bedroom.

It was in the shadows that Daniel Caulder waited for his woman. He waited till Ben closed the door. She stood there, waiting for something to happen, not sure what, but something.

"Toni," the voice was husky.

She was conscious of the scent of the man she loved and turned towards him. "Daniel" and she took a deep breath. "I thought I would never see you again!"

He turned up the lamp lights and stood there. His hair was longer, and he now had a moustache and beard. They had grown through darker than his hair. He'd lost weight, but somehow it suited him. Dressed in black jeans and a shirt open to the waist, he was the sexiest she had ever seen him.

Daniel looked at her. Her hair had grown out some and she wore a long, tight black dress. She had a glow about her, an inner radiance.

Toni was afraid to move. Why had he come back? Did he know? All she knew was that he stood in front of her. He couldn't know. Ben would not tell him.

Ben stared at his father. "For a man that's supposed to be dead, you look extremely good."

"Ben, I had to get you to take her out of there." And the two men exchanged looks. "So, you're marrying Toni tomorrow? Do you love her?"

"You know I do!"

"And, Toni, do you love my son?" he was so serious.

"He's a good friend." She was shaking.

"Not what I asked. Do you love him?"

She whispered, "No."

"Then why are you marrying him?"

She looked at Ben. He gave her no clue to go by. "I'm doing it for you. My uncle intends to find you…" She was telling the truth and could look him straight in the eyes, eyes right now that she could die for.

"That's what I thought. I knew if it was another reason you would tell me. One of you would. I have to go away, Toni, until all this calms down, and I couldn't go without seeing you one more time." He could hold his composure no longer. "Come here."

Toni almost fell across the room and into his arms. He held her there as if she would disappear and then he kissed her so passionately that she knew there was no one else in his life. He held her head and kissed her lips, then her eyes and down her neck. His feelings for her were so intense, and tears streamed down her face.

Ben left them then. She would always be his father's. He knew he had made the right decision. He walked out the door and took the elevator down to the lobby, giving them time to be together.

Back upstairs, Caulder's last few weeks of fantasies became a reality for him. He pulled the straps of her dress down and the gown fell to her waist. He cupped her breasts in his hands and kissed them, his head resting against her. She kissed his hair and felt the longing inside of her. Nearly three months pregnant, Caulder would never guess from her figure. He stood up and kissed her again and again, his kisses so desperate and urgent.

She pulled his shirt from him and then caught sight of his scars.

"Oh, my god, Daniel. Did Sung do that?" She clasped her hand to her mouth.

"Yeah, the night you left. Now you know why I sent you back. You could never have defended yourself. That's all over, Toni. It's the charges that worry me now. Your uncle is intent on getting revenge against me for taking you. But let's not dwell on that. Let's make this a night we can both remember. I have five hours till my flight leaves for….best you don't know."

"Daniel, don't leave me again! Take me with you. You're going back to Cameroon and Dana, aren't you? Somewhere you can be safe. Please, take me with you. I won't be in your way, I promise. Please," she begged him.

"I can't, Toni. It's not Cameroon. Your uncle's friends found me there, but with a little help I got out before he had me arrested. Dana is safe. Toni, your uncle carries a life long grudge. Sometime back…" He hadn't meant to tell her. He stopped. He hadn't wanted to tell that's why she was sent on the assignment in the first place. The Times newspaper had been a good cover for the Sinclair's all these years. No one had known the real people in the newspaper world.

"I know. I know what he is…" She knew the truth. All the pieces fit. Like one big jigsaw that had all come together. That's why the dossier was almost complete. It explained why he had sent his niece. She had reported everything back to him, direct. And it would explain why he was so angry when she went to the other side. He had this score to settle, and now was the time.

"Oh, Daniel, I'm so sorry." She pulled her dress up around her. "Go, get out, now. You should not have come here. There were men in the lobby. They followed us, Ben and me. They know you're here!"

"Honey, calm down. They don't know. Yes, they were following you and Ben. They were supposed to. You came here to meet a client. He's out there talking to Sam right now. Ben's with them. It's okay. We have a few short hours to be together." And he took her hands from the dress. This time he picked her up and carried Toni to the bed. "Silk sheets, honey, just like you wanted." He slid her dress from her and pulled off her underwear. He looked down the length of her body. The scars were healed and he had never seen such a perfect woman… his woman.

She needed no coaching from him to satisfy him. She ran her fingers down the scar. He never flinched, and she undid the belt on his jeans. She could feel his desire for her through the denims.

He wanted her so badly. She felt his muscles tense against her and she saw the lust in his eyes. How she wanted to tell him that she carried his child… And how she knew she couldn't.

He pulled her legs around him and she felt him inside of her. His body covered hers, and the heat was intense.

"Toni, I love you so much. There are so many things we need to say to each other and so few hours. I wish you could come with me. Maybe we could take you with us. Or you could follow at a later date. We'll get Ben in here later and see what we can do. Right now, I need you!" He turned on his back and pulled Toni with him.

This time she cried out and in the other room Sam turned up the television.

No one had thought to ask just how Ben knew about her parents.

Two hours later, Ben returned.

"Where'd you go? We were gettin' worried about you. Anyone see you leave?" asked Sam.

"No, I'm not stupid. I wasn't followed." He looked towards the bedroom. "They still in there?"

"Yeah, they have a lot of catching up to do." Sam studied Ben. "Must be hard watching your father make love to the woman you're going to marry tomorrow. Don't think I could do it! No, sir. Think that would be just a little more than I could take, even from Daniel Caulder." Sam was suspicious.

"All right! You made the point. I couldn't take it, that's why I left. Tomorrow, he'll be out of our lives. She has to have someone to love."

Sam rose up from watching television. "Sure she does, Ben, and it's not going to be you. Get used to the idea." He walked to the bedroom door and knocked lightly. "Mr. Caulder?"

Daniel pulled the sheets across Toni, and slipped on a robe courtesy of the hotel. Caulder opened the door. "Come in."

Sam went into the room. The door was ajar, but Ben could see them whispering. He could also see Toni swathed in silk. He knew then he'd made the right decision. Ben got up and joined them.

"Toni wants to come with me, or at least join me later. Ben, you still have to go through with this wedding. Sam, you and I should leave in an hour or so. I'll just spend some more time with her, and then we'll go. It's pushing it just by being here. They could arrest her, too."

Ben hadn't thought of that! The door closed behind them and Daniel and Toni once more became one.

"Honey, I have to leave you. God, I don't want to. I have something for you." He leaned across the bed and reached on the dresser. "Here, you left this behind. Don't ever take it off again," and he placed the ring on the third finger of her right hand. "That's how they do it in Europe, we are one for eternity."

"Daniel," and she clung to him, "there's something I wanted to tell you..." She looked into his eyes. He had a puzzled look. "Never mind, it will keep. Make love to me one last time," she begged him.

He climbed out of bed and took hold of her hand. "I have to go shower but not on my own." This time no one could hear them and Toni's tears were washed away in the warm sensuous waters that trickled down her body. When he put the soap on her, he wrote 'I love you' in the foam and on the mist from the shower door, she drew a heart. From behind, he made love to her and the heart became a blurred mess on the glass as her face pressed hard against it. As he dried and dressed, Toni couldn't drink in enough of him. Her heart told her to tell him the truth and her brain cried 'no'.

Finally she stood in the doorway to the bedroom. She had watched him dress and now he had to leave her.

"I'll see you again, Toni. You have my word that this is just for now. I'll come back for you. Ben knows that this is just a charade. Wait for me, Toni. Don't sleep with him..."

"Oh, Daniel, I don't want anyone else to make love to me, not ever. Please, make it soon, please! *We* can't be without you. I love you so much. Just till it's safe, right? My uncle will give up."

"No, Toni, he won't... not till one of us is dead. Your uncle is a clever man and me, well, I'm still one step ahead... so far. Goodbye, 'What'... I love you." He had missed the word *we*. He pulled her to him one last time, and kissed her mouth very gently.

Her hands shook and she let his fingers slip through hers. Daniel left her standing by the door, wrapped in the silk sheet and clutching at her ring. And Caulder and Sam left by the back entrance with bodyguards in tow.

Ben went into the bedroom and moved towards her. Toni was crying.

"Did you tell him? Did you tell him you're carrying his child?" he asked.

"No, Ben, I didn't. You know he would have stayed. Let's get out of here and go home. We have to get to a wedding!"

She had not told Daniel, but before the next day was out, someone else got the message across to him... loud and clear.

And Bryan's plan was still working.

Chapter 11

Inside Daniel's suite, Toni made ready for her marriage to Ben. She dressed in that suite because it was now hers. The very masculine room filled her memories of the last few hours with him. All she had added to his domain was her clothes, and her plants. Otherwise she moved in exactly as he had left it... on purpose.

The wedding was to be in the gardens of her newfound residence. Whether pronounced dead or alive, Toni now owned the Caulder mansion. Around two p.m., a few guests began to collect on the lawns. High security was very evident, men still loyal to the Caulder's. Ben was taking no chances and had every intention of keeping the enemy out... but who was the enemy? Certainly Sinclair? And then there remained the fact of his father. Toni watched from the bedroom window.

Ben had spent most of the morning by the pool, reflecting on last evening's events. Feeling sure he could handle it, when he was called upon, he had set the meeting between his father and Toni. He knew Sam had been goading him in the suite... but Sam was right. Ben could not accept the fact that last night his father had made love yet again to the woman he wanted. And Ben had no doubt in his mind that Sam had conveyed his feelings to Caulder.

Toni decided on a long black dress as a further reminder to Ben that this was a marriage of convenience. She tidied her hair, put on pearls, and high heels. No special arrangements for her, nothing to make Ben think this was anymore than an arranged marriage. Maybe now, Daniel Caulder would be left alone.

At three the justice of the peace arrived and the ceremony began to take shape. Flowers and balloons decorated the pool area, and music filled the air. Caterer's busied themselves most of the day with food preparation. Her wedding was not supposed to be like this. It was supposed to be romantic and wonderful, and to someone she loved.

Tony left the sanctuary of Daniel's rooms, and descended the stairs. A posy of wild flowers lay on the hall table. She picked them up and viewed them, and moved to the glass windows leading down to the lawns. Toni was afraid... afraid she could not go through with this charade. She watched the guests gathering in the chairs, and she saw Ben handing out orders like he owned the place. She came so close to running away from the whole thing. In her mind she could hear her uncle asking her that question. **'Which Caulder does the bastard belong to?'** He had to believe it was Ben's child and so did Daniel. And that meant betraying her lover. She and Ben would make believe it was theirs. Now it was her turn to convince Caulder never to come back, and that's the only way she knew how.

Toni clutched the flowers to her. She toyed with the ring on her finger and thought of her lover. "I can't do it! I just can't! I should have told him the truth. I can't play these games anymore," she murmured. She stared at herself in the mirror and tears clouded her vision.

Like a jolt of reality, the phone on the table burst into life. She looked around for someone to pick it up. There was no one in sight. Hesitantly, she picked up the receiver.

"Hello?" Her voice was low and uncertain.

A muffled voice on the other end spoke her name. "Miss Sinclair, do as I ask you. Go outside and get married. Do not look around you and do not speak. Just do as I ask."

She went to answer and he could hear her breathing change.

"Don't say a word! I'm sure the phone is tapped and I know for certain that the cameras are still working. Go outside and marry him, oh, and Miss Sinclair, your body looks stunning in that dress!" The line went dead.

Toni was shaking. She would recognize Caulder's voice anywhere. She wanted to spin around and find the hidden cameras. Were they all around the house? A thousand questions ran through her mind. Could he see her right now, this minute? Had he watched her dress in his rooms? And better yet, where the hell was he! Had he lied about catching a flight out? Was he going to make some grand entrance at the last moment? No... she thought not. He'd just told her to go outside and get married. But the emphasis was on 'go outside.' So, that's what she would do.

In the warm sun, Toni Sinclair walked across the lawn, down the homemade aisle, towards Ben. He looked so much like his father today that she was surprised she hadn't seen it before. He stood dressed in a black tux, and black silk shirt to match. With that jet black hair and arrogant attitude, no one would dispute that he was Caulder's son.

Toni suddenly felt totally alone except for the child she carried inside her. As she reached Ben, he took her hand in his, almost too tightly. He was too arrogant, as if he knew something she didn't. Did he know Daniel had called? Or was he aware of something she didn't know?

She heard the words the preacher said. She knew she answered back, but she had no clue what she was saying. Just repartition.

"I now pronounce you man and wife. You may now kiss the bride."

Toni felt sick. This was wrong, all of this. Something about today was radically wrong. She couldn't quite put her finger on it, but gut instinct told her something was going to happen. Her uncle had not shown up at the wedding... just as he said he wouldn't. Yet, somehow, she felt his closeness. A little too much closeness.

Ben kissed her.

She tried not to recoil.

They turned around and walked arm in arm back between the folding chairs.

"Well, Toni, what's it like to be Mrs. Caulder? Even if I'm not the right one." He whispered, almost mocking her. "At least now, your uncle can't touch you. You're my wife and you can never testify against me nor can you be arrested as being an accomplice of my fathers, even with all the pull your uncle has!" he smiled at the people either side of them.

So that was it!

"And whose idea was that? Was it Daniel's so that I shouldn't be arrested?" She stopped in her tracks. That wasn't it at all. "You made a bargain, didn't you? You made a bargain with my uncle and his friends. How long have you been in bed with the enemy? You're covering your own tracks! You traded your safety for your father's. And Daniel thinks that everything's okay. He told me to go ahead and marry you. He still trusts you. Oh, my god. What have I done!" She turned to run into the house, to escape, and Ben caught her by the arm.

"Oh no, my lady! You stay right here. You and I have an agreement. You have a name for your child and I have you. And as for any other agreement, I don't know what you're talking about, except I never will tell your uncle that it's not my child," he lied.

She turned to face him. "How can you hate Daniel so much? Is it because of the fact he never acknowledged you as his son till now, or is it because of me? I should have told him last night about the baby and taken my chances. I heard Sam telling Daniel you had left the hotel. Where did you go? To my uncle's? Daniel knows what he is. And you? How did you find out about my parents crash? Bryan told you, didn't he? But he won't catch your father because he's too far away and even you don't know where to find him, and thank god, neither do I. Now, let me go. You're hurting me!"

"He must have told you? He wouldn't leave without telling you? But we can discuss that later in the bedroom." Suddenly, Ben was a totally different person. He had the power to attain what he wanted. Or was it so sudden?

She got right in his face. "Bedroom? Whose bedroom? You have yours and I have Daniel's. You touch me… and he will kill you… son or not. Just when did you change sides, Ben? He trusted you with me, and this is the way you repay that trust?" She was beginning to panic but in no way could she let him see that fact. She pulled her arm from his hand. "So, you want to see this charade out? Okay, so how are you going to explain my attitude to your guests? Oh, something else, Mr. Caulder. You'll never be half the man your father is in bed!"

Toni walked away with her eyes fixed dead ahead. She had no idea what she was going to do. No Daniel, an uncle she could not trust and now Ben. She passed the caterers, and for one moment she thought she saw a face she recognized. He looked Brazilian. She looked again, and he had gone.

Toni walked through the dining room and towards the stairs. She had to get out of there. If Ben meant what he said, she needed to get out pretty soon. Then she remembered the cameras. She had been standing by the phone when Caulder told her she looked stunning. What if somehow he could see her? If she could get a message to him. Was it possible? There was only one way to find out. Clearly, he could not see into the ground or he would have witnessed the situation with his son. He had said the house. She moved by the phone. What did she think she was going to do… wave her arms at him? Her mind went blank, and Toni stood and tried to think. He'd told her not to speak. Did he mean on the phone or just not at all?

Then it occurred to her. Pick up the phone. Who would she be dialing? No one. If she picked it up and put it down two or three times, surely Caulder would get the message. But was he even watching and where was he watching from. Was he close enough to get to her? It was worth a try and the only option she had. She picked up the receiver three different times and then replaced it on the hook. The third time she hung up… it rang. She grabbed for the line and Ben beat her to it.

"I don't think so, Mrs. Caulder. The lady of the house doesn't answer the phone." The grin was maniacal.

Caulder watched on the screen in his chopper. He'd been on his way to Germany via New York. He'd figured to lie low for awhile, in his grandparent's old homestead, until he could return safely. But the whole time he'd been traveling, he'd had this doubt in his mind. It wasn't just Sam's suspicions of Ben; it was a lot of things. He was worried that Bryan would go after his own niece just to force him back. He knew Sinclair had to get him, even if Toni stood in his way… and right now she did.

He and Sam had disembarked the flight at New York and chartered a plane to take them back home. Andre went with them. Based in a small hangar in a private airstrip Caulder watched the proceedings. Out back of the hangar were a couple dozen of Caulder's men waiting for their instructions.

Sam looked at Caulder. "She's in danger, Mr. Caulder. She was obviously trying to tell you something. She figured you could see her where she stood. Look at Ben. Looks like he's threatening her." They listened and Caulder was staggered by what he heard.

"Okay, Mrs. Caulder, time to fulfill your part of our deal. I've kept your uncle off your back, and you got rid of my father with your lies. Funny, really, he did you the same way. Sent you packing with a huge lie. That's when I started to hate him. All that stuff I told you afterwards… I made it all up. I never stopped hating him. But you, you just turned against your uncle. No, that's wrong… he hated you… when he found out you were pregnant! Wouldn't have made any difference which Caulder was the father. But I have a feeling that he knows which one of us it is. He knows you better than you think. But the secret's safe with me, for now. Pity Daniel doesn't know he's about to become a daddy again. And now he never will because you'll never tell him. If he comes back for you, your own uncle is waiting. Ironic really. He still thinks that Caulder killed the ones he loved," and he laughed a cruel and almost sadistic laugh.

Caulder could not believe what he was hearing. His own son had betrayed him, but worse than that had set Toni up for the fall.

"Congratulations, boss. You guessed right when you said she had something to tell you. She was trying to stop you coming back for her. So, now what? If you go in, they will be waiting. Bet your life half the wedding guests are government officials." He handed the controls of the chopper over to the pilot.

"Where's Andre?" Caulder was quiet in his demeanor.

"Last time I radioed him he was by the bar. Want me to talk to him?" asked Sam.

"No, not yet." He leaned back in the seat. Toni was pregnant. How he had hoped, and right now, he wished he hadn't hoped so hard. It may cost her her freedom.

"You okay, boss?" asked Sam.

"Yeah, fine. Not every day you lose one child and gain another, is it?" he pondered, and then he returned to his normal self. "Okay, let's go get her out of there!"

Ben took hold of her hand. "Now, let's get back to our guests. Just make sure you're the dutiful wife." He looked around. "My father was clever leaving all this to you. I can't touch the house even though we're married. He's still retained enough money for himself between you and Dana. And he pays for good attorneys, oh, hell yes; he only ever has the best... of everything. He'll make sure that I only ever get my share..." His voice trailed off. Ben looked around again, and it was then he remembered the cameras. He turned to her. "He called you, didn't he? That was him, just... and I hung up on him. And you, how did you know how to reach him? He told you about the cameras, and you signaled him somehow. My, Toni, you've really learned a lot. Well, that's one thing we can take care of... right now!" and he walked to a panel and flipped a switch. "Now, he cannot see anything!"

"Damn! He figured it out. The screen's blank." Daniel thumped the monitor expecting it to spring back into life. "Call Andre and get him closer to Toni. Tell him not to let her out of his sight. Ben will either wait for us to arrive and use her as bait, or he'll take her and get out now. Did you give the rest of the men their orders?" He was so calm that he worried Sam.

"Yeah, boss."

"Okay, let's get this thing in the air and try to get to her. I have a feeling he's calling Sinclair right now. They'll know we can't see them anymore... what they don't know is how close we are to the house. Ben may think he has time to play with, but we know better. My guess is he'll stay put, at least for now. If he leaves without Sinclair's permission, he could run into trouble. He'll lose his ally. I don't think he can afford to alienate anyone else. You got the guns ready?" He turned in his seat to look, and reassured himself they were there.

"You think it will come to that, boss?" Sam looked worried.

"Absolutely! Only one of us can survive. And if it's not me... you get Toni out of there at any cost."

They swung up high into the air. The chopper turned north. Two more choppers followed. Three helicopters over Los Angeles were not unusual.

Back on the ground, Ben pulled out his cell phone. He dialed a number. "Yeah, it's me. Who else were you expecting? There's a problem... by the name of Daniel Caulder. He can't be too far from here because he's watched the whole thing through his security system. By now, he's on his way here from wherever. Your call, *Mr. Sinclair*. Do we go or stay?"

Toni simply stared at him.

He continued. "He saw me with your niece. I was discussing events and the baby issue came up in the conversation. Now he'll come back for her. Yeah, she's right beside me. Of course it's his kid. Who else's would it be? Mine?" and he laughed. "You are joking right?" He paused. "He wants to talk to you," and he handed her the phone.

Toni took it from him. Ben had lied to her the whole time and now he had just broken another promise. She listened.

"This is your very last chance. Get out now... the government is waiting for him. Caulder can't get out once he's in. He'll never get to you, Toni. I'm sorry, but it's my job!"

"Your job?" she screamed. "I always thought you were a newspaper editor. How much else was a lie? Were you in on Sung, too? Was I a plant or was I bugged for my trip to Cameroon? Which? You let me suffer with Sung, and when Caulder killed him, you just set him up. You know it was self-defense. You could stop this right now with just one phone call. You could do it! If you spare Caulder, I'll go away and have the child somewhere else. I promise I won't go near him!" She was crying, and her uncle was weakening. "I'll never let him see his child!"

She said the wrong thing!

"The hell he won't 'cause he'll be dead! He cost me dearly once and now again!" and Bryan slammed his phone down.

There was smugness about Ben. "You'll never have my father again. He's history, Toni. History!"

Toni realized the only way was to bluff through this. Panicking was not going to help.

"Somehow, I don't think so, Ben. Daniel's smarter than you think. So, he's on his way here. Don't you think he still has friends in this household? The people that worked for him still do. Once he's in, he'll find a way out. Maybe you should think of getting out now, before your father finds you! You're a traitor, Ben, to your father and to Dana. If Bryan will double cross me, what chance do you think you have? Think about it, Ben. All he wants is Daniel Caulder. When he has him you'll be of no use to my uncle or his friends. You're not the big fish; Daniel is!" She was trying to put him down and was succeeding. "You blew it! You could have had this house, me, the child, everything you wanted. All you had to do was stay on Caulder's side. Instead you switched. Now, he will kill you."

The idea was suddenly a reality. The girl was right. Caulder did still have friends at the house. But he had protection from Sinclair's friends. What if Toni was right and that was only a temporary attribute? Perhaps he should leave.

"Okay, you win! I'll go, but you're coming with me. Your uncle can take care of my father. Let's go! We'll take one of his precious Ferraris. I guess you never had time to drive one of those, Miss Sin.., I am so sorry, Mrs. Caulder. We'll drive up into the hills and out along the highway. I have a small two-seater plane up there. Keep it there for emergencies, and what more of an emergency can this be. By the time Caulder gets here we'll be gone. Get going, *Mrs. Caulder.*" He turned and grabbed his keys, pulled his gun from the back of his pants to check the clip, and in doing so dropped his cell phone which made a clanking noise on the floor.

Toni stepped forward and stood on it crushing it to pieces.

"You bitch!" and he hit her across the mouth making blood spurt from her split lip. "Let's go!" He pushed her out through the back door of the house and into the garage. He picked the red Ferrari. "Get in. We may as well take his favorite one," he laughed. "In fact, you can drive it." He hesitated. "No, maybe not. You'd crash the car on purpose."

She'd been here before. Blood gushed from her lip, and there was nothing to stem the flow with. Now, she was hardened to being hurt.

No one stopped them from leaving. The Brazilian wasn't quick enough to catch them, but he did hear the screeching tires of the car. Caulder's chopper circled over the grounds. It blew the linens on the tables, and it caused waves in the swimming pool. Wedding guests ran for cover. The whole place seemed to erupt in confusion. Caulder still, indeed, had friends in his household. They moved across the lawns towards his chopper, totally unaware they were surrounded.

"Take her down, Sam!"

"Are you crazy? Sinclair will have you arrested on sight! You can't do that... boss, look, out of the back gate! Your red Ferrari." Sam pointed to the car speeding away from the house.

"Up, take her up!" Daniel yelled. "Follow those cars. Don't lose them at any price." He could just make out two people in the vehicle. With the top down, it was easy to see Ben and Toni. "That sure isn't any honeymoon they're leaving on. Get the hell after them!" and he pulled his gun out. The chopper shot straight up into the air and headed in Ben's direction.

Andre took Toni's Mercedes and was not far behind them. Ben was driving like a maniac. If he managed to keep the car on the road... it would be a miracle. He'd spotted Toni's car; and then a noise in the sky made him look up and he saw his father's chopper.

"Damn, he's good! But then you know that, don't you?" The car swerved as Ben watched the chopper.

"Yes, I know that very well, Ben!" and she glanced up to the skies.

"Good god! Ben's going to kill her. Radio Andre in the Mercedes and tell him to back off a little." Caulder looked back at the house. It was like a war... his men against the world. And the world was losing, reducing the neighborhood to a battle zone. Aside from ground control, air power was enabled, too. As he turned his head around, he saw a sedan pull out of a side road and tail the other cars. This car was black, and sported tinted windows. No doubt Sinclair was on board. So, he hadn't been in the grounds... just biding his time outside. "Pull back... I know where they're going. We'll swing round and confront them."

The pilot did as he was asked, and the chopper looped around the hills, followed at some distance by one more craft.

Ben glanced up into the air, and the helicopter was gone. The Mercedes had dropped back and Ben could just see the sedan. "We had company on all sides, but your lover took off, Toni. Maybe he saw the sedan back there. What's the betting it's your uncle's people? Not sure who he's after now. They're still behind us, so I guess he's either trying to get you or he's pissed with me. Doesn't matter either way. Neither one of them is getting you back." Obsessed and crazy were the only words for Ben.

Toni watched him. He was a different man from the one she met three months back. She knew he was scared, probably more than she was, but she also knew Ben wouldn't kill her... not yet anyway. He'd have nothing to trade with. She doubted that, when it came down to it, that her uncle could kill her also.

They drove on, up the highway towards the small town of Cametta where Ben had his own plane. The highway was busy, and he weaved in and out of the traffic blasting the horn at anyone in the way. The Mercedes dropped way back and let the sedan by.

Caulder yelled above the noise of the helicopter. On the phone he called Andre. "Go back to the house, go into the safe, get any paperwork you can salvage, especially the girl's passport and some of her clothes. Bring all that and any of the men that you can to the airstrip. Have the plane ready and we'll meet you there as soon as we can. Be ready to take off!" Caulder disconnected the call.

The Brazilian understood most of what Daniel meant, turned at the next exit and headed back to the mansion. He would do the job... he had never failed Caulder.

Toni sat back in the car and used the end of her dress to clean the blood from her mouth. She had torn a large piece of it off, ripping it at the seam. The hemline was now up past her knees, and she kicked off her high heels leaving long tan legs in full view.

Ben glanced down. "What the hell are you doing?"

"Just getting ready for a funeral," she said calmly.

"Whose?"

"Yours!"

"I don't think so!" and he put his foot down on the accelerator. "They have to catch us first."

"Oh, they'll do that... one of them, anyway," and Toni forced a brave smile through cracked lips.

"Next time we stop for traffic, you can drive. At least while you're driving you can't be doing anything else." She was making him nervous and it reflected in his tone.

"Just as you wish, Mr. Caulder." She knew she was beginning to get to him. No longer afraid, Toni was adjusting well to the situation.

Within a few more minutes, they hit traffic. Saturday was always busy on the highway.

"Your turn. Slide over!"

"My pleasure," she replied. And she slid across his lap onto the driving seat.

As soon as she sat in the seat the traffic moved again. Ben dropped the glove compartment down. A gun was visible. He saw her flinch, and he laughed. "You should have known he'd keep a gun or two inside the car." And he pulled another one from under the seat. They were loaded like he knew they would be. "Bad slip, Miss... Mrs. Caulder! You could have dispensed with me way back."

She recovered quickly. "Wouldn't want to deprive your father of that pleasure!"

He jammed the gun in her ribs and she yelled in pain.

"That's enough! Just drive. Up here we turn off. Make a left at the next exit and head towards the beach." He motioned with the Smith and Wesson.

She did as she was asked. The sedan turned with them.

Ben looked at the girl sitting next to him. Her dress was open revealing far more than her knees. He reached over to her legs and stroked her thigh with the .357.

"Pity it wasn't me you fell for and not my father. But that's how it has always been. Any woman that came to the house wanted my father. And you, you're no exception. Except Daniel Caulder wanted you. But just like Dana's mother, you're going to die."

"What do you mean? What do you know about that? Daniel told me she died giving birth to Dana out in Cameroon. Didn't she?"

She glanced away from the road and the car swerved and the tires screeched.

"Watch what you're doing! She did... but she had help. Oh, yes, he went back to get someone for her. She did beg him not to go. That's all true. But, while he was gone she had a visitor... and lo and behold... she died! He didn't tell you because... he didn't know for sure. I found out by accident. One of the guys who was there loved her and couldn't let Caulder take her away." He had a wistful look about him.

"What happened to him?" She really didn't want to know.

"They found him with his brains blown out. Killed himself... so they say." The whole time he'd been talking, he'd kept the gun on her thigh like it was some sort of symbol to him and she didn't have to try hard to figure out what.

"So, why are you telling me this?" Then it sunk in why. He was going to kill her for the same reason. Only this time the child would die with the woman. There would be no son by her. But she wasn't giving birth, and this wasn't Cameroon. This was the highway road and they were heading towards the landing strip.

For a moment, she could see Ben was lost in thought. She looked ahead and stared in amazement. Coming up over the horizon, dead level with the top of the car, was the chopper. It faced her and its blades made one hell of a noise in the afternoon traffic. In the heat of the day the chopper shimmered on the road, its silver body glistening in the sun like a giant bird hovering over its prey. Traffic scattered in all directions.

Toni saw it before Ben did and she turned the wheel violently to the left and stalled the car.

"What the hell..." He saw his father and Sam leaning from the chopper, high powered rifles in their hands.

With the rifle Caulder motioned his son to stay where he was.

The sedan pulled slowly to a halt and two men leaned out of the windows firing shots at the chopper. The helicopter lifted back up into the air. It gave Ben enough time to grab Toni and pull her from the car. Dragging her barefoot down the embankment and through the surf, they took off running along the beach.

"Get me over there, right in front of them…his plane's not far from here," yelled Caulder. "Just go low enough so that I can jump. Destroy his aircraft and get that sedan, whoever is in it!"

Head on, they came. The chopper stood in front of the couple. Caulder jumped onto the sand below and faced his son; anger creased his face. His hair and clothes blew from the winds of the chopper blades and the surf churned around his boots as it washed ashore.

Ben pulled Toni in front of him and held her there.

"For god's sake, Ben! Be a man. If you love her…let her go. Do something right in your life." Caulder was yelling through the chopper noise.

The chopper lifted up and took off towards the little plane.

"What, like you did? You let her go, not once, but twice! And yet you claim to love her?" and he put the .357 to her head.

Toni squirmed in his grasp, and behind Caulder they heard the small plane explode. The whole disturbance was attracting attention. In the background police sirens became a reality, as Daniel's chopper once more appeared circling the party before landing.

For Ben there was no way out, and he called to his father. "You lost both women you loved, ironically both by the hand of someone else that loved them." Only the gun separated his face from hers.

Caulder watched helplessly as Ben gently squeezed the trigger.

"Drop the gun, Ben, or I will kill you!" Bryan's voice was clear and distinct right behind Ben.

Caulder had seen the chopper hold the sedan in abeyance. He watched as Sinclair climbed out. Sam let him go through…with his gun pointing at Sinclair's back. He had his reasons.

"I can't do that, Mr. Sinclair. Just like you couldn't let Dana's mother live…maybe not you specifically, but your brother's friends from the government." He didn't say which government.

Caulder's expression changed. "Did you kill her?" His face was black with anger and his voice loud. "Did you? And is that why you're so intent on killing your own niece, because she's pregnant with my child? Or is this one of Ben's sick ideas?"

"It wasn't me…but I know what happened. You know what you did. You remember that? My brother was under a different name back then… you knew him by James Simmonds. He had a good story going and Sung was his source. Sung was playing both sides… we all knew that! Always had been right back from Nam. Yes, I had someone on the inside help kill her. If my brother and his wife hadn't been covering that story of you and the girl, they would never have been in that place. After they died and so did the girl, I let it go! Then lo and behold, you came back into our lives when the governor, Sung's man, was overthrown. But no… this is not my idea. I didn't come here to kill Toni… only you!"

Toni stared at Caulder. He knew about the baby. She knew he was blamed for the crash. What no one had realized till then was that James Simmonds was Sinclair's brother.

Caulder raised his own hand gun and held it at his head. "Then why don't I do it for you? I didn't cause that crash. It was an accident. No one was to blame. But remember, you sent Toni to me. Why, Bryan? If you thought I was responsible for your family's death, why send in your niece? You knew I would want a girl like Toni! You set her up? Was it worth losing her to get to me?" He screamed at Bryan.

"Yes!" yelled Sinclair.

Toni's eyes widened in horror and as if in slow motion she screamed at him. "Daniel, no….." and she tried to break free.

Ben kept his gun on her. He hesitated just enough and then he pulled the trigger. But Ben's reactions weren't experienced enough and Caulder altered his target, pulling the trigger as he did. Bryan saw him change direction and he stepped to one side. He saw his niece's face as she turned her face side wards, and he hesitated. Then he fired… and so did Sam.

Ben dropped to the sand and the surf swelled around his body. Shot through the heart by his own father, Ben was dead on impact. Bryan's bullet was impaired by his vision of Toni and it hit Caulder in the arm. Sinclair had one of Sam's bullets in his shoulder and his arm hung by his side. His gun fell to the floor.

Toni stood like a marble statue. She felt no pain. Ben's bullet had not touched her as it passed her face. But she could not move. She could see and hear everything… but in slow motion. The surf lapped around the end of her dress and it clung to her legs.

Behind her, she could hear her uncle moaning in pain and in front of her stood her lover. In the background, the chopper engines roared into life. Sam took the helicopter up and crossed over the top of them, landing on the beach side of Caulder.

Caulder waited till the noise and the blowing sand settled. He was having a hard time adjusting to the fact that he had just blown away his son. But he knew that Ben would have killed the girl. He kept his gun ready, just in case.

"Toni… are you hit?" yelled Caulder.

No answer. She could feel Ben's body touching her legs.

"Toni! Get over to me! Come on… we have to get out of here, now!" He saw the two men step out of the sedan and start across the sands and then he saw Sinclair motion them to stay back.

"Toni," Bryan's voice was low. "It's over! Come home with me. Come back to your real life. You can have your job back at the paper… you can have anything you want. There's no obligation to this family now. Your husband is dead. You don't have to go with Caulder. I'll let him go, if you come back with me. He'll be a free man to come and go as he pleases. It's all up to you, Toni. You can set him free."

His words echoed in her head. If she went back to her uncle, Caulder would be free. She looked at Caulder. He raised his hand to her and beckoned her to him. Toni looked down at Ben and then back to her lover. She shook her head and the tears streamed down her face.

For a second, she hesitated. Then she turned around and walked back to her uncle.

"My god, no, Toni! Come back to me! He's lying to you. He'll never let me be free. You and I can fight this together. You and I, and our baby," screamed Caulder. He was frantic to get her back.

"Boss," yelled Sam. "We have to get out of here. The police are on the coast road and soon there won't be any way out! Caulder, come on!" He leaned as far out of the chopper as he could.

Somehow, Toni heard Caulder's words. There were no more secrets, no lies to be told. She kept on walking towards her uncle. The two men neared Bryan Sinclair. When she reached her uncle, he put his good arm out to her, and Toni bent down and picked up his gun.

"It will never be over." And she pointed the gun at her stomach. "You make me a promise right here and now in front of your men that you will never come after us again! Never, do you hear? You have the life of his son. Do you really want the life of another of his children and of your own niece? Is that what you want? If it is, then I will pull the trigger right in front of you." She watched his expression. "No? Then I will turn around and walk back to Daniel... and you will let us go. We won't come back here... not yet. Not till the time is right. You know he is telling you the truth. He had nothing to do with my parent's death. What is it, uncle? I always had this feeling there was something else. You were in love with my mother, weren't you? That's what this is about. You think that Daniel killed her. And now you know he didn't. Do I look that much like her? You lost her, and now you lost me!" She was so self assured. She handed him his gun. "I'm going. Then the only way to stop me... is to shoot me in the back!" She looked into his face, a look that would haunt him forever.

Bryan wept. "No, I don't want that. Go to him. You're right. I was in love with your mother, but she chose your father instead. Go, Toni. Go to your lover. I will keep these men here." He looked in her eyes for one last time. "Toni," he paused, "you were right, you were bugged. It was in your camera! I had it put there before you left. I swear I didn't know about Sung hurting you. I only knew when you had your camera with you. Toni, I'm sorry... dear god, I'm sorry..."

She turned away from him and never looked back. With dress clinging to her, the fallen angel moved across the sands and through the surf. She wiped away her tears and looked down at Ben's body.

Caulder crossed time to join her. He stood there for a few seconds and waited. She took his outstretched hand in hers and he gently kissed her. Then he slid his arm around her, and she nestled into his chest. He held his head high and looked across to her uncle. Caulder had won but it was a poor victory... only the spoils were good.

"Boss! Come on, let's go!" Sam jumped from the chopper and pointed to the road.

"All right. I hear you, Sam! Toni, get in the chopper. Our business here is concluded." Caulder pushed her into the aircraft and climbed in behind her.

She didn't look down as they took to the skies. And neither did Caulder. His son lay where he died.

Only Bryan cast his eyes upwards. "Goodbye, I love you," he whispered and turned to his men. "Caulder is dead. He's over there in the surf. Doesn't matter which one. He's dead and that's what counts... right? You understand me?"

They nodded, the men in the suits and shades.

And he lied to himself.

In the chopper, Toni was shivering. Salt water seeped up her dress but she showed little concern for herself.

"You've been hit!" She turned to him and ripped his shirt up his arm. "It's gone in one side and out the other. Sam, can you help him? Do you have bandages on here?" She was overreacting and Caulder knew it.

"Honey, calm down, I'm fine. I'll take care of it. Look at you, you're shaking. Slide out of the dress. Sam, pass her a jacket to wear." He held her arm.

"Seems I make a habit of running around barefoot and in other folk's clothes. Can't think why that is..." and her laughter turned back to tears.

Caulder pulled her to him and she clung there, not knowing how to do deal with all this.

"Let go, honey. Just let go. In a few more minutes we'll be at our airstrip. The plane is waiting to take us out of the country. We can fly back to Cameroon and live at the palace with Dana. He'll be so glad to see you and to know he has a little brother on the way."

She looked up at him. "When did you know?"

"Last night at the hotel. Today for sure. I hoped so much. Why do you think I left the house to you? Just to get it out of my name, I don't think so. I don't need that house. I have plenty of money in Cameroon for us to live on for the rest of our lives. Toni, I have something to ask you..."

"Boss, we're here!" Sam pointed to the airstrip as it came into view.

Beneath them lay the tarmac strips, and men waiting for orders.

"It can keep!"

"Daniel, I really didn't know about my uncle... I hope you believe me."

He laughed aloud. "That's what you think I want to ask you? Oh, 'What', how I love you. Will you marry me?"

Sam stared. He couldn't utter a sound.

Toni did the same.

Caulder had done a thing he had never done in his entire life. He'd asked someone to marry him. Even he was shocked.

In the noise of the chopper landing, Toni said yes.

Daniel took her hand and she ran barefoot across the tarmac and boarded the waiting aircraft... back into the luxury of his life.

On board the jet there was much to discuss.

Andre had managed to find passports, clothes and all of Caulder's paperwork. While Toni changed in the airplane bathroom, they commiserated the loss of Caulder's son.

Toni looked into the mirror. How her life had changed. How she'd changed. And how Toni knew they could never return home while her uncle was alive. She had chosen her life with this man. He was everything to her. Lover, friend, enemy, father of her unborn child, father figure... her everything. Now she returned to her seat and sat down next to her future husband.

The drone of the engines made Toni sleep most of the flight, but her dreams were not good. She took little consolation from the fact she had walked away with her life. She had few possessions, and that was the summary of her past life. Few possessions... but a great deal to live for.

Caulder watched over her. He held her close to him and pulled blankets around her. His arm was bandaged and he felt no pain... at least not in his arm. He'd lost a son. As he looked out of the aircraft windows, he felt some kind of remorse. He knew one day that this would all come to a head... it had to. How long could a mercenary expect to go on in that line of work? He just wished he'd had a chance to explain to Ben why it happened.

He looked down at Toni sleeping across his legs, and he held her body to him. Inside of her was his seed. A new child. One who would have both mother and father, and who would not have to flee from country to country. They would live in Cameroon and maybe one day, only maybe, would go back to the States. He'd watched Toni those days in the bush, and he knew that she would learn to love Africa the way he did. He knew that... the day they saw the baby elephant play with its mama. And the bull elephant that protected his family. There had been a look in Toni's eyes. Just like the one that Caulder had now. He was her protector.

Chapter 12

Finally, at daybreak, they arrived in Cameroon. Powder puff skies heralded their arrival. Yaoundé hadn't changed much as the plane touched down, except maybe for the better. Toni had been looking out the windows at the sun rising over Caulder's beloved Africa. She had a warm and comforting feeling as she saw Caulder's men waiting at the side of the runway. His power was still very evident.

It had been a long, tedious flight but with a good landing. When Toni disembarked, she felt as though she had come home. The sun shone down on her and she felt warm inside. Sam carried her belongings for her, and they walked towards the waiting cars. An unmarked vehicle drove them to the palace, unmarked that is, except for the Prince's flag flying from the antenna. This was a far cry from the last time she had seen this city.

Inside the car, Toni peered across the seat and into the driver's mirror. She fluffed her hair. Toni felt she was not dressed adequately to meet the new ruler. Caulder was amused.

"Toni, you look fine. Jeans and a T-shirt are okay. Will you stop worrying? It's only Dana we're going to see... not the king!"

"Oh, really cute, Daniel. I can at least look human for him. Did you tell him about the baby yet?" She rummaged through her stuff and found a bottle of perfume that Andre had thrown in with the clothes. She unscrewed it and put some on her wrists and neck.

Caulder could smell the fragrance as it filled the car. He reached for her and held her close. "No, thought I'd give him time to get used to 'us'. How do you feel... about the baby, I mean?" He realized that

that was the first time he had even asked her how she felt about the pregnancy.

"I'm thrilled and I'm fine... really. I actually made it here without throwing up," and she snuggled into him.

Tentatively she asked him. "How do you feel about another child?" And she looked up into his face.

"Do you really have to ask that? Isn't it obvious? I left you a damn house in the city for him!" Daniel smiled as he spoke.

She noted the 'him.'

The car sped through the streets with outriders on each side.

Toni was watching. "Daniel, with all this security... how did my uncle get to you?" She was serious.

"You told him... quite by accident... where I was... and he sent someone in after me. We thought the plane going down was enough to throw him off the scent, but when you kept insisting I was alive he, and Ben, believed you. So I just got out. Dana was safe. It wasn't him your uncle wanted... just me. But I couldn't go without seeing you. I was headed for Germany and my grand-parent's old homestead. Sam and I, and one or two others, just till the heat died down. But now that's all changed. Toni... I have to say this before we get to the palace. If, and I say if, your uncle tries to get to me or to you again... I will kill him. Make no mistake. Do you understand what I'm saying? Be very sure you know what I mean. If he does try again, I will win."

She hesitated before she spoke. "I understand you. He's not the man I thought he was. You have to do what you have to do just to protect us. Daniel... there is something I should tell you. On the beach... he told me the camera was bugged, so wherever it was... he knew what I was doing. When he told me, I asked him to make me a promise that he would never come after us and would just let it go. He used me to get what he wanted... to get to you."

He looked at her. "Did he make you a promise, Toni?" He knew the answer before he asked.

"No, he never did!"

Now, Caulder knew it was not over. It wasn't government business anymore... just personal between two men and the woman they both loved. The car drove through the gates and pulled up near the front door.

"Papa," yelled Dana, peering through the open door. "Oh, Papa. I was so concerned about you. I'm glad you came back. And you brought Toni, just like you said." He jumped into the car and hugged Toni. They cried on each other… and black met white.

Inside the palace Toni wandered around the great room. The winged trophy was still there. She fingered it, and it brought back memories. Everything was the same. Caulder left her alone with Dana and went to talk with Sam.

"Toni, come sit by me and tell me the news. Papa says that you will soon be married and that you and he will live here at the palace. I'm so happy for that. He also said there is another surprise. Can I guess, Toni? I hope it's what I wished for." He was effervescent. With his jet black hair growing again, this bright, bubbly child was an inspiration to the world.

"What do you wish for, Dana?" Behind her back she crossed her fingers.

"For a brother… or even a sister. That's my wish; and for us all to live here and be happy." He looked into her face… his deep brown eyes full of expectation.

She touched his hair and thought that if Caulder could produce a son like this, he could produce anything. "Well, guess what? Your wish may very well come true." She took his young hand and placed it on her stomach. "Inside there… is a baby starting its life. A tiny person… growing. Mine and your father's." She waited.

"Really, Toni? He'll be my half-brother." He was so excited. Then his tone changed. "Toni, about Ben. He was a stranger to me and possibly even to my father. No one knew that this would happen. Papa is dealing well with his death. Sam told me that papa killed him… to save you. Sam said he had no choice."

Toni realized that Sam was saying a lot in such a short space of time. Why? A thought ran through her mind. How far would Sam go for his friend? Was there some unseen connection between them all?

It was then that Sam entered the room. "Dana… your father would like to talk with you a moment… outside in the gardens. And Toni, he asked me to take you up to the new rooms."

That fact of rooms had crossed her mind. The old rooms had been completely redone, but she didn't think that Caulder would want to be in those... not after Sung's dramatic death in them.

Sam and Toni walked up the stairs. It was like going back to the old times.

"Sam, may I ask you a question?"

He cut his eyes at her. "Sure, go ahead."

"It's to do with Dana's mother." She paused. "Did you know the man who killed her? You heard the conversation at the beach, and I'm sure that you and Daniel talked about it on the flight. You did know him, didn't you?" She took the chance.

He glanced sideward at her. "Mr. Caulder's a lucky man. Not only is he getting your body but also your brains. I wondered if you'd figure it. The Times lost a very good journalist." He paused. "Yeah, we talked on the flight. The man who killed her... he didn't blow his own brains out... I did! He was also my cousin."

Toni stopped walking and stared at Sam. "Oh, my god. I didn't realize it went that deep. I thought you may have known him somewhere down the line... but your cousin? You killed your own cousin?"

"Yeah... I did... just like Mr. Caulder killed his son! No difference. All blood. So I know what the boss is going through. Caulder fell for the princess and my cousin was the king's aide. He was as American as I am, but he found a better life here. When he found out that Caulder was in love with her, the king planned to have the boss killed. I couldn't let that happen. My cousin wasn't a good man, neither was the king, and Caulder was. There was no choice. When Caulder went back for help... the king's party was waiting. He let the child live... just in case it was his child and not Caulder's... and then they killed her. Just to get back at the boss. They made sure Caulder never knew exactly what happened. The rest you know. Your father was covering events out here. The crash happened when the king's speeding convoy hit your parent's car. They died instantly, Toni. Bryan figured that Caulder had done the assassination which led to the speeding convoy. The convey had his body and were looking for the person that killed the king and his aide."

"Did they find out who killed the king?" She asked hesitantly.

"No, they didn't." And Sam looked at her. "They had their suspicions. But could never prove it. I managed to escape, along with the other guys. We just happened to be at that waterfall that day. It was sheer coincidence that we passed by their minutes after he killed her. My cousin still held her by the throat. In one day, a country lost a king and its princess, you lost your parents, and Caulder gained a son."

"My god, Sam. How can you go though all this. You never told Daniel what happened?"

"No. Why add to his pain? He never knew until Ben and your uncle told him their version. I guess Bryan told Ben what he wanted him to know. Toni, I have to say that your uncle will never let this go. He wants Caulder so badly... it's killing him, and really it's me he should be after. I caused the convoy to speed away. They were looking for me. To hell with the government. Sinclair made it personal... but I guess Caulder told you that already."

They stopped by the doorway. "Yes... he told me that. How long do you think it will take Bryan to get back here to us?"

"A week... maybe less. Depends who helps him. Your uncle is not so nice, Miss Sinclair... he's not very nice at all. He used you... all this time he waited, and when the time was right, he sent you in. He just didn't expect it to go like this. You remind him too much of your mother."

"You met her?" she whispered.

"She was a beautiful woman, just as you are."

"I only saw them when they returned to Los Angeles. They were gone so much that I felt like Uncle Bryan was my only family. He did love her didn't he?"

"If the question is did Caulder love the princess... yes, he did. If it's about your uncle and your mother... absolutely. That's one thing he didn't lie about. And you, you are her image. Bryan sees Caulder taking her, not just you. And Toni, I am truly sorry for your parent's death." He showed her into the rooms and then left her alone with her thoughts.

Toni knew he was right about Bryan. She hadn't wanted to believe it, but deep down she knew. That's why he'd sent her to do a man's job. He had used her the whole time. Toni cried. The next time she'd see her uncle she knew would be the last.

Caulder heard her crying from outside the bedroom door. He knew the toll it was taking on her; he knew the toll it was taking on them all. But he could never give her up…no matter the cost. She had become his obsession. He made a loud sweeping entrance into the room so as not to scare her.

"So, you like the rooms?" Daniel tried to change the subject.

Toni hadn't really looked. She knew what he was doing. She dried her eyes and looked at her new home. The words came hard to her. Her new home! No one ever told her she'd be living in a palace in Africa. Nor was it on the agenda that at twenty-four she'd be pregnant by a fifty-year-old mercenary and right now…that man wanted her body. Wound or no wound…that didn't stop his need for his woman.

No one ever told her that this was real life.

The wedding was to be that weekend. Last Saturday she was Mrs. Ben Caulder. This weekend…she would be Mrs. Daniel Caulder. Daniel did everything. He picked her clothes, brought in a priest, arranged the guest list, got catering at the last moment and most of all put his army on full alert. Yaoundé became a city under siege…a siege of wedding plans. When you had money…you could buy almost anything.

By Friday, all the plans were complete. Caulder didn't want his child growing up to be a bastard, not like the other two. But even though he'd broken his own promise never to marry, he had some reservations about the subject.

He and Sam sat on the back stairs veranda taking in the air… and the smoke from their cigarettes.

"This is the right thing to do, isn't it, Sam? I mean…look at the age difference. When I'm seventy, Toni will be forty-four. Is it fair to her?"

Sam leaned back in the wicker chair, the moonlight casting shadows across their faces. "Was any of it fair? She didn't ask you to fall in love with her, and neither did you ask her. It happened. And she didn't ask to get pregnant by you. You were the one that knew better. If that's what you mean?"

"Yeah, that's what I mean. Some of it anyway. I always vowed never to marry. What makes me feel so different?"

"You have doubts about loving her?" inquired his friend.

"Absolutely none. I would die for her!" His tone was sincere.

"Yeah, we all noticed that! Two or three times… we noticed that! So you want to know why this is so different? Because, my friend, you love her so much that you want her with you… always. You are devoted to her. You killed your own son for her. Devotion to another person is a wonderful virtue and sometimes destructive." The last sentence was said in a different tone.

Caulder had the feeling Sam wasn't just talking about the situation at hand. "Sam, about your cousin, I'm sorry for that. Truly sorry. I didn't know till the other day what took place. My god, why do these things happen?" He stood up and moved to the steps. He looked out at the moon hoping to find an answer.

"You knew about it?" Sam was surprised.

"I suspected it was someone in the government that killed her. And I had the feeling that you had a hand in killing the king's aide. All the pieces just kind of fell in to place lately. I just never asked you. If I hadn't been at the waterfall with her, and we weren't followed; you would not have become involved; that convoy would not have sped away with a dead king, and Toni's parents would still be alive! Maybe I was to blame in some kind of way. If I had thought with my brains and not my…"

"Boss, stop. It wasn't your fault. I know how much you loved that girl. You were the only thing she had. That government and the king were cruel to her. And these things happen because they're meant too. Just like you are meant to marry Toni tomorrow. She is your soul mate. I think you knew that right from the start, right from the first day you saw her, didn't you?" He followed him across to the steps and sat down beside him.

"Yeah, I did know that… right from that moment in the pool. She has guts and she has what I want in a woman. She is everything."

"Then you have answered your own question. Be happy with her. Who knows how long any of us have to live! My god, we could all be dead by next week. These are unpredictable times in our lives. At least you have a family and a woman waiting for you at night."

"Yeah. I've neglected her too long tonight and I need her." He stood up to his full height. His hair was even longer and the beard and moustache still stood untouched.

"How's the arm?" asked his friend.

"Fine. Just a scratch. Scratches don't get in my way… neither do uncles," and he left for his bedroom.

Sam sat a while longer reflecting on life's events.

That night, in Daniel's arms, Toni felt safe. Safer than she had felt for some time. She turned and looked up into his face. He was sleeping peacefully. His chest rose in time with his breathing and Toni fingered his scars. The hair on his chest was still dark like him. For Daniel… there were no shades of grey. Only black and white. She looked at the ceiling. The fan made a whirring sound as it spun round and round and cast long shadows on the ceiling. Slowly she drifted to sleep.

In the early hours Caulder awoke. Toni was rooted deeply to him, her arms tightly bound around his body. He gently kissed her nose and then her mouth and he felt her body move beside him. She wasn't quite awake and yet she felt him inside of her. She felt the ecstasy that she had come to expect and she moaned with pleasure as he came again. This time she was awake and totally enjoyed his lovemaking. Until daybreak they made love. Both had a need for each other, and neither could quench their thirst.

Toni leaned over Daniel and rested her body on his. "You trying to tire me out before the wedding?" She laughed. "I'm so looking forward to today. Today, I become your wife… and Dana becomes my family. He told me last night that he was glad I was going to be his new mother. He made me feel so welcome." The whole time she was talking she held Daniel's arms on the bed and her breasts rested on his chest.

"So, you think you have me prisoner here, do you? We'll see about that!" He turned her on her back in one easy move and pinned her down.

All Sam could hear was laughter from Caulder's rooms.

"Yeah, boss. That's why you're marrying her! She makes you happy!" There hadn't been laughter in this place for a long time. He knocked on the door. "Hey, boss, sorry to disturb you. But you did say to call you around now."

There was a pause.

Daniel collected his thoughts together.

"Okay, Sam. I'll be right with you." He turned back to his mistress. "It's about time we got out of bed. See you in the great room!" And he left their bed.

"Be right behind you, Mr. Caulder, just like I'll always be," and she ran to get showered.

The wedding was for set for four o'clock, with music, dancing, and food out in the grounds. It was done with purpose so that the evening shade would take on a new meaning.

At three Caulder received a message brought to him by Sam. One he did not want to hear. "Sinclair is in Cameroon."

"God damn him! Couldn't he let her have her day in peace? Is he alone?"

"Yeah, boss, he's alone. Traveling under the name of Benjamin. Couldn't let it rest, could he?" Sam was the bearer of bad tidings.

Daniel ran his hands through his hair. "Find him... and when you do... kill him, before he kills us! Thank god we are getting married in the palace church. He can't get to us there, but he can get near the gardens. Make sure that the army is on full alert. Damn him!" and he pounded his fist on the wall. Caulder paced up and down in the room. He was wearing the silks of Africa once more. Jet black silks and shades. "Sam. I'm going to ask you do something for me. Don't tell Toni. Don't tell her he's here."

"What if she sees him?" asked Sam.

"We'll cross that bridge when we come to it. Just promise me!"

"You have my word, Mr. Caulder. I won't tell her."

No one had to tell Toni. She had been coming down the stairs and was approaching the door when she heard every word.

She leaned back on the wall and rays of red sun fell across her long white dress. She brushed them away and they would not go. She brushed harder. And clouds cast shadows over the sun. Toni had run down stairs to ask Caulder to help her with the buttons on her dress. Daniel must not know she'd heard. This was their wedding day... if he could carry the burden, so could she.

There was no time for tears, only time to collect her thoughts. She rushed up the stairs and back to the bedroom. From the dresser she took one of Caulder's guns. She'd watched her lover strap it to his leg and now she did the same, only into her garter. She dropped the dress down over it and stood back. You couldn't even see the shape of it. She looked at the dress. What was she doing in white? Caulder had insisted. The dress had tiny pearl buttons up the back, and the front was totally plain. It hung from her breasts and gave an appearance of an angelic figure… something Toni was not. An angel with a license to kill.

There was a knock at the door. "Toni, are you ready?" a small voice asked.

She took one last look and was satisfied with what she saw. "Come in, Dana." Toni popped a garland of wildflowers around her hair.

"My, Toni, you look so pretty. My father is very lucky… and so am I. Is it okay if I still call you Toni… or should I call you mother?" He was considering the fact.

"Toni… is just fine. We're friends, Dana, and friends call each other by their first names. Okay, so let's go down and find your father. We can't keep him waiting, not today," and under her breath she whispered, "Nor my uncle," and with escorts of Daniel's men they made their way to the wedding

The tiny, old church was filled to the brim with people, some black and some white. Flowers adorned the railings, and an old world charm clung to the air. Dana and Toni stood waiting to go down the aisle. They waited for the music cue. Caulder turned to see her, and all he saw was a vision of his future life.

He removed the shades and stood tall and proud next to Sam.

"Did they find him yet?" he whispered to Sam.

"No, boss. Not a sign. Strange, I didn't think he'd let it get this far. Are you wearing what I told you to?"

"Yeah, I'm wearing it. You ever worn one of these? Damned uncomfortable. And it doesn't make me feel much like a man."

"Maybe not. But it'll sure help you live like one. Just get yourself married and let us do the rest. Andre is right behind the pulpit and there's more men mixed in all around. Did you arm Dana?" Sam's eyes darted round the church. He also sported the silks of Caulder's army.

"Yes. He understood why. He loves Toni so much. Good job he's not another ten years older." He was trying to break the tension. "Know what, Sam. I'm nervous. Me! Daniel Caulder nervous. I thought it was just because of the situation; then I realized I'm terrified of getting married. Can you believe that?"

"Somehow... yes, I can." Their banter was stopped by the music as Toni and Dana walked down the aisle. She was clinging to the child's arm.

When Toni reached him, Daniel offered her his arm. They stepped up together and to become man and wife. Once again Toni was marrying a Caulder. This time she knew what she was saying and why. He placed a diamond ring on her finger and the sunlight caught the stone. It sparkled down onto her dress and the light reflected there. Daniel brushed his leg against her and he felt the gun. His eyes shot up to Toni's and he whispered softly, "What the hell are you carrying a gun for?"

She put her face close to his. "For the same reason that you are! I heard, Daniel. I know Bryan is here in the capitol. And it's my turn to be ready. I want a father for my child."

Their words were drowned out by the organ grinding garish music in the background. Caulder glanced around. So far so good and they retraced their steps back down the isle as man and wife.

Outside on the lawns people stopped to congratulate the happy couple.

All except one.

He lurked in the shadows waiting for his opportunity. No one would suspect a man of the cloth. And no one would stop him either.

As the daytime shadows lengthened, the party continued.

"Mrs. Caulder, would you dance with me... and this time I won't send you away," he joked while encircling his wife in his arms, and together they danced till the evening took on shade. Toni leaned against him and she was tiring. "How do you feel? I keep forgetting you're pregnant. Me, of all people! I just think you can go on as before, 'What.'" He touched her nose with his finger. "You'll always be 'What' to me... but why are you carrying a gun? There's no need. We have everything covered. Why did you?"

"In case you miss. Then I will kill him," she stated.

As he held her in his arms he looked into her face. "No, Toni. You won't. It's not that easy. I know!"

"I will do what I have to do wherever and whenever the time arises. I am your wife and..."

He put his fingers on her lips. "Shush, Toni. You don't have to be so brave."

"No, I don't. But maybe between you and my uncle I have become like you both," and she laughed a sad and cynical laugh.

Toni wasn't brave at all. She was terrified!

Sam stepped up to them with drinks. "Mr. Caulder, bourbon? And for your wife?"

"Make mine the same... you know the drugged kind!"

"Don't you ever forget?" asked her husband.

"No, never... do you?"

"No!"

As the sun set over the West African capitol, bells sounded in the church. Drums beat in true African style and the crowd gathered to watch the dancing in the floodlit grounds.

All except one.

In the bell tower a lone gunman sat and waited... waited for the sun to sink and the party to be enhanced by firelight. He put together the rifle that he carried under his robe. He'd picked his target... And the opportunities were beginning to present themselves. Caulder never let his guard down. No one did. In the firelight he held Toni in his arms and she leaned on him, watching the children dancing. He slid his hands down onto her stomach to touch his child and he happened to glance down. He saw the red dot on her dress and he spun her around as the rifle shot rang out. She screamed and he fell on top of her. All hell let loose.

"The bell tower. Get up there! Kill the son-of-a-bitch!" Sam yelled. "Mr. Caulder, Daniel!?" He pulled his boss onto his back.

There was no reply.

"Daniel! Oh, my god. Is he...?" screamed Toni.

"No. Leave him there. Come on, Toni. Let's go." Sam pulled her up from the ground and dragged her with him.

"No, I want to…"

"No. You don't! Trust me." And he pulled her out of harms way.

"Daniel," she screamed and broke away from Sam. But she didn't run back to her husband. Toni had heard. She picked up the end of her dress and ran to the steps of the bell tower. Men were ahead of her and she pushed her way through, scrambling through the power. They had her uncle surrounded.

She faced him in the stony tower, the rifle resting by his side. He was laughing, hysterically. An unshaven, beaten man stood in front of her.

"I never promised you, Toni. Never. Look about you. He can't kill me now, because he's already dead and so am I." His face was distorted with hate.

"He can't. No… he can't. But I can!" She lifted the skirts of her dress and pulled out Caulder's gun from its holster. She held it with both hands and aimed it at her uncle.

He yelled at her. "You'll never pull the trigger! You haven't the guts. You can't have or you would never have betrayed Caulder to Sung." He smiled, sadistically.

"You said you didn't know! You said that. Oh, my god! You knew all the time, but how? You said the bug was in the camera?" She screamed at him, but the gun was steady. Slowly, she squeezed the trigger till it was almost there.

"I talked to Sung long after that. I was in touch with him right up until your husband killed him. What I didn't know was how much he hurt you. He lied to me. When the camera was near you, I knew everything. Your camera was not always close at hand and Sung only told me what he wanted me to know. And then Ben filled me in on the rest. He hated Caulder so. Daniel Caulder took you from me and that I could never allow. Go on, Toni. Pull the trigger. It's easy. Go on… do it!" He egged her on. "You can't… you don't have what it takes…" His eyes widened in horror and he looked over Toni's shoulder. "But he does!"

She turned and Caulder stood there. "I can't let you do it, Toni. It's not your job. You would go through with it, wouldn't you?"

"Yes," she whispered. "I thought you were dead."

He ripped his shirt open. All that saved him was the bullet proof vest that Sam had made him wear. "Needs more heat than this to dance with the devil."

And Sinclair stared. "You have nine lives, Mr. Caulder. And so do I! You leave me no way out. Remember, Toni. I loved you and your mother." And then he turned and jumped from the narrow stone window. As he did… a shot rang out.

Toni screamed and turned into her husband's arms. She saw the gun in Sam's hand.

No one could survive the fall… especially with a bullet in the back.

Sam replaced the gun in his shoulder holster. "Now it's over."

"Come on, Toni. Let's go down. Give me the gun. You won't need it now. Your uncle was a sorry man. You knew it had to end like this. Tomorrow is another day. One where we can live as a family and live in peace, maybe return home and back to the house." As he held his arms around her, he thought about the trees. He didn't know why he thought of them just then. "Maybe, I'll still get them trimmed, then the sun can shine on our days… and never block out the rays." He ushered her down the stairs and out into the grounds. They didn't stop by her uncle. They moved on by and the young boy-king joined them. Back into the cool of the night… and finally free from the heat of the day!